OLDER, YOUNGER

MICHAEL JOHN

Thanks to those of my friends who've helped me hone the text: you know who you are. Thanks of course also to my partner Ron for his love and support.

If you enjoy this book please tell your friends about it and leave feedback on Amazon. Michael John can be followed on Twitter @ mjohn6975, or contacted by email at: mjohn6975@yahoo.co.uk

PART ONE – NOCTURNAL MANOEUVRES

"WHEN I FIRST saw you I thought you were smiling at someone behind me," said the older man. "But when I looked around there was just this mirror here." He pointed with an unlit cigar at the wall next to where he was standing which was covered, as were most of the walls in this bar, with mirror tiles.

Terry laughed.

"Is it so hard to believe that someone might find you attractive?"

The older man looked outside, watching people walking past the front of the bar towards the plaza, with its colourful array of carnival attractions, as he considered the question. He didn't think of himself as particularly unattractive but he did wonder why a young guy like this, with all his obvious vitality and exuberance, would want to flirt with an old codger. Was he going to ask for money or was he genuinely interested? There was no hint of subterfuge in the face–a dash of roguishness perhaps, but nothing to suggest he was a robber or a thief. In fact there was a kind of openness to the features, an almost childlike straightforwardness–although the old man doubted that anyone who came to an establishment such as this could hold onto their innocence for long. The bar was called Hummel Hummel, and was a legendary pick-up joint for older gay men and their admirers. There were very few such places in the whole of Europe, but Hummel Hummel was one of the most famous–often mentioned alongside such fabled nightspots as the City of Quebec in London and J.J's in Benidorm.

It was early evening and the bar had only recently opened–the waiters were going around the tables lighting the candles, positioning the chairs and stools, arranging bottles of liquor on the shelves so that they would be within easy reach later when the place was crammed. There were a few other patrons there, nursing beers and after-dinner coffees, or drifting around outside the dark room where pornographic videos were played continuously. It was that time of the evening when expectation could be tasted on the air, people were emerging from hotels throughout the resort of Playa Del Ingles and strolling here, to the Yumbo Centre, to see what delights the night had in store for them.

Terry was well turned-out in brown leather moccasins, chino trousers and a grey cotton short-sleeved shirt which was open at the neck to reveal a little of his smooth, sunburned chest. The fit was on the trim side, and it was clear to even the most casual observer that he looked after his body. He was in his mid twenties, slim and reasonably tall with short, unruly blond hair and the kind of wholesome features that you might see on children's television, or in a boy band. His skin was quite fair and the strong sunshine of Gran Canaria had given it a ruddy sheen. The older man gestured towards his face.

"How come you've got sunburn when the weather's been so appalling for the past couple of days?"

Terry rolled his eyes.

"Unbelievable isn't it? I got here on Monday and because it was cloudy I thought I wouldn't need any sun cream–but of course like an idiot I forgot that the rays get through even when it's overcast. Thank goodness it rained all day today otherwise I'd probably have been burned to a crisp."

The older man sipped his brandy.

"I'm not sure those sentiments would be shared by the rest of the people who've come to Playa Del Ingles for their precious dose of winter sun."

"Of course," said Terry quickly, "I wouldn't want to spoil everyone else's holidays—but you've got to look on the bright side in these situations."

The older man was definitely warming to this boy. The hint of self deprecation, the way he spoke with a strong Lancashire twang and a northerner's straightforwardness—it was all rather beguiling. He was also pleased to note that there was nothing camp about the lad; the way he stood, the way he moved his body, the gestures, everything expressed a gentle masculinity. For Terry it was a familiar situation—trying to persuade older men that he really fancied them and wasn't just after what was in their wallets was something he had grown used to over the past few years. He could understand it because there were quite a few younger guys in bars like this who really were on the make. It was the reason he usually bought the first drink, and made a point of referring to his job as an engineer early on in the conversation—or talking about his family. They were all ways of saying: look, I'm not a threat, I'm not going to club you over the head and pinch your wallet as soon as we're alone. Terry could see the older man relaxing as they continued to chat—leaning on the bar, smiling, moving a little closer. The brittleness and tightness that characterised the first few moments of their conversation seemed to be behind them. To those who could appreciate such things, the older man was a particularly fine specimen with a beautiful head of white hair, combed back from the temples, and the sort of features which carry with them a natural authority—that would have been at home on the magistrates' bench or at a meeting of the school governors. He was about the same height as Terry, not quite six feet, broad of beam with a visible paunch, wearing an open-necked white shirt under a navy blue single-breasted blazer. He gave Terry a gentle, conspiratorial nudge.

"So what brings you to a place like this then?"

"Gran Canaria?" replied Terry, "or this bar?"

"Both if you like."

"Well—my best mate Rob works as a stripper at a club here," the boy nodded towards the brightly-lit plaza outside, "and a couple of years ago he invited me to come and stay. He and his girlfriend rent a villa down at Maspalomas. So it's a nice way to get some winter sun, catch up with my friends–and of course come to bars like this."

"But do your friends know about your... unusual predilections?"

Terry took a mouthful of beer and placed his glass back on a square cardboard coaster that had been laid on the marble bar top.

"Rob and Helen do, yes," he said. "But nobody does back home. You can't grow up in the kind of place I come from and go around shouting about it. People give you a hard enough time just for being gay–never mind fancying older men."

Terry was being honest about this. He'd grown up in a village in an isolated part of northern England where he still lived. His friends were the same friends he'd had since his school days, and everybody in the community knew everybody else's business. He had never admitted to his family that he was gay–it was so much easier just to drive to Manchester or Liverpool or even Newcastle on those occasions when he needed the scene, then return home on a Sunday night and resume life as normal, without rocking the boat. From time to time people asked why he didn't have a girlfriend, but he'd had a few in his teens and early twenties and that seemed to be enough to quell suspicion. As far as Terry could perceive he was just seen as a bit of a jack-the-lad, a young Turk who swilled beer with his mates on a Friday night and enjoyed the bachelor life. But as time passed he was gradually becoming less and less content with the way things were. There seemed to be a yawning void at the centre of his existence which was sucking the mirth out of him–despite the surface bonhomie and the good times with his pals, the feeling that everything was built on a sham had begun to weigh heavy. His sleep was suffering and he had even once or twice experienced waves of anxiety and panic that had engulfed him without reason or warning.

"I know what you mean," said the older man, nodding and staring greedily at the boy's lips. "It's a difficult situation."

"What about you?"

The older man decided to match Terry's frankness with an admission of his own. He kept his voice low.

"You may find this hard to believe, but I'm here with my wife."

Terry stepped back, shocked.

"You brought your wife to a gay bar?"

"Good heavens no!" The older man laughed. "She decided to stay in the hotel tonight and read her book–have an early night."

"So you took the opportunity to go on a little adventure."

"More or less, yes. We come to the Yumbo Centre for a walk every night and I've always liked the look of this bar, and the fact that there seem to be older guys in here as well as younger ones, and the music's not too loud–so I thought I'd give it a go."

"But what about your wife–does she know that you go for men as well?"

"Absolutely not–I've never done anything like this in my life, but in Playa Del Ingles you see so many men together and the more I thought about it, the more it intrigued me. To tell you the truth I just came in here to test the water." He took stock of Terry's slim figure and shook his head. "Never thought for a second that I'd get chatted up by a terrific guy like you."

Terry ignored the compliment. He wanted the older man badly, but thinking about his own closeted life back home had slightly knocked him off his stride. Now he wanted to find out if there was anything in the older man's experience of life that might help him deal with his own situation. He kept smiling but his voice was serious.

"Have you always known that you like men, or is it something that you've just realised recently?"

"Oh," the older man looked down at his feet. He had never been asked about this before, and wouldn't necessarily have chosen to talk about it–but Terry was so natural and disarming he felt he could admit to something that he'd never once discussed in the thirty or so years since it happened. And talking to a stranger–particularly a rather seductive one–often gives a person the confidence to reveal things about themselves that they would normally keep under wraps.

"Many years ago, not long after we got married, Marion and I went on holiday to Switzerland–a place called Lugano. We met a lovely couple at the hotel and became friendly, spending a lot of time together, eating at the same table each night, going on a few excursions–that kind of thing. But once or twice when the husband and I were swimming together in the pool during the day, I felt an urge to reach out and touch him, and I'm sure he felt the same way. It was just something about the way he looked at me. Nothing happened, and I never said anything to Marion, but I suppose that was the moment when I realised that it was possible."

Terry thought about what had been said, comparing it with his own situation–trying to imagine what it would be like to live a married life while experiencing homosexual feelings. Eventually he spoke up.

"But how could you feel attraction for that man–know that you wanted him–and not do anything about it?"

The older man shrugged.

"Times were different then, it wasn't something you did. I got on with life, and Marion and I have had more than thirty happy years together."

As he spoke one of the waiters, who was bored by the lack of customers at this early hour, sauntered towards their end of the bar. He picked up a clean white cloth and gave the tall stainless steel draught beer taps a wipe, then minutely adjusted the position of a pile of drinks coasters on top of the bar–all the while singing "Love Is In The Air" under his breath. Terry and the older man stopped talking and regarded the rascal, both smiling but at the same time making it clear that he was intruding. He winked at them and wandered off, twirling the white cloth around in his hand. Above the bar there were two television screens suspended from the ceiling, one of which showed a continually changing series of still pictures of naked younger men, while on the other were displayed a sequence of similar pictures of older men. The images were downloaded from the internet, and had been assembled into these slide-shows for the enjoyment of people sitting at the bar. At that moment a photograph appeared of a fit young guy dressed in a pair of skimpy sports shorts, that perfectly followed the contours of what was underneath.

"Now that is pure sex," breathed the older man. "How can you prefer an old thing like me, with my pot belly and my wrinkles, to someone like that? He's beautiful."

Terry examined the image.

"I can see that he's an attractive guy but he does nothing for me. I mean, have you ever stopped to ask yourself exactly why an image like that excites you?"

The older man swooshed the brandy around inside his glass and took a swig. At the beginning of the evening he had certainly not bargained on having a conversation like this.

"Because I find it sexy, that's all."

"But what makes a person sexy?"

"I don't know–vitality, virility, things like that."

Terry moved a little closer, maintaining eye contact and keeping his voice low.

"When I look at a handsome older guy, it's the same qualities that I find attractive. I look at the face and I see vitality in the eyes and the smile, experience in the brow, and virility in the way you look at me, the way you seem to want me. These are the things that I find sexy."

The older man put down his brandy glass and clapped his hands quietly.

"Bravo," he said. "And I suppose that's what you tell all the old crocks."

"Pretty much." They laughed. The old man looked at his watch.

"Way past my bed time. I'd better go before you pick my pocket– or flatter me to death."

If he was to pull off his seduction, Terry knew he had to act quickly. Despite the obvious flirtation and the interesting conversation, it had felt a bit like he was leading the older man by the hand through a minefield and a sudden sprint towards safety at this stage, tempting though it was, could blow the whole enterprise. But of course he was just as likely to miss out if he held back too much, especially now that the older man had signalled his intention to leave. Terry decided to chance his arm and go for the direct approach.

"Where are you staying?"

"The Princess Hotel in Maspalomas," said the older man. "I should be getting back soon, or Marion will be sending out a search party."

"I'm staying not too far from there–fancy a quick nightcap?"

An hour ago the older man would never have imagined that he'd end up being propositioned in such a way–but now after a few drinks and a pleasant chat with this sexy young guy he felt that anything was possible. His wife would probably be asleep anyway, and he could always tell her he'd gone to the casino for a couple of hours. After all–just how often would he get the opportunity to do this? It felt to Terry as if everything around them stopped momentarily as the man made up his mind–even the music and chatter seemed to fade for a fraction of a second. The older man smiled.

"Why not? Another hour or two isn't going to do any harm."

Terry finished off his beer–suddenly aware of a slight ache coming from his bladder. He'd been so involved in the conversation that he had forgotten to go to the toilet.

"Do you mind if I just pop to the loo?"

"Not at all," said his companion, flagging down the waiter so he could pay for the drinks. Now it's often said that lust can be a fickle thing, and so it was in this case. No sooner had Terry disappeared around the corner on his way to the gents, than a slender young charmer called Clive materialised out of the shadows and began talking to the older man. The bar seemed to have been designed to allow patrons to flirt with one another discreetly, using the mirrors that had been attached to the walls, the pillars and even the ceiling in some places. Together with the subdued lighting, these meant that if you were careful you could lurk near someone and examine him, maybe even make contact with him, without being noticed by anyone else. An expert in this kind of subterfuge, Clive had positioned himself in a spot where the older man would see him if he looked in the mirror behind Terry's head–which was more than likely to happen at some point while they chatted. He'd then rather shamelessly stared at the guy, smiling whenever they caught one another's eye, and more or less just waiting for the opportunity to move in. Clive was dark-skinned with something of the gypsy about him, short black curly hair, a black goatee beard and deep-set, brown eyes. He wore a pirate's gold hoop in his left ear. If Terry was the boy next door then Clive was definitely the mysterious stranger–the young showman who turned up with the travelling fair for a few weeks, gave the locals the ride of their lives, and then disappeared without a trace.

Poor Terry! While he'd been gabbling away, trying gently to coax the older man towards a liaison, picking his moment, the older man had been looking over his shoulder, taking stock of Clive and exchanging the occasional flirtatious glance with him. And he had started to think that, although Terry was undoubtedly very attractive, there was something about this dark and brooding stranger that suggested he would be more interesting in bed. His comments about having to leave had in fact been a ruse to allow him to go outside and wait around the corner, in the hope that Clive would follow him. It's a universal truth of pick-up joints all over the world that while some people procrastinate, others take direct action–and usually succeed. By the time Terry came back from the toilet the job was done, Clive had whisked the older man away to his suite in a nearby hotel, which as luck would have it was empty that night because his extremely wealthy boyfriend was spending an evening at the opera in Las Palmas. Terry stared in disbelief at the empty brandy glass, the vaguely obscene stub of the unsmoked cigar lying next to it, abandoned, on the bar top. The young waiter saw the expression on his face and approached. Terry looked up at him.

"What happened... has he gone?"

The waiter was Dutch and like most people from the Netherlands he spoke excellent English. He looked a bit shifty as he spoke, not wanting to break the bad news.

"Yes—a young guy came and spoke to him and they left."

"Did you see the other guy... what did he look like?"

The waiter was clearly nervous about providing more information—love spats and jealousies were common in this kind of place and the staff were careful to separate themselves from such intrigues.

"Come on," urged Terry. "I'm hardly going to start a punch-up the next time I see him! What did he look like?" The waiter scrutinised Terry's face for a few seconds and finally smiled. Working in the bar trade had given a keen sense of the way people were, and he could tell that Terry wasn't the kind of guy to cause a scene. He decided to be a little more forthcoming than usual.

"About your age, slim, dark hair, with a beard. Comes in here every night. English I think."

Terry shook his head.

"Clive—the sneaky bastard. I should have known. Oh well, not much I can do about it now." He sat down at the bar, long faced, staring into space. The waiter rapidly cleared away the brandy glass and the cigar stub and gave the counter a wipe with his cloth—erasing all the evidence that the older man had been there. He slid a fresh beer mat onto the marble in front of Terry.

"Can I get you a drink on the house?" he said.

"Oh... cheers. Very kind." The waiter poured a small draught beer from one of the tall, stainless steel taps behind the bar and placed it on the mat. He then pulled out a small shot glass and poured himself a schnapps. They clinked glasses and drank.

"You know you shouldn't be upset," said the waiter quietly. "A gorgeous guy like you—you can have anyone you like."

Christ, thought Terry, that's all I need right now. A guy my own age trying to chat me up and then most likely giving me an earful of abuse when I tell him that I'd rather sleep with his grandfather! He looked at the waiter and smiled.

"Very kind of you to say so, but I'm not that bothered, really."

The barman seemed to sense what Terry was thinking, and laughed.

"It's okay," he said. "I'm not trying to seduce you–I know you only go for the older guys. I'm just saying that I think there's something good for you, just around the corner. People like these," he waved his hand dismissively towards where Clive and the older man had sneaked out of the bar, "you don't need to waste your time on them." At that moment a noisy group of four or five Germans strode into the bar and shouted across to the waiter–who hid his schnapps glass behind the counter and leaned forward, whispering into Terry's ear. "It's true–just wait and see." He then turned and walked away, greeting the new customers enthusiastically in German and getting a raucous response. Terry finished his beer and swung his legs around, sliding off the tall bar stool. He stretched, touched his pocket to make sure his wallet was still there, and then walked outside, heading in the direction of the plaza and the huge stage that had been set up in preparation for carnival night. He turned around and saw the barman watching him while pouring drinks for the Germans. Terry gave him a quick salute and then continued on towards the gathering crowds of revellers.

*

AT various moments during his childhood, long before he had experienced anything that could really be described as a sexual feeling, Terry had felt drawn to older people. Each summer when he was a boy his family would go to a hotel somewhere in Britain for their annual two weeks holiday. His parents would try to find a place where children would be welcome, where there would be other youngsters–possibly even activities laid on for kids–but Terry was rarely found socialising with his peers. While his sister was in the swimming pool or the games room playing table tennis he would be in the lounge, charming all the old ladies into giving him fifty pence for an ice cream. The small town in which he was brought up offered plenty of fuel for Terry's nascent desires. He remembered being fascinated by the local butcher: who seemed somehow majestic with his salt-and-pepper hair, ruddy complexion and thick, pink fingers–one of which was missing because of an accident with a meat cleaver during his apprenticeship. And the jovial chatter inside the shop, with its shiny white tiled walls, marble slabs and scored wooden chopping surfaces, gave Terry a much deeper pleasure than anyone–especially the butcher–would ever have imagined. The barber was another source of private thrills. Most young boys hated having their hair cut, but not Terry. He looked forward to going to the old fashioned shop which was split into two halves–one run by the husband, the other by the wife. The female half, called a salon, was all done in shades of pink and had a row of those big, space-helmet hairdryers against the wall. There was a carpet, floral wallpaper and piles of clean towels. He remembered the strong smell of hairspray and the occasional glimpse through a half-closed sliding door, which acted as a partition between the two worlds, of women sitting around with curlers in, gossiping over large mugs of tea. The male half had worn-out linoleum covered in stray bits of hair, overflowing ashtrays and a calendar with a different topless woman every month. Cutthroat razors and combs were stored in a big jar of blue disinfectant called barbicide–there were plastic combs for sale, a dizzying array of scissors and electric clippers, and a drawer full of something called Durex that customers often bought with a wink and a nudge on their way out. All this was fantastic but for Terry the crowning glory was the barber himself–a small man with white hair swept back from the temples, whose eyes flashed as he spoke with a foreign accent about football and horse racing. At the beginning of the hair cut there would be the simple pleasure of him running his fingers and comb through Terry's unruly mop of hair, then there'd be the tickle of the electric razor as he did the back and sides. When the barber came to doing the boy's fringe he would have to lean across, and Terry would feel the weight of the old man's body pressing gently on his arm as he caught in his nostrils the exotic, masculine aroma of cologne mixed with traces of cigarette smoke. Finally there was the excitement as the barber used the cutthroat razor to finish off around the boy's neck. He'd slap a bit of after shave on and there'd be the exquisite coolness, the fresh feeling of air on skin that had been covered for weeks by downy hair. These were some of the early highlights of Terry's sensual life, and he still to this day chose to get his hair cut at a traditional barber's rather than the trendy hairdressers used by his pals. The interesting thing was that despite the strength of these feelings, and the fact that they went back as far as he could remember, it was fairly easy for Terry to drift into an apparently conventional adolescence. When his fellow pupils started expressing an interest in girls, Terry did too. Almost before he knew what had happened, he was going out with one. Strangely, it was at this time that he first fell in love with an older man–but more about that later. In the future Terry was to meet old codgers who would say they always knew they were gay, but chose to get married because it was what everyone else did in those days. His own experiences in his teenage years would allow him to understand that this was not so much of a charade as it appeared at first glance. These men could love their wives, construct a home with them, have children–and the fact that they were homosexual would have no discernible effect on their family lives at all.

But this was not to be Terry's destiny because his mind was simply too active, too curious, to keep ignoring his urges. It was only a matter of time before he would step through the mirror into looking glass land. It happened while he was at university. One night, after five or six pints in the bar at his hall of residence, he had gone to a payphone a few hundred yards down the road, to make absolutely sure that he wouldn't be heard by any of his fellow students, and telephoned the local gay switchboard.

"Hello? I wonder if you can help me. I'm eighteen years old and I've just started at the university and... well, I think I like older men. Can you tell me please if there are any gay pubs where they go?" The operator sounded intrigued.

"Do you mind if I ask how old, exactly?"

"Oh, from about fifty-five up. Perhaps with grey or white hair."

"Bloody hell! Trust me to be stuck in here when there's a dish like you out looking for an older man. But I'm probably not old enough anyway. Typical!" Despite the apparent annoyance in the words, the voice was friendly and comforting. Terry smiled into the receiver. It was his first brush with the gay world, and this kind of banter would always make him feel at home.

"So do you know of anywhere, then?"

"Well, you could go to the Magic Clock, or the Brewer's Arms. Anywhere really, I'm sure they'll be delighted to see you wherever you go." His tone changed, adopted a wistful quality. "Eighteen–the mind boggles." Terry laughed.

"Thanks a lot. Maybe sometime I'll see you out."

"I certainly hope so, darling!"

So Terry's first experience of going on his own to a gay bar was in the Magic Clock. He felt his heart beating as he walked towards the door and heard loud music coming from inside. For a fraction of a second he considered bailing out; worried as he was about what might confront him, but it had just started raining and besides–they'd stuck coloured fairy lights to the window frames, which gave the place a festive, cozy look. And how appropriate, he thought, that some wag had removed the 'l' from the sign hanging outside. As the door closed behind him, dozens of pairs of eyes gave him the once over. The music was coming from a large sound system that had been set up in the corner, which was being presided over by a fat drag queen with spiky hair, dressed all in red. As Terry took stock of the place, the drag queen picked up her microphone and turned down the music slightly.

"Evening darling," she shouted in a voice that was way too gruff. "How's life on the rent?" There were titters as Terry, red-faced, scuttled over to the bar and ordered a pint from the extremely friendly barman. Above the bar there was a huge, old-fashioned clock face built into the wall, its pointers spinning slowly backwards. Terry assumed that this was the clock after which the place was named. He was unnerved by what had happened but as he stood there drinking, the drag queen took verbal pot shots at other people walking around the bar. Clearly it was nothing personal and everybody was fair game. Within a few minutes he was laughing along with all the other punters. Eventually, nerves bolstered by a couple more pints, he went and stood near the man he considered to be the most appealing in the place. He was a plumpish, balding fellow with glasses who was dressed in a jacket and tie. There was a liveliness about him–despite his size he seemed light oh his feet. Terry had seen him laugh a couple of times at comments his friends had made, and the change in facial geometry that constituted a smile was one of the most beguiling things of all. As he hovered around nearby, feeling a little helpless (it would be a while yet before he would learn the finer arts of cruising), Terry heard the man discussing cars with one of his friends. It transpired that he had an old Ford Granada that he parked in the street outside his house, and one night some vandals had snapped off the radio aerial. His friend was advising him to get a new aerial that stuck to the inside of the windscreen, so that the vandals wouldn't be able to do it again, but the handsome guy felt that this would spoil the appearance of his car.

"I mean look," he spoke with a strong Yorkshire accent. "I'd have to stick a rubber grommet in the hole, or cover it with filler–and it never looks right if you do that." One of the man's other friends, who had been listening to the conversation, suddenly chipped in.

"Long time since you stuck anything into a hole, eh Trevor?" The others laughed but the handsome man was unfazed.

"Fuck off Charlie, at least I can still get it up without using a pump." There were hoots of laughter and the banter continued for a few more minutes. Presently, though, the conversation moved on and the handsome man was no longer the centre of attention. It was the opportunity Terry was waiting for.

"Excuse me," he said. "I couldn't help overhearing what you were saying before. Ford make an electric aerial for the Granada, you know, one that goes back in when you turn the ignition off. You could fit one of those easily, and it'd solve both your problems." He paused. "Or if you like I could fit it for you. I know quite a lot about cars."

The older man looked at Terry as if he'd just landed in a space pod. Terry thought to himself, as soon as this little disaster has unfolded I'm going straight outside, getting on the first bus that goes past and forgetting about the whole thing. But then Trevor grinned.

"Now then young man, why exactly would you want to do that?"

Terry's heart stopped, but he had nothing to lose–and the beer had made him bold.

"Because I think you're attractive, and I'd like to help you," he said quietly. It's worth mentioning that if Terry had been speaking to someone with the usual hang-ups about getting old, things could have become quite difficult for him at this point. Many older men, filled with insecurities about what the passing years had done to their bodies, would have been wondering why such a handsome lad was coming onto them. They would assume that Terry was a rent boy or someone who was just trying to wind them up. But Trevor was not that kind of man, and age did not weigh heavily upon him. He had zest for life and knew he still had plenty to offer, and he'd been around the gay scene long enough to understand that there were people out there who found older men attractive, and to accept their interest without questioning it. He took hold of Terry's hand.

"You know, I might just have to take you up on that offer–but what can I do for you in return?" Terry looked at his shoes.

"Take me home with you?" Trevor laughed.

"I was hoping you'd say that." He turned to his friends. "Night chaps. I'm just giving this young lad here a lift home." As they walked away, Terry heard one of them saying "That sly old bastard. How does he do it?" Later, as he sat on the edge of Trevor's bed taking his clothes off, Terry paused.

"Look," he said, "there's something I should tell you. I've never slept with a man before. Do you mind?" Terry couldn't see the older man behind him, smiling from ear to ear.

"You mean I'm to be your first? Well, that's an honour I'm more than happy to accept." Trevor lay down on the bed. "Help yourself, lad, do whatever you like."

*

ALAN Reid and George Hope entered the Yumbo Centre through an alleyway opposite their hotel, which brought them around the back of an amusement arcade on the second floor. The centre was like a cross between a huge open-air sunken garden and a multi-storey car park; roughly square in shape with each side about a hundred metres long. From street level, visitors looked down upon a landscaped plaza surrounded by several floors of shops, bars and restaurants. Each of the upper floors had an open-air walkway from which balconies looked down at the central square. It looked to George like an enormous oblong amphitheatre, ablaze with neon light from top to bottom. He wondered how many times they'd walked down these cracked and worn-out marble staircases. A big outdoor stage had been set up in the middle of the plaza for carnival week, and the evening's entertainment appeared to be some sort of talent contest. The compere spoke rapidly in Spanish, and his comment about the act that had just been on the stage drew laughter from the audience. Because the place was busier than usual, Alan and George were unable to get seats outside one of the bars where they usually had a coffee, before starting the evening's boozing. As they walked along looking for a table, George eyed with disapproval the people sitting in prime positions, making their drinks last as long as possible so as not to have to pay for another one. Neither he nor Alan was in a particularly chirpy mood, because it had been raining all day.

"Bloody tourists," he said. "I thought they'd all stay in because it's been so miserable. Do you think they'll do us a coffee at the Block?"

Alan's response was gruff.

"For customers as loyal as us they should lay on free Champagne."

George laughed at the absurdity of the idea as they turned the corner. He was the shorter and more robust of the two, with a round face and naturally cheerful features. His upper front teeth were widely spaced and protruded slightly, and when he smiled his tongue would appear momentarily underneath them. He had a dark complexion and his moustache accentuated the Mediterranean look. For most of his life he'd had coarse black hair that grew in curls, but in the past few years, as he approached his late sixties, it had thinned a bit and gone grey. He'd always been vivacious, and even now there was a certain spring to his step–a liveliness and a sense of mischief that the years hadn't subdued. In contrast, Alan had more of a regal, ponderous air. He was about six feet tall but he seemed bigger, because the unruly bush of white hair that he spent so much time combing back from his forehead tended to spring up again from his scalp at the slightest provocation. He looked like a renegade professor from a university arts faculty, who most probably shared a barber with Albert Einstein. The round, gold-rimmed glasses perched on the end of his nose added to the impression of bookishness. Aware of how pale he would seem next to George, he had put a bit of false tan on his face before heading out that night, and some of it had seeped into the hair at the edge of his forehead, giving it a slightly yellowish tinge. Walking along jabbering away at one another as they usually did, George taking two steps to Alan's one, there was something Vaudevillian about them, as if they were the two halves of a comedy double act that had spent years touring the music halls. The asphalt glistened under their feet, still wet from the afternoon's downpour–the reflections of a thousand coloured neon lights smeared across the greasy surface. Market stalls had been set up temporarily all around the plaza, selling the usual fairground paraphernalia: brightly-coloured trinkets, plastic lizards, sweets, toy guns and teddy bears. Alan saw excited faces lit by the rows of lightbulbs strung along the fronts of the stalls, as people inspected the goods and tried to win prizes. Cash and merchandise changed hands–candy floss, toffee apples, and beer in waxed-paper cups. Alan and George arrived at the Block, where most of the tables outside were empty. Tonight, presumably because of the carnival, the staff were all wearing Halloween costumes. The waiter had on a rubber skull mask that covered his whole head, a black skin-tight body stocking with the bones of a complete skeleton painted on the front in a pale phosphorescent colour, and a long black cape.

"Is that my lovely Juan under there?" asked George, peering up at the mask. It nodded. "Well," he said, "I'm sure it's a very nice costume and all–but it means we're not going to have the pleasure of looking at your gorgeous face." Alan had known that it was Juan, because the boy was always chewing gum, and the rubber death mask could clearly be seen distorting as his jaw worked up and down. After a few seconds he stopped chewing.

"I have... scythe," he said quietly, holding up a scythe made out of crudely painted cardboard, that was already bent in several places and starting to fall apart. Alan and George laughed heartily as they bumbled their way to a table.

"I think we'd better watch ourselves old chap," said Alan, "it doesn't do to mock The Reaper–particularly at our time of life." Once they'd settled down, the boy explained in broken English that, to commemorate the carnival, he and his colleagues were offering something called a Flaming Inferno: a special cocktail of spirits that was set on fire before being served. Alan looked at George for confirmation.

"Two coffees and two of those then, eh? I could do with a little sharpener." George nodded and raised a finger towards the waiter.

"But don't light them too early–we don't want to lose all the alcohol."

"Or burn our bloody lips off," said Alan, prodding the skeleton in the ribs. A subtle change in the shape of the rubber mask suggested that the boy was either smiling or scowling. Alan often wondered what the lads at the Block made of him and George. The waiter would probably walk back into the bar and say: "It's those two old buggers back again, why do they keep coming here?" A boy from Salford ran the bar on behalf of a reclusive German, who took all the cash but chose not to interfere in the business. The manager's name was Peter, and he always made Alan and George welcome. One evening he had confessed earnestly that there had been a big age gap between himself and his ex-boyfriend, but the way he had said it suggested that the difference wasn't particularly huge, and that he was just trying to put them at ease because they were significantly older than most of the bar's clientele. It was a nice gesture though.

Alan got up from the table and passed through a chain-link curtain into the relatively dark interior of the bar. Three or four customers were sitting on stools watching a lightly sadomasochistic porno movie that was playing on a television set attached to the wall. In the far corner there was a large cage, inside which the stripper would perform later. The walls were painted black and the only lighting was ultra violet, augmented by candles burning in red glass containers that were dotted around the place. The serving area of the bar was a big black slab of heavy material, like granite or polished concrete, attached to the ceiling with thick chains. As usual, they were playing thumping dance music at a volume which most people Alan's age would have twisted their faces at. Strangely, though, he and George enjoyed the music here–although they tended to avoid the sort of clubs in which it was normally played. Juan walked back into the bar, and Alan could see that in the pure ultra violet light his costume was actually quite effective. The black body stocking was no longer visible, and all that could he seen were the glowing bones of a walking skeleton. Peter, who was dressed as a witch, was sticking miniature sparklers into the links of the chains–he and his colleague would light these up at the climax of the stripper's act, filling the place with bright light. Seeing Alan, he smiled and laid the packet of sparklers aside, and they shook hands across the bar. Peter nodded towards Alan's jacket.

"Looking smart tonight." Alan grimaced.

"It's so bloody cold."

"The weather's been shocking," said Peter. "No good for the carnival at all. I'm amazed by how many people are out. At least it's stopped raining though, and it's supposed to be sunny tomorrow."

"We'd heard that a stretch of the beach was washed away last night."

"Yeah, although I don't think the damage is as bad as it was two years ago," said Peter, wiping the bar top. "But look, if you're feeling the cold, come back later–we've got a show that'll warm you up."

"I hope he's better than the one you had on Tuesday. He was handsome enough, and he was a good dancer, but when he took everything off there wasn't much down there." Alan glanced at his own crotch. Peter picked up the sparklers and continued attaching them to the chains above the bar, looking slightly sheepish.

"A lot of people complained about that," he admitted, "but he had 'flu and he said afterwards that he'd taken some medicine that may have interfered with his... performance."

"Maybe I should lend him some of George's Viagra." Peter laughed.

"Maybe–but you'll like the one we've got tonight. Rob from Macclesfield. He's a right dirty bugger."

"I'm not sure I understand what you mean, young man," said Alan, lifting his nose in mock disdain and shuffling off towards the toilet.

Outside, George had caught the gaze of a swarthy man among the crowds of revellers who were walking past. He was dark-haired and trim, probably in his late thirties, and dressed in tight blue jeans and a white cotton shirt. George's eyes took in the slim body as the stranger floated back into the stream of people, glancing back once or twice. He was starting to conjure up a pleasant daydream about giving that lovely taut bottom a few slaps when Alan sat back down and nudged him.

"Hoy! The waiter's here, and he wants to be paid–or perhaps you hadn't noticed." George looked down to see that their coffees and liqueurs had been placed on the table. Blue flames danced lightly on the top of the dark liquid, and the surface near the rim of the glasses bubbled and hissed. George handed over a note, blowing the flames out as he waited for his change. The boy dressed as death stood over him, rummaging in a small black leather pouch attached to his belt.

"Strange, really, to be waited on by such a fellow," said Alan, examining the skeleton costume closely. George glanced at the scythe leaning against the wall near the door.

"Maybe we should leave him a tip." He dropped some coins onto the plate and stirred his coffee thoughtfully as he spoke. "When death really does come, I doubt that we'll be able to buy him off with a handful of euros."

"Christ," shouted Alan, "that reminds me–I forgot to take my pill at dinner." George smiled.

"I know–you were too busy flirting with that young waiter."

"I was not flirting with the waiter! As a matter of fact, my attention was diverted by that old josser and his toy boy sitting at the table behind you. They were holding hands and gazing into one another's eyes like a couple of teenagers at the back of the school bus. It was embarrassing–especially in a dining room full of heterosexual people." George decided to play devil's advocate.

"Hang on though old chap," he said. "Maybe they're in love." Alan rose to the bait.

"Pah!" he spat, waving his hands about in disgust. "You expect young people to fall head over heels in love–but that bastard's older than I am! There's nothing worse than a man in his dotage, sitting there gazing into some young chicken's eyes, especially when you know the kid's probably only interested in the money." George shook his head.

"You're overreacting. I mean, I've reached the stage when I don't particularly want to fall in love any more, because it's too much trouble, but that doesn't mean other people our age can't give themselves over to it if they want to."

"I think it's pathetic," said Alan. "If I start acting like that, I want you to put me out of my misery." George smirked.

"Well look, before you have a heart attack, do you want to take your tablet?" He pulled out one of those packets of pills with foil on one side and transparent plastic blisters on the other. Alan's face lightened.

"You picked them up!" He took the packet and held it up to the light, squinting to read the tiny lettering, and then squeezed a pill out and put it in his mouth. He washed it down with a swig of his Flaming Inferno.

"I feel better already. Now I think it's time for your medicine." Alan removed an old fashioned hard spectacles case from the inside pocket of his jacket. It was a battered thing, and in places the brown leatherette had been scratched off to reveal the metal beneath. There were some faded gold markings on the top–but the name of the optician who had supplied it was no longer legible.

"Ah, the magic glasses case," said George. Alan opened it and extracted a long and perfectly-rolled joint. They had found that the case was the ideal receptacle for carrying an evening's supply of the things, because it stopped them getting crushed. Smoke and flames billowed out of the end of the spliff as Alan took huge puffs to get it going, his eyes twinkling through the fumes. He spoke as he exhaled.

"Can you remember how we first discovered the joys of dope?"

"Oh yes–that young painter who came to decorate your place the year after Marjorie died, who used to work all day with his shirt off, in those little blue nylon shorts." Alan stared wistfully into the distance.

"Another hunk who slipped through our fingers."

"He may have slipped through your fingers, old fellow." George was smiling. Alan looked astonished.

"What? How did you manage that?"

"Well, one afternoon when I was there you were outside in the garden talking to your next door neighbour, and he was up a ladder in the bedroom. He called down and asked if I would come and hand him one of his brushes. When I did, my face was about level with his crotch, and I don't know what came over me, but I just started blowing on it, like you'd blow on a hot drink. So this thing inside started getting bigger, and he stopped talking, so I stopped blowing. And he said, oh, please go on. Of course eventually I just had to take it out. When you came back in about ten minutes later, it was all over." Alan held out the joint.

"All over your face?"

"There's no need to be crude."

"I don't know," said Alan. "It's the quiet ones you've got to watch." He took a sip of his coffee, gazing at the people walking by, lost for a few moments in his thoughts. "But don't you find it amazing that these young guys can find wrinkly old things like us attractive? I mean, when I was their age, the thought of going to bed with one of us would have horrified me." Just as he felt the first warm licks of the dope starting to massage his brain, George spotted the man who'd wandered past earlier, walking slowly back towards them.

"Not at all," he said. "I'm just glad there are people like that around." The stranger was only a few feet away, and as he returned George's smile, Alan was amazed by the whiteness of his teeth. George asked if he wanted to sit down.

"How can I say no to an offer like that?" He spoke with a broad Midlands accent.

"I could have sworn from the way you looked that you were a native," said George. "What a superb tan."

"Thanks," said the stranger. "Everybody thinks I'm Spanish. I just need to go out in the sun for a couple of hours and I go mahogany. Mediterranean blood, I think."

"I'm George, and this is my friend Alan." He waved casually at an empty chair with the hand in which he was holding the joint. "Please, have a drink with us."

"Mark," said the stranger, shaking their hands and sitting down. Alan was impressed by the firm grip and by the confidence in his face, which seemed to light the place up a little. He marvelled at the sheen of the skin, the pleasant lines of the eyebrows and nose. Then he realised that he was getting pretty squiffy off the joint, and was probably gaping like an idiot. His friend, who had obviously had enough too, held the thing up in Mark's direction–and then withdrew it, looking worried.

"Oh I'm sorry–perhaps you don't smoke dope." Mark laughed.

"Who doesn't these days? But what are two respectable gents like you doing with this?"

"One of our boys grows it in his broom cupboard," said George. "He has the full setup–hydroponics, special ultra-violet lights. We've found that it does wonders for our aches and pains." Alan nodded in agreement.

"Medicinal use only, you understand." At that moment Mark, who had taken a huge drag and inhaled it all, began coughing. Smoke billowed out of his mouth and nostrils. Alan handed him the Flaming Inferno and he drank some, but then reeled back as the combination of liqueurs hit his throat. He spluttered and coughed again, tears streaming down his face. George slapped him on the back and he slowly managed to regain his composure, eventually managing to speak in a hoarse, semi-whisper.

"Don't you think it might be a good idea for you guys to take things a little easier?" Alan nudged George playfully.

"Do you hear that? He wants us to be siting in our bath chairs in a quiet corner with a blanket over our knees, sucking peppermints." George laughed.

"Of course he does–but he's the one who looks like he's on his last legs, not us!"

"Here's to that." Alan raised his cup, noticing how well Mark's powerful-looking thighs filled up his trousers, and how beautifully the white cotton shirt rolled up at the sleeves accentuated the dark hairiness of his arms. He'd felt a pang of jealousy watching George pat the younger man on the back. Now the lad was looking across the plaza at a fairground ride not far away that had been set up for the carnival. It was called the Sky Rider and was designed to fling a spherical steel cage with two people strapped inside high into the air. The cage was suspended on cables between two enormous metal columns, lit by multicoloured neon lights, which towered above the surrounding buildings. At their base was a contraption that looked to Alan like the pipes of a church organ. It consisted of hundreds of metal springs–and was used to increase the tension of the cables. Once the cage was secured in place on a platform between the two columns, and the passengers had been fastened into the padded chairs inside, these springs would be slowly stretched. Then, at the moment when the tension reached its peak, the attendant would push a big red button and the cage would be catapulted into the night sky, flying high above the columns, before zooming back down between them and then bouncing up again. This would happen a few times before it came to rest, still some sixty or seventy feet in the air, bobbing and spinning above the crowd until it was lowered back to the ground. Mark shook his head, a wistful look in his eyes.

"My boyfriend Paul loved fairground rides. He'd have had me on there straight away."

Alan hated that kind of thing, and was happiest with both feet planted on terra firma. Just watching it shoot into the air made his heart beat faster. But if he accompanied Mark on the ride, he might be able to use it as an opportunity to invite him back to the hotel. And after all—how frightening could it be? He'd seen children going on it, so it couldn't be that bad. The alcohol and the dope coursing through his system helped complete the decision, for better or worse.

"Do you fancy going on it with me?" he asked. One of the attendants was running around among the crowd, trying to persuade someone else to have a go. George realised immediately what his friend was up to and chuckled bitterly.

"You're scared out of your wits by things like that, you silly old fool," he muttered. 'The last time you went on one you were as sick as a dog."

"Nonsense," said Alan. "I absolutely adore them—you've just never had the guts to accompany me."

"I'm not that keen to go on it anyway," said Mark, looking nervously from one to the other and suspecting that trouble was brewing.

"Really?" said Alan. "A fine man like you? I bet you're not scared of much." Maintaining eye contact with the younger man, Alan leaned forward and started rubbing and patting one of his legs. George thought for a second that he might start drooling on the faded denim. He found it quite an embarrassing display with a hint of desperation about it—and it seemed a bit rich too given that only moments before Alan had been criticising the old queen staying at their hotel, for making eyes at his young boyfriend in the dining room. Across the plaza two more people had been strapped into the Sky Rider, and were about to be sent on their way. As pumping dance music played the cage was enveloped in a cloud of smoke that hissed from an unseen nozzle, a strobe light flashed and the attendant pushed the red button, causing the thing to leap into the sky. The girl on board was a real screamer, letting out a piercing yell as they went up and not stopping when they regained their equilibrium and bounced around gently, high above the party crowds. For some reason the cage was left spinning and bobbing in mid air for longer than usual, and as it did so the pitch of the screaming kept changing, like the Doppler effect of a passing siren. Then with a jerk the cage was lowered back to the platform and the couple got out. The boy was laughing but his girlfriend wasn't very pleased–some of the people in the audience cheered and clapped as they walked down some steps and disappeared into the crowd.

"She obviously didn't think much of it," remarked George sniffily, finishing his coffee and placing the cup back on the table. Mark heard the disappointment behind the words and felt awful about the way things were going–but he had to admit that of the two he found Alan more attractive. George was very handsome but his friend had an extra allure that was difficult to explain. Maybe it was the air of corrupted authority he seemed to exude–the louche quality that lurked behind the posh accent and smart appearance. George sighed, adopting the expression of a long-suffering martyr.

"You go on lad–perhaps we can have a drink later."

"Okay then," said Mark. "I know I'll probably regret this, but why not?"

'That's the spirit!" Alan downed the last of his Flaming Inferno and jumped up, nearly tipping the table over as he did so, but managing to steady it with his hand. He turned around and advanced across the square towards the Sky Rider, waving some money at the attendant and shouting "Hey, boy!" at the top of his voice. Mark looked across the table and shrugged.

"Hope to see you later." He stood up and held himself erect like a man preparing to face his destiny with courage. George managed a smile.

"Yes I hope so too." He sat and watched as Mark headed reluctantly across the square and the crowd parted to let him walk through to the ride. It was so typical of Alan that in order to pull off a seduction he would end up going on some ridiculous Heath Robinson contraption that was bound to scare him half to death. Most people walked into a bar, picked out someone who seemed interesting and started chatting to them, but not Alan–never the easy way for him! George looked around for the waiter and waved to him.

"Night Juan," he called as he stood up and set off towards the crowd. As Alan and Mark were ushered through a gap in the metal barriers that had been set up to keep people back, George squeezed through the spectators until he was standing in front of a large video projection screen next to the ride. On it he could see a CCTV view of the interior of the metal cage, and through a loudspeaker nearby he could hear Alan talking to Mark as they clambered inside. He realised that there must be a microphone in there as well as a camera, so that the people on the ground could listen to the victims as they watched them go through their ordeal. The attendant leaned in and told them to keep their hands on the bar in front of them, even though they were held secure by padded harnesses that came down over their heads and were locked in place between their legs. He then rolled the cage backwards so that the two men were on their backs, looking directly up into the night sky. He stepped back, pushed a button, and an unseen mechanism began to pull the springs, building up the tension. Mark's eyes were tightly closed and George could see from the whiteness of his knuckles how tightly he was gripping the harness. Alan in contrast seemed quite happy, his eyes wide with child-like excitement as he looked around at the machinery. He smiled directly at the camera and the crowd cheered, delighted by the gameness of this plucky old bird. George could hear the metal springs making little pinging noises as they were stretched. Standing this close, he felt that the machine was more like a living creature, the stretching of the springs resembling a massive inhalation. The cage stirred slightly as the tension increased, and one of the attendants stepped forward to adjust its position slightly, making sure that it was perfectly balanced. George was fascinated that human beings would pour so much scientific knowledge into creating something designed to give such fleeting pleasure. The strobe started flashing and there was a hiss as smoke poured into the capsule, obscuring the view on the video screen. The crowd joined in with the attendant as he counted down from five, his thumb poised next to the big red button—then he pushed it.

What surprised George most was the lack of noise when the thing lifted off. There was a muted click as the locking mechanism disengaged, and then the cage took to the air with a sort of slow-motion poetry, like the faces of two people coming together to kiss. He caught an improbably glimpse of one of Alan's trouser legs flapping around his bare ankle as the cage shot upwards out of the smoke, then on the screen he was watching the lights of Playa Del Ingles fall away behind the two men. Inside the cage, Alan found the sensation of the ascent delightful. Down at ground level it had seemed quite noisy—there were the sounds of the machine itself, the cheering crowds, the music pumping out of the bars and the carnival show that had begun on the outdoor stage in the centre of the plaza. But as the cage rose those sounds became faint and all that could be heard was the cool air rushing past and the slight creaking of the contraption itself. Alan wished for a second that their ascent towards the stars would continue; that they would just fly up into orbit and leave everything behind. And what a view it was! He could see the whole of Playa Del Ingles stretching out in all directions, glittering at the foot of the dark mountains like a secret horde of treasure. In the distance the sea was a vast quicksilver lake illuminated by the intense moonlight, and he even made out the tall lighthouse of Maspalomas, standing proudly at the southernmost tip of the island. Alan was lost for a moment in the wonder of it all, but then he remembered where he was—and how much he hated heights. The elasticity in the springs had all been used up and the cage was now left bobbing around, pitching backwards and forwards like a rowing boat on a stormy sea. Alan tried to control the rising sensation of nausea by staring at his shoes but it didn't help. He caught a glimpse of the crowd far below as the cage rolled forward, then a fraction of a second later he was on his back again looking up at the stars. He swallowed hard to stop himself being sick, trying to forget the large meal he'd eaten earlier that night at the hotel, the copious drinks that had both preceded and followed it, and the marijuana he'd smoked. Mark, who was obviously unaffected by this kind of motion sickness, seemed unconcerned by what was happening.

"That was wonderful," he enthused. "Much better than I expected. How are you doing?" Alan's face was a rigid mask the colour and texture of raw tripe. He spoke through his teeth.

"Enjoyed the first bit, but all this hanging around is making me ill. Can I hold your hand?" Alan could see out of the corner of his eye that the younger man was smirking.

"Of course not—but I'd rather you held onto something else." Down on the ground the spectators tittered. George had seen and heard enough. The attendant pushed another button and the cage began its short journey back to the ground—but by the time it reached the platform George had disappeared into the crowd.

*

GEORGE Hope started his national service in November 1954. He was sent to Hillsea Barracks in Southsea for six weeks of basic training. He arrived along with a couple of dozen others at Portsmouth railway station—his suit too big for him but his shoes well polished. The ragged little group was soon blasted into shape by the powerful gush of air that was coming out of the sergeant major's mouth as he yelled at them on the platform. Throughout his life George would swear that his hair was blown back flat against his head by the force of it, as if he'd stepped into a wind tunnel or onto the deck of a ship during a particularly violent storm. It was a blustery afternoon and for the first time that year George felt the teeth of approaching winter in the chilly, damp air. There were grim faces all around when the conscripts saw the camp. Inside the perimeter fence a forlorn collection of surprisingly flimsy-looking buildings was spread out across a dank, monochrome landscape. There was an enormous concrete parade ground, and roads that disappeared off into the murk. As they got out and walked into the mess hall he caught the scent of fresh mud, and was reminded of the sports fields at school. George and his new band of comrades were assigned to a wooden accommodation block made up of four dormitories and a big communal bathroom, all joined together by a central corridor. The mood was bleak because this was the first time most of the lads had been away from home, and also their first brush with military discipline. Some withdrew into themselves, heads down, simply going through the motions of what had to be done, while others tried to kindle some bonhomie among the young men they would be living with for the time being. George had been in the school cadets so he already had a good idea of what was to come. His was an optimistic personality, and to him this whole experience was just another adventure, like a scout camp or a few days' hiking in the wilds.

One particular evening, several weeks after his arrival at Hillsea, he was sitting on his bed polishing his boots. The radio was tuned to the Home Service and a few of the others were lying on their bunks–smoking, reading or cleaning their gear like George. Some of the lads had gone to the NAAFI club. Going through his evening routine George achieved a sorted of contented, meditative state. They spent their days being shouted at and pushed to the limit by the instructors, so the few hours of peace and quiet were most welcome. Wood and coal burned in a small stove in the middle of the dormitory, warding off the coldness coming from the ground, a few feet beneath the wooden floor. George finished his boots off and laid them under the bed, as he did every evening. He was now ready to have a shave–after which he would come back and lie on the bed and smoke and read. His stubble grew slowly enough at that age to allow him to shave each night instead of having to jostle with the others for a basin in the morning. He stripped down to the waist and hung his towel around his neck, then took his washing bag out of the metal locker next to the bed. George had always been whippet-thin but in the past couple of years he had started to fill out and now, although he was still slim, he had quite a lithe, well-shaped body. Out in the corridor it was cooler and there was a strong, musty smell. The floorboards had seen better days, and getting a splinter in the foot on the way to the toilet was such a hazard that it was worth putting your boots on if you had to go to in the middle of the night, even though you would probably wake everyone up as you clumped down the corridor. As he walked to the bathroom, he could see into the other dormitories and hear snatches of conversation, laughter and men moving around. George always felt a deep sense of harmony when he was surrounded by men. He had been brought up in a small terraced house in Warrington with three elder sisters, and although he loved them very much, the constant exposure to females at close quarters often left him yearning to get away. He and his father would go fishing or walking together and not say anything for hours, and it gave them both immense pleasure. Throughout his life he would have these odd moments–such as sitting with a pint of beer in a bar full of blokes, or lying in a Turkish bath listening to the gentle sound of conversation in the hot room next door, when that same sense of contentment would return.

The bathroom was empty, as he'd hoped it would be at this time of the evening. The sinks were lined up against the wall, and he chose a specific one near the far end because he knew that although the mirror above it was cracked like all the others, the damage wasn't quite so bad and he would be more able to see what he was doing. He turned the tap on and swooshed his palm around the cracked porcelain, feeling the imperfections in the bowl, then he stuck the plug in and there was the usual frantic babbling sound as the basin filled up and he splashed the water around briskly. He took out his shaving soap and brush and started to work up a lather. Just as he was beginning to smooth the foam onto his face another man came in. The fellow smiled and said hello as he strode directly over to the showers. George watched in the mirror as the stranger unfurled the towel wrapped around his waist and threw it with a flourish over a peg sticking out of the tiled wall nearby. The lad turned on the shower and shrieked loudly.

"Christ," he said, "no matter how much I try to prepare myself mentally before I come down here, it always takes my breath away."

"I know," said George, continuing to apply shaving foam to his chin. "What we need is a tin bath that we can put in front of one of the stoves, and fill up with hot water from the kettle."

"Sounds fucking marvellous," said the stranger, soaping himself down. He was taller than George and he looked quite dashing with his wet hair all standing on end, stark naked and smiling across the bathroom. There was a certain confidence, almost a brazen quality about him. George looked him over slowly and placed his shaving brush back down on the rim of the sink, choosing his words carefully to keep them neutral.

"I find that if I stay in there for more than five minutes my whole body goes numb." The stranger turned off the water, grabbed the towel, and started rubbing himself vigorously. Red marks appeared on the firm, smooth skin. He kept his eyes on what he was doing.

"It makes your private parts all shrivel up," he said. "When I come out, I can't see what I've got anymore." George glanced downwards as the lad moved the towel over his thighs. He spoke quietly.

"It doesn't look all that shrivelled up to me." The stranger stopped what he was doing and stood up straight. His smile had become a smirk.

"You should see it when it's warm. That would bring a tear to your eye." George was suddenly unsure about this. The other lad's comments about his private parts could be read as signals–but there was always the chance that this was a set-up, and that if George went too far he could get himself into trouble. But there was something about this chap's friendliness–the way he smiled when he came into the bathroom and the way he stripped off so unashamedly–that seemed to suggest there was no danger here, so George decided to take a risk. If things went wrong, he could always claim that there'd been some sort of misunderstanding. After all, he wasn't the one flashing himself about.

"Maybe you'll have to show me some time," said George. The other was still smiling.

"Would you like that?"

"Might do."

"What if I wanted to see yours in return?"

"I'm sure that can be arranged." The lad stepped out of the shower.

"Look–I'd better stop distracting you or you'll cut yourself to ribbons." He wrapped the towel around himself and walked forward to shake hands. "My name's Alan by the way, Alan Reid."

"George Hope–pleased to meet you." Alan stepped back and looked at the door, speaking with his voice lowered.

"Not here, eh? Too many other people about–but we'll get our chance I'm sure."

Their sexual encounters were always rushed because even when the dormitory block was quiet, there was always the fear that someone would come in and catch them. Full sex was of course impossible, but both would have loved to try it. Once or twice they managed to arrange things so they went out on night patrol together, but the danger of discovery was still there–remote as it may have been. The instructors liked to sneak up on recruits during their stints on sentry duty, to see if they remained alert in the small hours, when the body's defences were at their weakest. As it was, close friendships were not necessarily seen in the military context as evidence of homosexuality, so George and Alan were able to shield their affection from public suspicion with plenty of boisterous tomfoolery. The new recruits had two instructors who often groped each other but no one thought anything of it, because there was always a steady flow of background chatter about women. Girlfriends, prostitutes, sisters of friends–even mothers of friends–nobody cared what kind of woman you talked about, as long as you made it clear that you had some kind of experience with the opposite sex.

Once their training finished they got posted to different places. George went over to Northern Ireland and ultimately got his commission, Alan ended up at a Central Ordnance depot in Shropshire, looking after thousands of pieces of military equipment for the Army. But despite the separation they stayed in touch, often writing long letters. Other men in George's platoon used to kid him about having an affair with a secret girl, and it would have been completely unfeasible to tell them he was in fact writing to another man. He and Alan were unable to meet up until two years later, when they went on a camping holiday together in the Lake District. They were blessed with the most fantastic weather, and fit and strong as they were, managed to cover a huge amount of ground. Sca Fell, Helvellyn, Haystacks, Great Gable, they climbed them all. They drank pints of bitter in the local pubs, ate heartily, and slept together in the way they had always hoped to. But as they caught the train home each had different feelings about what had passed. To George the experience had been a revelation, and he knew then that what he wanted more than anything else was to share his life with another man. He had no idea how it was going to happen or even if it was possible, but that was what he would aim for. Alan on the other hand was gripped by doubt. He did love George but the concealed nature of the romance irked him, and ultimately the physical consummation had left him with a vague sense of disgust. A few months earlier he had met a girl called Marjorie, and they'd started going out with each other. It was wonderful to be intimate in public, to hold hands or kiss and to know that people would see nothing wrong with it. Marjorie was brilliant company–she made him laugh, she spoke of things that interested him, she made him feel like a man for the first time in his life. Alan saw other men look at her and felt delighted that she had chosen to be with him. Of course George knew all about Marjorie, because Alan had told him in his letters. He knew they were sweethearts, and he had probably understood deep down that they would get married in the end, but such knowledge can exist alongside a certain amount of self-delusion. In George's case, the glorious Lake District trip served to fuel that denial, and made him disregard the weight of evidence that proved where his friend's affections were going.

And so when Alan asked him to be his best man some weeks later, George was unprepared for the wave of desolation that engulfed him. Alan broke the news of the wedding to him in a pub in Shrewsbury. Marjorie and a group of her friends were there and the mood was quite naturally one of celebration. As he accepted Alan's invitation, it took every ounce of George's inner strength to mask his feelings. He thought he'd done a pretty good job, and decades went by before Marjorie told him one night that he had in fact turned a bluish-white colour when he heard the news: a change of hue that gave the game away somewhat. The wedding took place the following year. There was an expectant murmur at the reception as George stood to give his speech. He ran his fingers through his hair and spoke with a slightly resigned air.

"Well, I don't know about you chaps, but I have to confess to feeling a trifle jealous of the bridegroom." There were cheers and a round of applause, and afterwards people said it was one of the wittiest speeches they had ever heard. But later George left the dancing and the laughter and the light behind him as he headed out into the gardens to get some air. He sat down under a tree with his back to the hall where the party was going on, and lit a cigarette. The music provided a welcome accompaniment to his thoughts. He no longer felt sad about Alan getting married–in fact, in the months leading up the wedding he realised that it probably was the best thing for his friend. He had also decided that fighting against the progression of events could only lead to isolation and bitterness. But the nature of the occasion, one of the milestones of life, did force him to meditate on his own existence. Alan's decision to get married did not anger George–but what did seem unjust was that his friend had been presented with a choice, when he had not. For George the only option was to accept his homosexuality. He was not physically drawn to women at all, and to allow a relationship to develop with a girl when such an attraction was absent seemed inexcusable–the masquerade would permeate and subvert everything that followed. Evidently Alan's sexuality was less clear-cut, and he had been able to fall in love with Marjorie. George imagined that his friendship with Alan would fizzle out somewhat–after all, Alan now had the duties of the married man to attend to. In the years to come there would be children and anyway, the social life of married couples generally involved other married couples. And George believed that on some level Marjorie sensed the way he had felt about her husband–and was ever so gently pushing him away. During the evening, many people had asked George when he intended to marry, and of course he had said vague things about meeting the right woman, and how he would do so in good time, but what he really wanted to say was: "never". That was the basic problem–he was surrounded by love but the people who loved him had expectations that differed vastly from his own. So his choice boiled down to staying in the midst of all this and living half a life or admitting that his future lay elsewhere, and preparing to move on. But where to? Did the way of life he needed exist anywhere? As he considered the thought he noticed the glow of a cigarette, in the darkness some way off among the trees. The pinprick of orange light became more intense for a few seconds as the person smoking it took a drag, then it fell back to waist level, more subdued once again. George decided to try an experiment. He stretched out his arm and waved his own cigarette in a big arc above his head. Immediately the cigarette in the trees was lifted up and moved back and forth in the air. George wandered over–and thought he could make out one of the bride's cousins, a nice-looking chap who was in the Merchant Navy, standing behind a bush. They had exchanged lingering glances in church, so George wasn't particularly surprised that he was here. The lad had probably seen him leaving the hall and followed him outside. George smiled as he approached. My future, he thought, starts now.

*

GEORGE drifted around the Yumbo Centre, passing bars he and Alan often visited. Because they all opened out onto the central plaza he could see clearly what was going on inside each one as he walked by. From a distance they looked like a row of stage sets, each differently lit and with its own scene being played out–variations on the same theme. Young waiters and waitresses zipped back and forth between candle-lit tables, their trays filled with cocktails, jugs of sangria, and slender glasses of cold beer. Expectant faces looked out at those who walked past while simultaneously the passers-by looked in, trying to decide if a particular place was worth a visit. As George walked along the music from one bar gave way to the music of the next, so he heard a bit of pop, then some salsa melding into pumping dance music–then jumping out and striking an altogether different chord, a Strauss waltz. It was like a free-form eclectic DJ mix; a queer soundtrack to accompany the workings of his mind, but somehow it worked because there were a lot of different things going on in there. He was angry that Alan had hijacked his attempt to seduce Mark–partly because of the betrayal itself, but also because he felt that he'd been deprived of a chance to spend the evening with a decent guy. Throughout their lives, very little had come between George and Alan, and yet here they were suddenly at odds with each other. He wondered if all the attention they received in Gran Canaria was doing them any good. Back in England they were plain old Alan Reid and George Hope, two affable buffers; stalwarts of the British Legion and the Over Sixties club who were treated with respect by most of the inhabitants of their small village. But here in this strange gay scene of Playa del Ingles, where things were turned on their head and it was the old buffers who became the sex symbols, they were like stars in front of an adoring audience–in the spotlight, puffed up beyond all recognition. A few nights earlier, someone had told Alan and George that Gran Canaria would be incomplete without them. And although it was meant as a compliment the comment disturbed George because it implied that somehow they had become part of the island, nothing more perhaps than two attractions in a neon-lit menagerie. How much of their old selves had they already sacrificed? He was reminded of the faded and peeling poster stuck to the tiles above the urinal in Hummel Hummel that had printed on it: "Attention! The dark room is not controlled by the waiters, so please be careful of your values." A slip of the pen, committed no doubt by someone whose grasp of English was less than perfect, but it raised a valid point–had they been careful of their values? The answer was less than clear.

George smiled as he walked along, wondering why he was being so serious. This was just a holiday resort where people came to let their hair down in the sunshine for a couple of weeks. And it was impossible to stay angry with Alan for long. The poor chap had been through such a miserable time over the past few years, George could hardly begrudge him sex with Mark–even if he had been angling for it himself. The night was still young and there would be more opportunities. He turned the corner and saw the dim interior of Hummel Hummel. The tables outside were already quite full; the murmur of dozens of conversations in different languages reached his ears. George had always thought the name of the bar had something to do with those little porcelain figurines called hummels that some people collected, but then someone told him that hummel was also the German word for bumble bee. The implication was that the people in the bar were like bees buzzing around a honeycomb. George liked both explanations, but the hum of conversation as he approached certainly fitted more with the one about the bee hive.

Several young men watched him closely as he walked under the awning and squeezed his way through the tables towards the bar. He felt their eyes upon him but he looked straight ahead, remembering a comment Alan had once made about smiling so much one night at strangers in Hummel Hummel that he had started to get cramp in his face. He needed a drink but he decided to have a quick look around before he settled down. The bar itself was in the centre of the room, so that people could sit all the way around it. He walked through to the back, where there was a stage and the entrances to the video rooms and toilets. Sweeping aside a thick curtain rather like a patchwork quilt, he found himself inside a narrow chamber about five feet wide and fifteen feet long. Alan had a penchant for giving things nicknames and had called this room the Cabinet of Doctor Caligari, after the old black and white German horror film. It was L shaped, so that there was an area at the far end that was around the corner, out of view. The walls were painted black and the flickering screen of a large and dilapidated television mounted on a bracket high up in the corner provided the only illumination. There were tall bar stools arranged along the wall on the right hand side, and the far end was mirrored so that one could just–if the image on the TV was fairly bright–get an idea of what was going on around the corner. George could see an indefinite number of bodies there, a cluster of shadows shifting in the warm dimness. He heard the clink of a belt buckle being undone, some heavy breathing and a gasp. It seemed pretty packed and George had no desire to linger. The porn films they showed in this room all featured older men, and so held no attraction for George–but even so it was always worth checking in there because over the years he had met several nice young men, genuine aficionados of the mature male body, sitting alone watching the films. That was more likely to happen later, when Hummel Hummel was quieter and most of the customers had moved elsewhere. He pulled the curtain aside, touching it gingerly because he had seen people wiping their hands on it as they left, and emerged blinking back into the bar. To his right and left were the backs of men sitting on stools, hunched over their drinks. A couple of men were leaning against the wall, monitoring who was going in and out of the video room. That was the most effective technique, to hang around until you saw someone nice going in and then pounce–because at least then you got a good look at the person you hoped to liaise with in the darkness.

George decided to try the other video room. It was larger than the first because in there they showed the films featuring younger men–which were more popular. The room was oblong in shape with a higher ceiling, and stools around three of the four walls. At the back was another curtain which led into perhaps the strangest room of all, tiny and pitch-black, always infernally hot and crammed full of writhing bodies. Alan called it the Chamber of Horrors, and George never bothered with it because the only time he had gone in, a thief had taken his wallet from the pocket of his trousers when they were around his ankles. George could see in the bluish, insubstantial light from the television screen in the corner that most of the stools were occupied. He recognised the faces, because the same people were always in here. They arrived like night watchmen coming in to relieve the day shift and sat watching the porn films, their heads all swivelling in unison whenever someone moved the curtain aside and entered the room. It seemed alien to George to refuse to take part in the social interactions going on in the bar outside, and instead sit in here waiting. These poor fellows had obviously never experienced the thrill of the chase. George went back outside and found an empty stool at the bar. As he sat down a waiter materialized in front of him, wiping the marble bar top and laying down a couple of coasters. George ordered a large beer and then looked up and saw, on a television screen fixed to the ceiling above the bar, an image of a naked older man. He wrinkled his face in disgust, cursing himself for having sat at the wrong end yet again, and looked around. The place was like an ancient chandler's shop that someone had converted into a gay bar, but that was what gave it so much charm. The interior had been panelled with wood decades ago, but more recently large areas had been covered with mirrors. In fact, the whole bar was a bizarre mixture of things that had obviously been there since the beginning, and things that had been added over the years. Part of the ceiling had a fishing net attached to it, with spotlights above beaming down to the floor. In another area there was a hi-tech steel mesh frame with hundreds of fluorescent streamers hanging off it. An old ship's anchor hung in a dark corner, while above the bar tiny illuminated fibre-optic strands sprouted from the ceiling, changing colour in the way that coral undulates as the sea's currents pass over a reef. Above the stage was a large glitterball that had stopped spinning. The myriad beams reflected off it were frozen in time–splaying outwards towards table tops, walls, the cigarette machine and the velvet curtain behind the stage. The many different types of lighting were underpinned by ultra-violet, which seemed to get stronger in certain areas, intensifying the contrast between white hair and dark suntans and making teeth glow in improbable colours.

When George was younger he used to try to project himself onto places like this and the people inside them. If he saw someone who looked appealing he would initiate a conversation, or at least smile and try to attract his attention. He used to enjoy being the one who took the action, rather than being acted upon, but now he was content to sit back and watch the faces, to read the crowd. Invariably when George did that some kind of opportunity would come along. It was like drawing a magic circle or a pentagram on the ground and waiting for a spirit to coalesce inside it. At that moment he realised it was happening already. A young man at the other end of the room was smiling at him. When he was on his way through the bar George had seen the lad sitting on a high stool at the circular table tucked into the corner. He had thick eyebrows, black hair, and vaguely Arabic features and he was wearing a brown shirt made out of a heavy material that looked as if it would be velvety to the touch. This was unbuttoned in a rakish way, revealing a deeply tanned and hairy chest. George smiled back at the stranger, thinking that these things always began with a smile—but seldom ended with one. The man slid off his stool and approached.

"I don't believe someone as good-looking as you can be here alone," he said with an obvious German accent. "May I join you?" George looked at his watch.

"I'm meeting some friends later, but by all means join me for a drink." It was unwise to appear too keen.

"Thank you," said the lad. "My name is Manfred." George gave his large and slightly clammy hand a shake. Manfred flagged down the young barman and ordered a mineral water. "Would you like a drink?"

"Just bought one, thanks."

"I saw you going into the video room," said Manfred as he sat down, "and I thought, damn it, another one I've missed out on. I don't like it in there because you can't see anybody properly and if anything happens you end up surrounded by voyeurs. For me it is truly awful." He sliced his hand through the air as he spoke the last few words, to emphasise the point he was making.

"I know," George replied. "I only go in to see what film is on." Manfred chuckled.

"One of the waiters here occasionally goes into the dark room to make sure there are no glasses lying around. He takes a torch with him like a cinema usherette. So when he goes in there's a commotion, all these people thinking that maybe the police have arrived, or suddenly seeing for the first lime the person they are with and not liking it. Very funny."

"Yes," said George. "People arrive here and go straight into the video room without buying a drink, and don't come out again until the place is about to close–it seems like a strange way to spend the evening." As he spoke, George noticed that Manfred continued to look around the bar. He possessed what Alan would call a restless eye. Perhaps he was looking for something better. George had a strong dislike for bad manners and decided in that instant that sex with him was out of the question–but there was no point in being unfriendly.

"Have you been here long?" he asked. "I don't think I've seen you before." Manfred took a sip of his drink. "I'm here with my lover, Max. We arrived yesterday. He is still a bit tired so I came out alone for a drink, and then of course I met this very handsome Englishman." He winked. "Is this your first time in Gran Canaria?"

"Oh no–my friend Alan and I have been coming here for a couple of years now. Last year we came twice, in February and November."

"I always like to come twice," said Manfred, repeating his wink and breaking into hearty laughter at his own crude pun. George smiled but said nothing. "This friend of yours," Manfred continued, "is he as sexy as you are?"

"That depends on how you define sexy. He's in his sixties and has white hair, like me. He used to be very handsome." A great big grin was spreading across Manfred's face which George found slightly unnerving.

"Would the two of you be interested in coming to live with me?"

"What?"

"I want you to live with me, but not as a lover. I have an idea for a business that I want to set up and I think you could be part of it."

George thought: I must stop smoking this dope because when I do conversations always seem to take a turn for the surreal.

"I'm not sure that I follow you," he managed eventually.

"I want to provide a service for people with tastes like mine–who love only older men." Manfred leaned forward and lowered his voice, as if he was about to let George in on a great secret. "Let's say you're a business man or woman and you find yourself staying alone in a big city. If you want some company for the evening all you have to do is pick up the phone and call an escort agency, and you can have a nice young man knocking at the door within an hour. I know that's something a good-looking man like you has probably never had to do." George laughed.

"Flattery will get you everywhere."

"I hope so. But you see, these places never have older men on their books, men with silver hair. They think that if you ask for an older man, you want someone in his forties, not someone in his fifties or sixties, and that's a big gap in the market. Think about all the guys in bars like this one, who would be more than happy to pay for the company of a fine older gentleman. Well, I intend to be the first person to offer that kind of service." Manfred went on to explain that he intended to buy a big house in Berlin or Cologne and refurbish it with a bar and pleasant accommodation, like a high class bed and breakfast. The older men he recruited would be allowed to live there and through some kind of arrangement would receive a salary to provide services to customers. Any surplus money would be re-invested in the project. "I'm going to take from it only the money I need to live," he concluded. "What do you think?" George let the idea wash around for a few moments.

"It sounds interesting–but what makes you think that we would want to give up our lives back home to come and be your... whores?" Manfred waved his arms above his head.

"What have you got to lose? If you're no longer working then it's no problem. You could keep your house in England or even rent it out. Or you could spend a few weeks working for me and then fly home to relax in your own place. You could be as flexible as you wanted about it."

"Have you managed to persuade anyone to get involved?"

"Of course! I've already got a retired librarian, another guy who used to be a lorry driver–and even a man who was once the mayor of a small town in Bavaria. At the moment I'm looking for suitable places to set it up."

"The mind boggles. Well, I wish you luck. You certainly sound like you've done your research, but I can't see Alan wanting to get involved with that. He has a grown up family, and isn't quite as comfortable with things as I am." Manfred looked disappointed.

"And you?"

"I don't know. It's a lot to take in. I've got a good life and I'm not sure I want to disrupt it."

George had to admit that his life did lack something–but could this really fill the gap? These other men who had signed up obviously thought so. It was certainly a radical solution to the post-retirement blues. His doctor had recommended that he get plenty of exercise and take up a new hobby, but George doubted whether working as some kind of courtesan was quite what he had in mind. Manfred took out a business card and laid it on the bar top.

"Think about it. I'm here in Gran Canaria for two weeks, and if you decide that you want to try it out once you've gone home, you can call me or send me an email." George looked down at the classy cream-coloured card, with its embossed gold lettering. How many people had these been presented to... and how many had taken up Manfred's crazy offer?

"I will," he said, thinking that it was high time for another look in the video room.

*

GEORGE had only had one live-in lover in his whole life. He'd met Jason one day when he was in the city, taking care of some business. It was nearly an hour until the next train back home, so he popped into the pub at the back of the railway station for a quick pint. The main post office was nearby and many of the Royal Mail workers came in during the afternoon when their shifts ended. Jason walked through the door wearing his postie's uniform, relating lurid details of how he was trying to seduce a woman who worked on the switchboard–all bold and manly in the way he dumped his bag near the bar and slapped one of his friends on the back. The rough and tumble of the episode seemed a trifle staged and there was something in the way the lad, when he looked across the room, maintained eye contact with George for just a fraction of a second longer than he should have. George had nothing planned for the rest of the day so on impulse he decided to linger in the bar, sitting in the corner with his pint and his evening paper, to see how things developed. Gradually Jason's friends dispersed, and within an hour he was standing on his own at the bar, smiling across at George. They chatted, and it transpired that he had worked at the post office for a couple of years, living with his aunt and uncle. He'd never known his father, and his mother had died of cancer when he was in his early teens. There was a slightly brittle quality about the way in which he explained the circumstances of his life, an indicator perhaps that all was not well beneath the surface, but in every other respect he seemed like a smashing lad: funny, fresh and full of life. On a whim George invited Jason over to the house for dinner, and that was how the affair began.

At first they met only at the weekends. Jason would arrive at the tiny railway station a few miles from George's village on a Saturday afternoon, smiling from ear to ear when he saw the older man's bright red Triumph TR4 parked at the kerb, then laughing in the passenger seat as they zoomed back home, the top down, George piloting them expertly through the twisting lanes. Jason would stay until Sunday evening, when they'd return to the station, the car moving somewhat slower, its occupants a trifle subdued. Six months later Jason gave up his job and moved in. But despite his charisma and the fact that he was some of the best sex George had ever had, he was a young man in the grip of demons. He hated being homosexual, and ultimately what for George was the perfect situation was for Jason a constant reminder of a side of himself that he would rather have been able to forget. The fact that he was suddenly out here in the country, away from his friends and the underpinning routine of his work at the post office, made things worse. The plan had been for him to help out with George's market gardening business, but that proved difficult because he often argued about what should be done. Within a year George was being rudely awoken from his great dream of gay domesticity. Jason came to help out at work less and less frequently, and took to lying in bed until the late afternoon. Occasionally he would go into the city and disappear for several days–and there would be no telephone calls, no clue at all as to where he had gone. There were bouts of heavy drinking, tantrums, and even violence–although fortunately he was physically no match for George, who was usually able to restrain him before he did any serious damage. It all came to a head one night when George had some friends over to dinner and Jason lay in bed upstairs, refusing to come downstairs, incoherent on booze and pills, banging on the floor and screaming for George to bring him a glass of water. The next day George asked him to leave. When Jason realised he was serious he became spiteful, saying he intended to tell his relatives about what had been going on, and claim that he'd been made to have sex against his will by the older man–but George's suspicion that this was an empty threat was borne out by the fact that nobody ever came around to the house to challenge him. George was terribly depressed about Jason's departure–his usually buoyant temperament swamped by the fundamental bleakness of what had happened. He had continued to love the lad through all the ugliness–hanging on despite everything to the memory of the bright young guy in his postman's uniform who smiled at him across the bar. The affair had given him a glimpse of the life he craved but left him feeling more than ever that it was out of reach, that it might always be unattainable. But despite the sense of desolation and loneliness, he carried on from day to day, working, eating and sleeping, doing his domestic chores–forcing himself to keep going.

One Sunday the following June, Alan Reid telephoned to ask for George's help with an old petrol-engined lawnmower that he had found in the shed and was trying to get going. Alan explained that he'd taken the machine to pieces and cleaned off all the thick lumps of dried grass and muck–but he could make no sense of the torn and faded instruction manual he'd discovered rolled up in a jam jar on the window sill, and so was not only unable to work out why it wouldn't start, but also incapable of putting the components back together. George was never happier than when he was in his garage, his fingers blackened with grease as he dismantled things, replaced their worn parts and re-assembled them so they ran better than ever before. He had spent the morning working on the TR4 which, during the sparkling early days of their romance, Jason had christened Doris. The car was now standing in the driveway all cleaned and polished, with the oil changed and the hydraulic systems bled and topped up with fluid, so that the clutch and brakes would be nice and crisp. The work had made him hungry so he decided to eat some sandwiches and have a cup of tea before starting out. It was one of the first really sunny days of the summer but there was also a heaviness about it as if a storm was brewing. There'd been a lot of rain in the past week and the leaves on the trees seemed to have an especially intense greenness about them. As he walked back to the house the sound of the birds was incredible, the sweet smells of sap and pollen contributing to the thickness of the air, the fecundity of the atmosphere. Strange patterns danced before his eyes as he moved from the brightness outside to the comparative dimness and coolness of the house. He washed his hands but left his overalls on, because he was in all likelihood only going to end up getting mucky again in Alan's garden shed. As he sat alone eating, George's thoughts turned to sex. The arrival of summer had left him hopelessly randy, and Jason's departure meant that he was more or less unable to get it fully out of his system. He'd been cottaging a few times, but his heart wasn't in it. Those encounters could provide a short-lived relief but in order to have really satisfying sex George had to develop some kind of rapport with the other person. Just a few words would do; it didn't have to be a candle-lit dinner or anything like that. Plus the element of danger that seemed to excite everyone else–the possibility that at any moment the police might appear–was a big turn-off for George. And there was Doris. There weren't any other bright red Triumph convertibles knocking around in these parts, and if people spotted the car parked outside a certain public lavatory or abandoned in some notorious lay-by, tongues would wag. He suspected that it was this kind of complexity that drove most homosexual men to move to the city where they would have a certain degree of anonymity, but he loved the country and the idea of giving it up held no appeal at all, especially on a day like this. Besides, his business and his best friend–the two mainstays of his life–were both here. He was pleased that Alan had invited him over for the afternoon because it had been a few weeks since they'd met up, and it was always nice to see Marge and the kids. It was also a real pleasure to take Doris out for a spin on a Sunday when the roads were quieter. It was mainly psychological he knew but the car always felt tighter, somehow smoother and more sure-footed, after he'd been working on it. He washed up his dishes and headed back out into the sunshine. George put the old leather doctor's bag in which he carried tools onto the passenger seat, then slid in behind the steering wheel and pushed the starter button. The engine roared into life. In the years to come he would own cars with electronic ignition that didn't start as well as Doris.

"Keen as mustard," he said to himself, grinning as he released the handbrake and headed towards the gates. Turning left onto the lane, he resisted the urge to push the car too hard because it wasn't fully warmed up yet. The exhaust sound was like a fat black insect buzzing just behind his left ear as he climbed through second gear into third, slowing down again as he approached the main road. There were no other cars coming so he pulled out without stopping, the wind starting to rush around his head as the car smoothly picked up speed. Up ahead he saw a bus lumbering along, making heavy weather of the road's slight uphill gradient. Zipping up through the gears, he was approaching the rear of the larger vehicle within seconds. There was nothing coming from the opposite direction so he was able to overtake it without lifting his foot off the accelerator, the speed climbing now up to seventy miles an hour–which felt pretty fast in a car so close to the ground–at which point he flicked the switch on the top of the gear lever, activating the overdrive. There was a barely perceptible lurch as the higher gear kicked in and the sound of the engine dropped from a growl to a purr. Such a manoeuvre always made George feel invincible, as if he was the king of the road, rocketing along in this wonderful machine with its gleaming paintwork and chrome, its rasping steel exhaust and its fan heater blowing smells of petrol, leather and engine oil up his leg.

Alan and Marge lived on the outskirts of the nearest town, which was reached from the east by a road which wound its way through farmers' fields, woods and several small villages, before straightening out for the last few miles. Not much traffic came in from this direction, so the road had never been upgraded. There were plenty of twists and turns, giving him the opportunity to test the car's handling, changing down a gear and pushing his foot to the floor, keeping the power on all the way through the bends. The tarmac was dry so he was unlikely to come unstuck–unless of course he lost his nerve and lifted his foot off the accelerator. Closer to town the road straightened out, but for the last mile or so it traversed a series of small hills, the result of subsidence caused by the mining that once took place in the area. Coming out of the final curve before this stretch, he allowed the needle on the rev counter to rise almost to the red line, then changed up to fourth and continued to accelerate. The car would be forced downwards at the bottom of each dip, the G-force compressing the suspension until George's bottom was only a few inches the ground, then he would zoom up towards the crest of the next hill, where the car would almost take off and he'd experience an instant of weightlessness that seemed to make his genitals float for a fraction of a second inside his underpants before gravity was restored. At the end of the straight stretch, within sight of the speed limit signs at the outskirts of the town, he slowed down. The whole journey took less than ten minutes but it always left him in a good mood. He passed a caravan site, allotments, a sports pitch, and a small wood in which men were rumoured to hang around looking for sex, but where George had never met anyone except once, when he came across a bunch of young lads of no sexual interest whatsoever, who'd set up a rope swing between the trees and lit a fire. Hardly Hampstead Heath, thought George as he turned into Alan's road. He tucked the car in expertly right next to the kerb, grabbed his leather bag and jumped out. The house was a three-storey affair built at the end of the previous century that looked as if it could do with some repairs. The window frames, which were blistered and peeling, needed to be stripped and painted, and in places the masonry ought to have been re-pointed. The tiny front garden was overgrown and the front door, which was painted a dismal maroon colour and could also have done with some TLC, was open. Alan was standing at the gate in his shorts and a ragged summer shirt looking out into the street, his face creased with seriousness as if there was something weighing on his mind. He waved and called out as George approached.

"Car's looking good!"

"Thanks. I washed and polished it this morning." Alan laughed.

"The usual Sunday routine, eh?"

"The usual routine. What are you doing out here? Don't say you've been waiting for me–surely the lawnmower situation isn't that desperate."

"Of course not! I was just seeing off Marge and the kids. They've gone to visit the in-laws for the afternoon. They'd only just left when you came around the corner." George reached the front steps and they shook hands.

"Shame. I was looking forward to seeing them."

"They were sad to miss you too. But the visit to Marge's parents was arranged last week and they had to get going."

"Not to worry. Why don't you bring the family over to mine for tea next weekend?"

"I'm sure they'd love that." They walked into the house and Alan closed the front door. "Do you want something to drink or shall we go straight down to the shed?"

"I had lunch before I left so I'm okay for now," said George, noticing how well Alan looked. "You've got good colour."

"Thanks. Took the kids down to the coast yesterday. It was absolutely gorgeous. I hope we get a few more days like that before the summer's out." George followed Alan along the hall and into the kitchen, where they continued through a side-door into a wood-framed conservatory–then out into the garden itself. "How are you doing?" George shrugged.

"Things have been a bit flat since Jason left, but I'm getting on with life. I keep myself busy. You know what they say about idle hands and all that." Alan laughed and stuck his tongue out in a slightly coquettish way. There was something nervy about him, an air of preoccupation.

"Been getting any sugar in your tea?"

"Not really," said George. "I don't go to the pubs or baths very often, and you know cottaging was never my scene." Alan nodded but said nothing. They reached the shed and he yanked the door open. The hinges made an agonising squealing sound and a bank of hot air which smelled of creosote and compost hit them full in the face. The sunshine on the tin roof had turned the place into a miniature oven.

"Christ," said George. "I hope you don't keep anything flammable in here!" Two flies, stupefied by the heat and exhausted by buzzing at the window, flew lazily out of the dim interior into the open air. Alan walked through the door and gestured towards the dismantled lawnmower, which he'd left in the far corner, and leaned on the workbench at the other end of the shed. George stooped down for a closer look, sliding his fingers over the flaking green enamel paint that had been sprayed onto the metal chassis of the machine. It needed a thorough clean but was actually in pretty good condition, with only a few patches of rust. The blades themselves were still quite sharp. George began going though the mental checklist he always applied to mechanical things that weren't working. Was the flywheel moving? Was the fuel line blocked? What condition was the spark plug in? Within a few seconds he was totally absorbed, and it wasn't until he turned around to get something out of his bag that he saw Alan standing there naked. He wasn't entirely surprised because of the way his friend had been behaving. He stayed on his haunches and smiled up at a face heavy with sexual need. Alan's voice had a slightly frantic edge as he spoke quietly through his teeth, almost pleading and unable to make eye contact.

"Come on George, I really need this and I know you do too. Just once, eh, for old time's sake?" George stood up and unbuttoned the front of his overalls, then moved to where Alan was standing. Dirty fingers made contact with warm skin and their lips came together for the first time in fifteen years.

*

ALAN Reid walked briskly up the Avenida Tirajana towards the Yumbo Centre, hoping to catch his friend George before he disappeared off with some young man for the night. His liaison had not been a success. He and Mark had taken a taxi to the lad's apartment, which was at the far end of the Avenida, near a large luxury hotel called the Riu Palace. Alan had felt fine as they walked to the taxi rank, but when the car doors closed and the short journey began, a weight seemed to descend upon him. The fact was that although the idea of casual sex appealed to him, when it came to the crunch he developed a kind of stage fright and all the erotic potential slipped away. He knew that George too was not a fan of the darkrooms and the sand dunes of Playa Del Ingles–those places where anonymous sex happened largely without words, or indeed any communication. But he also knew that George, in the right circumstances and with the right people, was more than able to enjoy casual sex. But for Alan it was not so easy. He worried constantly about the fact that he would be unable to perform, and this anxiety itself brought about the impotence he feared. In the short time it took for them to get to Mark's flat Alan had already been overtaken by his insecurity, and knew that he would be incapable of getting turned on. Mark made them a drink and they sat on the balcony for a while, chatting and smoking–but in the back of Alan's mind was the fact that he had lured this guy away from George with a false promise, when George would have been a much better bedfellow. Alan's guilt only served to make the situation worse. They had eventually tried to make love, but it was a disaster. He had rather awkwardly made his apologies and rushed away. Mark said it was no problem, that he understood and he hoped to see Alan again, but his bonhomie merely increased Alan's acute sense that it had been a fiasco–and he cursed himself for having seized George's chance and then squandering it. He so wanted to open himself up to this world–but time and time again he found himself lacking the ability to do so, and successive abortive attempts seemed to worsen the problem. Maybe if he had a younger lover, someone he could actually get to know over a period of time and maybe even share his life with, things would be different, and the psychological blockage would clear. But it was a classic catch-22 situation: in order for this to happen, they'd have to meet each other at least a few times—and why on earth would a gorgeous young guy of the kind that he fantasized about want to stick around long enough to become acquainted with an old crock who couldn't even get it up?

Across the road and a few hundred metres away from Mark's apartment block Alan slowed down, walking past closed and shuttered shops, quiet bars with locals inside watching television, dim light reflecting off glasses on tables, vinyl tablecloths and satellite football. What on earth was he doing here? Chasing something... but what? He felt that he needed more than the occasional fumble in a darkened room, but when the opportunity to take things further came along the psychological blockage always returned. A black man walked towards him, carrying at his chest a shallow plastic box hanging from a strap around his shoulders which was filled with watches, pens, key rings and other glittering paraphernalia. As Alan looked down at the pavement, he caught a glimpse of the tiny red dot produced by an unseen laser pen. The pencil-point became a shimmering straight line, which shot across his body as the man walked past saying good evening and showing big, white teeth.

"Hey granddad, you wanna buy something? Etwas zu kaufen?" Men like this patrolled the streets and commercial centres of Playa Del Ingles each evening, trying to sell their trinkets and novelties to the tourists, who were mostly English or German. Alan quickened his pace and heard the man laughing behind him—a sinister, deep sound. He came next to a hotel that had a dance floor at street level. Through the open windows Alan heard a live band playing the Stevie Wonder song, "I Just Called To Say I love You", and saw heterosexual couples of his generation moving slowly to the rhythm. He knew that not so long ago, he and Marge might have been among them. Now he was out here with the sellers of trinkets and the stray cats and dogs, the warm night wind blowing scraps of paper about his feet. He felt a wave of remorse and considered going back to his hotel room, closing the door and spending the rest of the holiday minding his own business, drinking cheap brandy and smoking cigarettes on the balcony. The hotel was in sight, a few hundred yards ahead of the next roundabout, its name spelled out in red neon. But just as he was about to reach the corner he heard the blast of a horn, and a large black Jeep pulled over next to him. What was this... robbers, the police? He felt almost ready to submit to anything. Then he heard a voice calling to him in English.

"Hello there! Where are you going? Can we offer you a lift?" As the vehicle drew up, Alan recognised the people in it as a couple whom he'd seen on the beach and in the bars. The older of the two, who was driving, looked to be about sixty years old, and was sturdily built with close-cropped hair, a lean face and a short grey beard. His companion was probably about thirty. The young guy looked as if he did a lot of swimming, certainly something to keep him nice and slim. The older man wore a white and blue checked shirt with short sleeves. Alan spotted in the light from the street lamps the familiar logo of a famous clothes designer, and saw that the man also wore gold rings on his fingers and a gold chain around his neck. He obviously had money, but at the same time there was something rough about him. The younger man, who was sitting in the seat closest to the pavement, smiled and said hello. He had flirted tentatively with Alan for the past week or so but the older man had always been there when their paths had crossed, and so Alan had felt disinclined to investigate further.

"I was on my way back to the hotel, actually," he pointed. "It's just up here." The older man laughed.

"Not going home already, are you? Things don't really get started until about now." Alan looked from the older to the younger man– and saw once again in the eyes of the latter that sense of promise, the silent communication which spoke volumes.

"I suppose you're right," he said. "But all these late nights do catch up with you after a while." The older man snorted.

"Speak for yourself. I reckon there's plenty of time to recover when you get home. Why don't you come for a nightcap with us?" The young man continued to smile but said nothing. He really was handsome–and what harm could it do?

"Okay then," said Alan. "Why not?"

"That's more like it!" The young guy opened his door and climbed out of the Jeep, swinging the seat forward so that Alan could clamber into the back. His companion turned and stuck out his hand.

"I'm Frank by the way and this is Steve." Alan shook his hand.

"Alan," he said, settling down. Steve pushed the seat gently back until it clicked into position. Alan saw that he was wearing a shirt made by the same company as his friend's, and that he also wore a gold chain around his neck that matched Frank's. In his current mood of self-pity it seemed to Alan to be an almost sickening display of togetherness. Steve climbed back in and shut the door.

"All aboard," barked Frank. He revved the Jeep's engine and pulled out onto the quiet road. As they drove up the Avenida Tirajana, Alan noticed for the first time that the local council had turned on the festive lights that had been suspended from the lampposts running up the entire length of the street, in readiness for the carnival. Playa del Ingles was hardly the most attractive town in the world, but such touches gave it a splendour that made Alan smile. He'd walked up and down this road so many times, but to see it from a new perspective, all beautifully illuminated like this, was surprisingly pleasurable. As the warm breeze rushed around his head he realised how long it had been since he'd ridden in an open-topped car. It was probably George's beloved Triumph TR4, Doris–which had been stolen decades ago when he'd gone into the city one night for a few pints. In those days the gay bars had not been in the better part of town. George had never seen the car again–and had subsequently accused the police of not doing enough to try and track it down because they suspected he was gay.

Frank had talked continuously since they started off; telling him about how he and Steve always stayed in Maspalomas because it was nearer to the beach, and how they rented a Jeep each year so they didn't have to rely on taxis and buses–but Alan was only half listening. He started to wish that the ride would continue and that they would keep heading north out of Playa del Ingles, and join one of the roads that went up into the mountains. He imagined the steep climb, the hairpin bends with huge drops on one side, the coolness of the mountain air and the twinkling lights of the town seen in the distance far below. They reached a big roundabout and turned left, driving along one of the roads that surrounded the Yumbo Centre.

"You could park in one of these spaces here," ventured Steve, interrupting Frank's monologue, and gesturing towards a lay-by they were about to drive past.

"Nonsense," said Frank. "The taxi drivers use those." Alan knew that the lad was right and that the taxi rank was actually on the other side of the road, further along next to the crazy golf course, but he decided to keep quiet. Steve offered no argument and Frank manoeuvred the Jeep into a space and turned off the engine.

"Better put the top up at this time of night," he said. Steve jumped out and swung his seat forward, then stood holding the door open for Alan, like a nobleman's page. Alan smiled as he climbed out, feeling pleased to be attended on in such a fashion. Back at the Yumbo Centre now, near the music and party noise and the colourful neon lights, he felt his confidence returning. The unfortunate incident with Mark was fading away quickly, becoming less significant by the second. As he moved past Steve, almost without thinking, he reached out and lightly patted the boy's bottom, enjoying the curvature and bounce of it against his hand.

"Nice," he breathed–almost too quietly to hear. Steve giggled and started pulling the canvas roof over the Jeep's protective roll cage. He then leaned back inside to fasten the catches that secured it to the top of the windscreen. Frank pushed a button and the indicators flashed to show that the alarm had been switched on. He looked at Alan.

"Right then–which fleshpot are we going to first?"

"I'd quite like to go to Na Und if you don't mind," said Alan. "Earlier on I told my friend George that I'd meet him there."

"Great," said Frank. "That's where we normally head anyway." By coincidence they had parked at the top of the staircase that led down to the corner of the plaza where Na Und was situated. Like most places in the Yumbo Centre, the whole of the front of the bar was open to the elements, and when they reached the bottom of the stairs, they could see that there was a big crowd of people standing outside, watching the dancing. Earlier in the evening it was generally quite subdued and sophisticated, with the patrons sitting at candle-lit tables having a quiet drink, but there was a different bunch here now, a later crowd, more boozed-up and boisterous. German pop music was blasting out of heavy-duty loudspeakers, as Alan walked through the crowd with Frank and Steve. The smallish dance floor was improbably full of waltzing pairs of men, and the heat being generated by all the moving bodies in such close proximity was intense. As usual George was sitting on a stool at the bar, with his back to the dance floor. Alan approached from behind, laying his hands on the smaller man's shoulders. George turned around and when he saw who it was his face lit up.

"Darling, how lovely to see you! How has your evening been?"

"Pretty dire so far, but I think things may be looking up. I bumped into some friends on the way here. What about you? Marvellous, I expect."

"It was... different. I'll tell you about it later." Alan pulled out his wallet.

"Anyone like a drink? This is Frank by the way, and his friend Steven." George shook the older man's hand, surprised by the bone-crusher grip. He had quite a lot of strength in his hands though, and gave as good as he got.

"A pleasure to meet you," he said, and then turned to the younger man. "And as you can see, I've reserved this stool here specially for you, my dear." They all laughed as Steve sat down. He looked around, taking in the sheer energy of the place with a big, childlike grin. There were eyes everywhere–especially in the shadows and the dimly-lit corners. But whereas discreet cruising and after dinner drinks were the order of the day at Hummel Hummel, here the revelry was much more in your face. At this time of night it was a bump and grind kind of joint. Alan flagged down a waiter and ordered four large beers. The waltz ended and the dance floor cleared. A slow Spanish ballad that was ideal for a smoochy dance came on the sound system.

"Oh I love this," said Steve, grabbing George's arm. "Would you dance with me?"

George looked over the top of his spectacles at Frank. He had no desire to inflame any jealousies or tread on anyone's toes.

"Do you mind?" he said.

"Not at all, you go ahead. We'll keep your seats for you." They stood up and began to dance, moving slowly and holding one another close. Alan passed Frank a beer.

"How can you do that?" he asked.

"What?"

"Allow your friend to go off with another man."

"They're only dancing! I might feel differently if they started taking each other's clothes off, mind you." Alan looked at Steve and George. The younger man had his hands clasped around George's back, and they appeared to be speaking to one another as they moved. As his face span into view and he saw that Alan was watching, George smiled and winked, clearly enjoying himself–then a fraction of a second later they were looking at the back of his head again.

"But there's something very sexual about dancing," said Alan. "It's like a form of courtship. If I had someone like Steve, there's no way I'd let anyone near him."

"It's just a bit of fun," said Frank. "And besides, Steve's not going anywhere–he's lived with me since he was eighteen and he's never done a day's work in his life. He needs me. So I know that even though he may have the odd dance now and then, he'll be coming back sooner or later. And anyway, I trust him."

Alan smiled.

"That's an extremely enlightened point of view." Frank leaned forward and touched Alan's arm, spoke confidentially.

"I think it's the only point of view, particularly here in Gran Canaria. I mean, look at it this way–you fancy my friend, and he likes you. I can see that but I'm not going to rip your eyes out and send him home to bed. He knows which side his bread is buttered on. And you? Well, bless you, you're so old-fashioned that you'll probably be too scared even to lay a finger on him. That's lovely, because a lot of these guys in here would take him from right under my nose if they had half the chance. But look, if I'd told you to sod off when you touched his bum upstairs, we wouldn't be standing here having a pleasant chat–this good atmosphere wouldn't exist. There'd just be something negative instead, and that would be a shame, because I like you."

Alan was perplexed and slightly unnerved by what Frank had said–it seemed like a strange blend of magnanimity and menace. He was embarrassed that Frank had seen so clearly what was going on, and amazed that he could be so understanding. When the tune ended Steve and George came back to their stools, laughing and sending up some of the more effeminate dancers. George picked up his beer and had a drink, a few beads of perspiration visible on his forehead. Another song, "Something Stupid" sung by Frank and Nancy Sinatra came on, and Steve looked at Alan.

"This one's great too–will you dance with me?" Alan looked unsure.

"Oh yes," said Frank. "Go on–take him away. Give me a few minutes of peace." They walked onto the floor. Alan was pleased he'd put some leather-soled shoes on which were perfect for this kind of dancing. The young man responded well and as they started to move in time to the music Alan could tell he had good rhythm. Steve spoke in his ear.

"I'm pleased you're leading me, because I really haven't got a clue what to do."

"That's not true, you're doing very well." Alan thought about the last time he had danced like this. It was with his wife at a New Year's Eve party, about four years ago. He really loved to dance, and doing it with an attractive young man gave it a wonderful new twist. Steve sniffed the older man's neck.

"I like your aftershave," he said. Alan moved his hands a little lower.

"It's called Sporting Chance. I thought it was rather appropriate for this place–but maybe I was being a little optimistic." Steve laughed. Even though it was a slow tune, several German couples carried on waltzing anyway, barging around the floor at completely the wrong speed, almost as if they were determined not to acknowledge the change in tempo. Every so often they would spin alarmingly close, but they were pretty good dancers and managed not to crash into anyone. Alan ignored them, concentrating instead on the feel of this young body in his hands, the way it rubbed against his own as they moved together. As they span around, he avoided looking at Frank and George, even though he felt sure they would be watching. He spoke in Steve's ear, half aware that what he was about to say could ruin everything, but somehow unable to stop.

"I think you're a lovely guy and I'd love to go to bed with you." Steve half-smiled and shrugged, nodding towards the bar.

"It's difficult for me."

"I know. Your boyfriend's got all the angles covered–and I can't say I blame him. Just my luck."

"Sorry about that," said Steve. "I like you too."

"It was a bit of a long shot–but you never know, we may get our opportunity."

"Yes maybe," said Steve. "There's always a sporting chance." He giggled. The song ended and they separated. As people dispersed around them, Alan took hold of Steve's hand as if he was going to shake it, then put his left hand over it and clasped it tightly.

"Thanks. Thanks a lot," he said. As they approached the others Frank looked at Alan with mischief in his eyes.

"You danced beautifully together–but now it's my turn. Come along young man." Another slow tune had come on and they moved onto the floor, sliding into one another's arms and instantly taking up the rhythm. Alan saw in a flash the depth of their relationship–saw how close the years had brought them. It was all in the way they moved together. George turned to him.

"Drink up, squire, it's way too hot in here and we've got some catching up to do. Let's go for a stroll." They waved goodbye and squeezed their way through the crowd, out towards the cooler air. Nothing was said as they walked past the vaguely building site-like façade of the bar next door, which was called Construction. George took a smallish joint out of the magic glasses case and lit it up.

"Pleasant couple," said Alan, still thinking about the feel of the young lad's firm bottom in his hand. George made a puffing sound, blowing a large quantity of smoke out of his mouth.

"The boy's an absolute dish I grant you–but I thought the friend was a bit full of himself. While you were dancing he started telling me how much better off we'd be staying in an apartment rather than a hotel. Then he told me he didn't think I suited a moustache. Cheeky bugger."

"Fortunately, the older one doesn't feature in my plans."

"Glad to hear it." George passed the joint to Alan. "Anyway darling–what's the story with you? I saw from your face the moment you walked into Na Und that things hadn't gone so well." Alan looked at George strutting like a cat amid the sparkling lights and the music, exchanging friendly glances with people coming towards them. In the past few years George seemed to have really come into himself. After a life of gripes and groans, of dramas and letdowns, he had finally kicked back and decided to let it all hang out, and the transformation had been remarkable. Now men who wouldn't have looked twice at him a decade or two ago were queuing up, and George just took it in his stride as if it was all meant to be. Alan, in contrast, had gone the other way. The companionship he had enjoyed with his wife had made him complacent, allowing him to view the ups and downs of George's life from the elevated vantage point of his marriage. Now he found himself back down in the foothills, having to navigate the terrain that his friend had already mastered.

He sighed.

"I don't know–for some reason whenever I meet someone pleasant, I don't seem to be able to make it work like you do. I find them attractive, I chat to them, but when it comes to the crunch it's always a disaster."

"You mean you took Mark from under my nose, scared him half to death on that ride, but when it came down to it you couldn't get it up?"

"Well, yes." Alan was clearly ashamed. "That's about the height of it." George shook his head.

"Deary me," he said quietly. Alan took a drag on the joint and grimaced–feeling the strength of it in the sweetness and density of the smoke. He held it up to the light. It was beautifully made; tapering smoothly down to a narrow mouthpiece that had been expertly crafted out of some thin cardboard and inserted into the end. He knew how bad his friend was at making these things.

"Where did this come from?"

"Those Dutch boys we met at the shopping centre in Maspalomas yesterday. It's pure skunk, dear, so do go easy or we may have to get one of those gorgeous ambulance guys over there to give you the kiss of life." Alan laughed.

"Even if one of them did I'd probably screw it up."

"You're a complex case, there's no doubt about that–but at some stage you'll have to let that go and allow yourself to enjoy the rest of your life. That's what I pray for–for you to come to me and say, 'You know what George, I've met this smashing bloke and I really don't think I'll be coming with you on holiday next year, because the two of us are going to go away on our own.' That's what I'd like." Alan was touched.

"Do you really care about it that much?" George looked surprised.

"Why do you think I allowed you to walk away with Mark earlier tonight, even though it was me he came to speak to? I mean, I was a bit miffed at first but then I thought, what the hell? The man has to take his chances." He shrugged. "Of course, I should have realised that you'd make a pig's ear of it." Alan looked at the pavement.

"Sorry to be such a dead weight, old chap."

"You're not a dead weight at all. You're wonderful company, but we're like this odd couple. It's almost as if I've been married to you all these years and I'm not sure it's healthy. We both need some new blood, some romance in our lives. And here is the place we can get it. If we stayed at home there'd be dinner parties, church and the Over Sixties club—and a few years down the line, a lonely old death." As they walked, they passed more stalls being set up for the carnival. A swarthy man in a striped shirt and trilby hat was cooking shrivelled things that looked like kipper skins, on a brazier full of hot charcoal. The flesh was brown and crispy and the smell was abominable. Alan pointed at the makeshift griddle.

"We'd better watch out, though—because if we stay in the sun too much our skin will end up like that."

"I think my liver already is," said George, and they both laughed. "It's no joke. I mean, if you stayed here for a whole winter you'd look like an old leather hide left too long in the tannin, your gizzards would be pickled by all this cheap beer, and your genitalia would be red raw."

"Aye," said Alan wistfully, "but you'd be smiling from ear to ear."

"For sure. Go down with the guns blazing, that's what I say." They walked on in silence for a few moments, and then Alan spoke.

"I've told you about my disastrous evening. What happened to you?" George thought for a second as if he was trying to dredge up a long-forgotten fact. Then his eyes lit up.

"My dear," he said. "I was propositioned by a pimp." Alan giggled.

"Doesn't surprise me in this place—but I hope you told him that you've never had to pay for it in your life."

"He wasn't touting for business, at least not in that sense. He was asking if I wanted to become a prostitute." Alan considered this.

"Darling," he said, "you know I'm your biggest fan, but aren't you getting a little long in the tooth for that kind of thing?"

"Apparently not. In fact, he wanted to know if you'd be interested as well. He's recruiting as it were for a new business venture."

"Goodness. Why us?"

"He thinks that people may be willing to pay for old crocks– and actually, looking around this place, I think he could be onto something."

"So what did you say to him?"

"I turned him down–politely of course."

"Glad to hear it!"

"But he gave me his card and told me to think about it, and to ring him if I changed my mind." Alan shook his head.

"A brothel full of fossils. I wonder what Over Sixties would make of that."

"Perhaps we should get him over to England to do a talk on it. I'm sure it'd be more interesting than those dreadful slide-shows we usually have to sit through, and he might get more takers than you'd think."

"You sound like you're actually coming round to the idea."

"Well I don't know. Obviously I'm not going to up-sticks and emigrate to become a strumpet, but it has captured my imagination to a certain extent–and it's quite complimentary in a way. I think if he'd been a bit better looking and not so bloody cocksure I might have accepted." They found themselves back at the busy part of the Yumbo Centre where they hadn't managed to get a table earlier in the evening. It was thinning out now, but it was still pretty busy. The joint had made Alan's mouth unpleasantly dry, and left a foul aftertaste. It had also made him acutely aware of the eyes of all the people sitting at the tables watching them. He needed a drink, but felt disinclined to give these bars the trade. He glanced across at his friend.

"Fancy going upstairs for a quick one?"

"You read my mind," said George.

*

ABOUT six months after his wife died, Alan visited a gay guesthouse for the first time. Everyone kept telling him that he needed to get away from home for a few days, so eventually he had asked George to recommend somewhere. Because he was so used to concealing his homosexuality, he made the booking under a false name: Fred Smith. It was a beautiful, sunny afternoon when he stepped of the train in Brighton. Alan decided not to tell the taxi driver the name of the hotel, so he just asked to be taken to the street where it was. He waited until the car drove off before he walked up the steps and rang the bell. The door was opened by an unkempt man in his fifties who was accompanied by a docile golden retriever that wagged its tail slowly back and forth. In the hall there was a doormat decorated with a ship's wheel and the greeting: "Welcome Aboard". He was shown into a lounge that was very much like someone's living room, with a sofa and armchairs and a television in the corner with the volume turned down low. On the coffee table there were books, newspapers and a bowl of fruit. Sunlight streamed in through the net curtains. A few guests were there: two older men watching the television and a couple of younger guys, smartly dressed and probably in their twenties or thirties, on the sofa reading magazines. They all greeted him. One of the older gents turned to the other and spoke.

"Well, Wally, we're not getting any younger sitting in here, so I'm off for a walk. See you downstairs later." He winked and left the room. As they heard the front door being opened, the other shouted after him.

"Stay out of the bushes, you mucky old sod!" The man who had met Alan at the door came back with a wad of leaflets in one hand, also carrying a small tray with a cup of coffee and some biscuits on it. He signed Alan into the hotel while telling him about the town; where the gay bars and the sauna were, when the drag shows and various other entertainments happened. It was all very thorough, and the man rounded it off by giving Alan a card with the hotel's logo printed on it.

"This is your poofter's pass. If you show it at most of the places marked on the map, they'll give you a discount. The honeymoon suite was already taken, so I've given you room nine, which is on the second floor. The steam room will be open from six until seven thirty."

Alan went upstairs and put his bag on the bed. He was full of excitement and dread, nervous but also thrilled to be in such a situation after all these years of marriage. He'd had mixed emotions about coming here. His wife had only been dead for a short time but he had begun the grieving process while she was still alive, during the long months she spent wasting away in a hospital bed. And although some people grieved for years, something inside him was pushing him to continue with his life, to not waste the years that he had left. He and Marjorie had had a good sex life right up until she became ill, and he had never been unfaithful to her–except when George was desperate. So he was here to explore this impulse that had remained under the surface for so long and it was a strange, unsettling feeling. He sat on the edge of the bed, which gave way as if it had seen quite a lot of action. He thought about the sort of things that might have happened in this room over the years, and suddenly had the urge to go downstairs, pay the man who had signed him in, walk outside and go straight back home. But what would that achieve? All these questions would remain unanswered, and now that he was here he might as well make the best of it. He threw himself into the task of unpacking, hanging his shirts up in the wardrobe, and laying out the contents of his wash bag around the sink. There was the toothbrush, the deodorant, the razor, the shaving foam and the cologne that Marge had bought him just over a year ago, while they were on their last holiday together in Venice. All were little slivers of familiarity in the midst of an alien world. A whole weekend in front of me, he thought, and I have no idea what I'm going to do. It was still sunny, but actually going outside and walking around seemed like too much at this stage. Alan decided to take a nap, and so he lay back and allowed the sagging mattress to engulf him. He dreamed of his wife, and then was woken up by a voice coming through the radio built into the bedside table, telling him that the steam room was open. He went downstairs to a small, dimly-lit changing room in what had once been the cellar. Inside a locker he found two soft green towels–the smaller of which he wrapped around himself, the larger he would use later when he'd finished and had a shower. He pulled open the heavy glass door and went into the steam room. He couldn't see very much because he'd taken off his glasses–but he could make out at least two indistinct human shapes sitting in the hot, moist darkness. There was a gentle conversation going on about something that was in the news. Alan was unsure of what kind of decadent scenes he had expected to be going on in here, but the civilised nature of it all took him by surprise. He sat down on the warm ledge near to one of the dark shapes, which moved along slightly to give him a bit more room. The hot steam closed in around his body, made him feel almost as if he had disappeared. After a short time there was a movement to his left and he felt a hand come lightly to rest on his thigh.

From that moment on the weekend was a triumph. Occasionally in a small hotel the guests seem to gel with each other, as if a mutual friend has invited them all to a big house party. That weekend at the bed and breakfast in Brighton was one of those occasions. Alan hadn't come across such camaraderie since he was in the forces. The group ate out together, they went to the pubs together, they visited the sauna together–and in fact had so much fun that they all agreed to come back the following year at the same time, during the August Bank Holiday weekend. For Alan, one of the main reasons the stay was such a success was a thirty-year-old Parisian called Charles who as luck would have it was staying in the room next door. Even now, thoughts of Charles would make Alan smile. On the face of it the boy wasn't his type at all–he was tall and gangly, with jet-black hair and a comedian's bold features, a big nose, big mouth and big ears. He was also covered in tattoos and had his ears and nose pierced. Hardly the boy-next-door type that Alan had always fantasized about. But Charles had such a wonderful personality–and of course when they had met for the first time, in the steam room, Alan was unable to see what he looked like. All he had really been aware of as the vapour swirled around them was a sweet and seemingly never-ending kiss, and the feel of a firm young body. Charles was also one of the most frank people Alan had ever met. He was utterly fearless when it came to telling the truth. On the Saturday afternoon, after they had been for a long walk on the seafront, they went back to the hotel and ended up in bed together. Alan got up to go to the toilet, and when he came back to the room he stopped at the sink to wash his hands. Charles was lying on the bed behind him smoking a cigarette (which somehow contributed to the charming seediness of the whole experience). As he turned on the tap, Alan looked at Charles in the mirror. He was actually hoping that the younger man would say something encouraging, loving even–but when the words came they were a rude awakening.

"Why do you dye your hair this blonde colour?"

"I beg your pardon?"

"I asked you why you dye your hair. Why don't you just leave it to be the way it is?"

"I don't know," said Alan hesitantly. "I mean, it always used to be blonde and I just thought it would make me look younger if I put some colour back into it." Charles continued to puff away on his cigarette.

"Let me tell you that people will find you far more attractive if you let it go back to being its natural colour, white. It's so much more distinguished, so much sexier."

Alan had been annoyed by this, as he had been when they went out the previous evening, and Charles had ridiculed the black leather jacket he had bought a couple of weeks earlier, because he thought it was the sort of thing that would go down well in gay bars. But Charles was adamant that he was not trying to be hurtful–he was just making it clear to Alan that he was attractive enough in his own right and had no need to try to make himself appear younger. Alan dried his hands and turned around, his eyes suddenly bright with anger.

"You could try being a bit more sensitive," he snapped. "My wife died six months ago and I'm trying my best."

"I'm sorry about that, I really am. But the fact that you've lost her doesn't mean that you have to start looking like a fool."

Charles was a perplexing character–full of compliments one minute, full of insults the next. Alan couldn't work out whether it was just part of his Gallic nature, or if the lad actually suffered from some kind of mental imbalance. Either way he had turned out to be an interesting companion for the weekend, and had also taught Alan an important lesson, which was not to try to be something that he wasn't. And in the years to come Alan and George would go to gay bars and meet older guys in jeans and trainers, squeezed into designer T-shirts, with earrings and dyed hair, who wondered why they were getting no interest at all from the younger ones–when he and George walked in wearing jackets and ties and ended up having to fight them off. Alan had gone back to the guesthouse the following August Bank Holiday, but it was nothing like the previous year. He knew that Charles would be absent, because he had received a garbled letter some months before, in which the Frenchman explained that he had met a retired stockbroker and they'd disappeared to the Dordogne together, to live a life of rural bliss. Alan smiled as he imagined Charles strolling into the local farmer's mart with his tattoos and his piercings and his talk of exotic Parisian nightspots, and wondered how successful such a venture would be. A couple of the others were also unable to make it–and a small group was booked in the second time around who kept themselves to themselves, creating an us-and-them atmosphere that was nothing like the openness of the year before. On top of all that, the weather wasn't quite as good. Alan had taken George with him the second time–and it was in Brighton that someone in a bar had told them how much they would enjoy Gran Canaria, and they'd hatched the plan to visit the place the following November. So in the typical manner of things, as one door closed another was opening.

*

TERRY was sitting outside Hollandaise, a small café bar on the first floor of the Yumbo Centre that was sandwiched between an electronics shop and a place that sold belts and shoes, with his Danish friend Alex and Alex's younger lover Dieter. As they drank coffee, Alex was regaling them with an anecdote about something that had happened to him during the Second World War. Although Terry had heard the story several times before, he still found it exciting. Alex was a robust man in his eighties, with sharp eyes, a hooked nose, and white hair which was swept back from his forehead. Perched on the edge of his stool, the light glinting off the lenses on his gold-rimmed spectacles, there was something of the bird of prey about him. He had made a living carving tombstones before the outbreak of the war. After the occupation of Denmark, he became a member of the Danish Resistance. One night he was captured but before he was interrogated he managed to escape from a police station, disguised as a woman. Making his way to safety along a country road he was offered a lift by a Nazi officer, who had a penchant for big-boned nordic maidens and proceeded to run his hand up the inside of his passenger's skirt.

"Another inch and I'd have been dead for sure," said Alex–who had apparently managed to persuade the German that he wasn't that kind of girl. He sat back and winked–an octogenarian swashbuckler in his dark suit and crimson shirt, telling these wide-eyed youths what life at the sharp end could really be like. Terry met Alex during his first visit to the island. As a young man on the gay scene, he'd come across quite a few larger-than-life characters who had tried to talk him into bed with their drunken tales of derring-do, but while a lot of these guys were making it all up, Terry realised quickly that Alex was the genuine article. For his part, Alex was delighted by the way the young lad–perhaps emboldened by the drink he'd consumed–walked straight up and started chatting away, his eyes and his smile as bright as the neon lights outside the bar, and their message plain: I want you. Alex had moved to Gran Canaria after he retired because he knew that it was one of the few places where older men weren't laughed at when they went into the gay bars, but he had become frustrated that even here in such an enlightened environment, people often treated him as the venerable old statesman–a figure to be respected rather than someone who could arouse other responses. Now here was Terry, obviously interested sexually–but at the same time slightly irreverent, gently mocking the older man's grandiose way of talking, almost as if he was letting him know that he wasn't just going to roll over onto his back, like a little dog waiting for his belly to be tickled. When they finally got back to his bungalow, a few miles away in the resort of Puerto Mogan, and he was making the drinks, Alex–smiling mischievously but with his back to the boy–had shrugged his shoulders.

"Of course," he said, "I don't even know why I've invited you here. I don't find you attractive, you've got nothing up here." He tapped his head with a finger. "There's no reason for you to be here at all." He turned and watched Terry's face for a reaction as he handed the drink over, then leaned down to whisper in his ear. "Apart from this overwhelming tenderness I feel towards you." Terry had stayed for several days, and his visit had done wonders for Alex. Before Terry, there had been a series of abortive encounters which had made him start to suspect that perhaps he really was getting too old, and that romance might have become a thing of the past. Terry, whose lovemaking was gentle and easy, had put him back in touch with his sexual nature–indeed, Alex was surprised by how virile he could still be when offered the right stimulus. He would have loved this new relationship to develop, but he knew that Terry had a job and a life back home, and would be unlikely to want to give it all up and come and live here. And there was a sense in their conversations that Terry, despite his apparent directness and straightforwardness, was holding things back. Perhaps there was a lover at home in England or, even though he seemed a bit young for it, a wife and children. On Terry's last night they went as usual to Na Und and had another splendid time together. As they said goodbye, Alex gave him a piece of paper with his address and telephone number written on it–but a large part of him expected that he would never hear from the boy again.

Terry traveled home with a heavy heart. While he had been with Alex he'd tried to minimize the significance of what was happening, telling himself that it was just a holiday fling, but now with each mile the plane moved further away from Gran Canaria, the feeling of loss seemed to increase by a notch. He knew he'd met a very special man, and glimpsed a life that could bring him a huge amount of happiness and contentment. It was already getting dark when his plane touched down back in England, even though it was only half past three in the afternoon. It was also bitterly cold with grey sleet falling and slush underfoot. He'd put on a jumper before they opened the aircraft doors because he knew what the weather would be like, but outside the airport as he bundled his case into the back of a taxi the wind blew straight through the woven wool as if it wasn't there. This was all in stark contrast to the balmy warmth and golden sunshine of his afternoons with Alex on the terrace at Puerto Mogan. Sitting in the back of the car, travelling through the semi-industrialized landscape on the outskirts of his home town, past landmarks that were all too familiar, Terry resolved to telephone Alex as soon as he was back home. But when he unpacked an hour or so later he was unable to find the scrap of paper. He hunted and hunted, going through his suitcase and rucksack, his wallet, his dairy, the book he had been reading—anywhere he might have slipped it, but all to no avail. Later he tried to ring Na Und to leave a message, but the music was too loud and nobody knew what he was talking about—and he was ashamed to discover that he didn't even know Alex's surname. They might as well have lived on opposite sides of the universe!

At first Terry told himself it was probably for the better that he had lost the address and that his life would soon settle back into its normal routines, but those logical and sensible thoughts did nothing to ease the hollow ache that came upon him whenever his mind wasn't fully occupied with other things. He put a brave face on it, but people knew something wasn't right. Then, the following weekend when he was in the pub getting drunk with his friends, the solution came to him in a flash. He would simply go back to Gran Canaria at the same time the following year, despite being unable to contact Alex in advance, and explain himself in person. He felt sure that Alex would understand and even if he didn't, at least it was a plan of action, an objective to be working towards rather than a passive acceptance of fate. So the following day he went into town to book the holiday.

"Wow," said the girl in the travel agent, the same one who had arranged his first trip. "You must have really enjoyed yourself." Terry could hardly muster a smile.

"Yes—I think perhaps I had too good a time." The girl laughed.

"I wish all our customers felt the same way." Terry went home with the spring back in his step, thinking that it was only ten and a half months until he would return to the island. His life resumed its normal rhythm and the weeks began to slide by. The thought that he and Alex would be re-united less than a year in the future became the thing that kept him going–like the fire in the kitchen stove which keeps the whole house warm throughout the winter. In quiet moments he remembered certain things about Alex, the best things, so that in his mind's eye, Alex gradually became a huge, almost mythical figure for whom he was carrying a torch, and was most delighted to do so. He felt sure that it would all work out in the end.

Alex, meanwhile, was rather saddened not to hear from Terry. They'd had such a marvellous time together–it had felt different, significant somehow. At first he thought, well, the lad has to get on with things–I'm sure he leads a busy life in England, but he'll ring eventually. Then he started to accept that the call would never come. He did consider the possibility that Terry had lost his details but dismissed it as wishful thinking, the delusion of an old man who wanted to believe that there was something deeper there than there actually was. After a while his frustration subsided. He still thought about Terry, but there was no bitterness. Similar things had happened to him before, it was all part of the experience of being a gay man–especially one who lived in a place like Gran Canaria.

But this being a holiday resort, as one set of visitors was leaving others were arriving–and it was only a matter of time before the inevitable happened. Alex was sitting in Na Und in more or less the same position he had been in when he met Terry, when Dieter walked up to the bar, stood next to him, and ordered a drink. Whereas Terry had initiated conversation immediately, Dieter was somewhat less forward. He smiled and said hello and he waited for his drink, then moved away from the bar to a stool behind the dance floor, out of the way of the action. But every time Alex looked over in that direction, the young man was looking back and gave him another smile. So after a while Alex went over and they started talking. Dieter–who lived in Berlin and worked as a chef–was well spoken and charming in his own quiet way. They danced together a few times. At the end of the evening Alex invited Dieter back to his villa, where they stayed until the younger man's holiday came to an end. Unlike Terry, Dieter did not lose Alex's details–and in fact was on the phone the night he got back to Berlin. He was able to return to Gran Canaria six weeks later, and then made the journey out to the island a few more times in the coming months. The following summer when the Canarian heat became unbearable, Alex flew to Germany and stayed at Dieter's flat for three weeks. Their relationship deepened and in the autumn Dieter gave up his job and came to live with Alex. He quickly found work at a restaurant in Maspalomas. So in the twelve months that Terry spent waiting to return to Gran Canaria, the rest of his life in stasis, Alex's world was completely transformed.

On his first night it was with a feeling of dread that Terry walked into Na Und–almost as if he knew somehow through a subtle change in the fabric of the place that things were not going to turn out as he'd hoped. There was Alex, sitting in his usual position at the back of the bar. He looked bigger somehow and there was a sheen about his skin and a contentedness in his face that hadn't been there the year before. As they embraced, Terry spotted the half-finished beer and the packet of cigarettes on the counter in front of the empty stool next to the one Alex was sitting on. The older man didn't smoke, nor did he drink beer. The implications were still sinking in when Dieter returned from the toilet a few moments later, smiling but clearly intrigued by the new arrival. Alex introduced them, noticing how badly Terry disguised his disappointment. Later, on the dance floor, Terry spoke into the older man's ear, shrugging his shoulders as he thought about what might have been.

"I'm really pleased for you. It's what you needed–he's a lovely guy."

That had been a couple of years ago and now as Alex finished his story about the Danish Resistance he put his hand on his lover's leg.

"Of course," he said quietly, "I've found my own way of paying the Germans back for all the shit they put me through." Dieter looked at Terry and raised his eyes.

"Yes... I think if I hear that story one more time I'll die of boredom." Terry watched the two of them sharing the joke and was suddenly jealous of their rapport.

"Enough of my nonsense," Alex said to him. "Tell us about the meeting you had earlier this evening." Terry was caught out and he blushed.

"How do you know about that?"

"We have our spies out all the time–you should know that by now." Terry laughed. After he'd left Hummel Hummel he had gone off to watch the drag show at Ricky's Revue Bar to take his mind off what had happened with the older man. Standing watching the performance he became aware of a nice-looking guy in the crowd, who kept smiling and winking. They'd gone for a drink together at a leather bar and ended up in the dark room. Terry was just in the process of explaining all this when Alan Reid and George Hope turned the corner and sauntered past, opening the door and going straight into Hollandaise. He stopped in mid flow. Alex waved a hand in front of his face.

"Something caught your eye, young man?" Terry looked confused.

"I think I know one of the men who just went inside. From a long time ago, when I was at school."

"So while all your friends were playing games in the school yard, you were off trying to play with their grandfathers? I can picture it."

"Well, no it wasn't quite like that," said Terry, suddenly not in the mood for jocular banter. "Do you mind if I just pop inside and have another quick look at him?" Terry went to the door and pushed it open slightly, peering inside as if making sure the coast was clear before going in. The bar was pretty small, about the size of six broom cupboards. Moroccan music was playing quietly in the background– the lyrics in French. Alan and his friend were sitting with their backs to the door, talking to the man behind the bar. The toilet was in the far corner.

"I can't believe how much that little memorial someone planted in the dunes last year has grown," Alan was saying. "You know–the cluster of shrubs and flowers near the place the Germans call the Hauptbahnhof. It can't be getting any nutrients because it's like a desert out there." Terry knew the voice, and there was now no doubt in his mind about who it was.

"It's rained more than usual over the last few months," said the barman. "Maybe that's helped the new plants to get established." Alan's friend leaned forward on his stool.

"It's obvious what's keeping the plants alive," he told the others. "They're being nourished by love, by the feelings of whoever planted them in the first place."

"How romantic," scoffed Alan, taking a swig of beer. "I once knew a woman who kept her dead husband's ashes in an urn on the mantelpiece. Every so often she'd get pissed and sniff a pinch of them, like snuff. Then one day her friends–who were absolutely appalled by this, as you can imagine, said to her: 'Why on earth do you do that?' So she says with a wistful eye: 'That was the only hole he was never up.'" He burst out laughing and started coughing uncontrollably as the others shook their heads.

"Dear oh dear," said his friend. "You can always be counted on to lower the tone." As they laughed Terry slipped through the bar. The toilet was a darkened cubicle with a couple of porcelain urinals attached to one wall and a tiny hand basin in the corner. There was no room for anything else. It was separated from the bar by a pair of louvred, spring-hinged doors, like the saloon doors in old cowboy films. Because they reached neither the floor nor the ceiling, Terry could clearly hear the conversation as he had a pee. The barman spoke next.

"So what have you two disgraceful old farts been up to since we saw you last?"

"Nothing much," said Alan's friend. "Casanova here flew off into the night sky with some gorgeous hunk, and I got propositioned by a pimp." There was a pause while the barman apparently digested this information, and a muffled, drunken giggle.

"What are you talking about?"

"He took a guy he was trying to seduce on the Sky Rider." Another pause. Terry moved to the basin and ran the cold tap over his hands, staying back in the shadows while he looked over the louvred doors and out into the bar. He felt sure that they couldn't see him. The barman eyed Alan as he polished a tankard with a white cloth, clearly waiting for some kind of explanation. Alan emptied his glass.

"It was a disaster. I was nearly sick and completely failed to get into his trousers. I did get a smashing view of Playa del Ingles, though." They all laughed again as Terry watched from the shadows. Alan had already gone grey when Terry had known him, seven or eight years ago–but now that his hair was bright white he seemed even more handsome. The face was pretty much as it had been, a trifle more wrinkled perhaps–but that too served to increase his appeal, rather than to diminish it. As Terry dried his hands he cast his mind back to that time when, as a teenager, he'd been forced to acknowledge consciously his desire for older men for the first time. Then the door opened, and several other people came into the bar. Alan and his friend stood up, and there were hugs and hellos. They obviously all knew each other. Terry took the opportunity to leave as discreetly as he could. Once outside he pulled the door closed behind him without looking back, then sat down and lit a cigarette, staring pensively at the lighter in his hand once he'd done so. Alex gave Dieter a serious look, sensing trouble.

"Anything to tell us?" he ventured. "You look like you've seen a ghost." Terry exhaled and leaned back.

"Well–in an odd kind of way I have." Something about his tone of voice suggested that he was not keen to discuss the matter further. He looked at the door, clearly concerned that the person in question was going to emerge at any moment. Alex decided that a tactical retreat might be the best plan of action.

"Shall we move on then?"

"Good idea," said Dieter, intrigued about the mystery man but able to see that now was not the time to delve any further. "I feel like a dance." They finished their drinks and stood up. Terry hung back.

"If it's all the same to you, I might go and get something to eat. I didn't really have a proper dinner this evening and I'm starting to feel a bit peckish. I'll catch up with you later." Alex placed a hand protectively on his shoulder.

"Yes of course. You do what you have to do. Are you all right?" Terry smiled.

"I'm fine thanks, really. I'll see you in Na Und." Alex and Dieter set off down the stairs that led down to the main plaza, while Terry turned and walked along the corridor, heading towards an all-night café on the first floor which he went into most evenings. Back inside Hollandaise, Alan and George had finished telling their two friends about what they'd been up to. Alan had just recounted the details of his disastrous meeting with Mark.

"I can't understand it," said one of the friends. "You seem to be so unlucky in love, and yet only a few moments ago the most gorgeous young man was staring at you when he walked through here." Alan looked up.

"What gorgeous young man?" George shook his head–for a gay man his friend was shockingly unaware of what was going on around him.

"I saw him too," he said. "An absolute dish, and he was definitely giving you the eye."

"For God's sake you lot, stop taunting me!" Alan waved a hand in front of his face as if he was trying to swat away a fly. "If I missed him, I missed him–and if he was that interested he'd have hung around."

"Don't worry," said the barman. "Playa Del Ingles is such a small place that you're always running into the same people again and again."

"Unless, as usually happens to me, they're flying home the morning after you meet them." Alan's tone was defeatist. George slapped the bar with his hands.

"Well you may be content to let this go, but I'm not."

"Bravo!" shouted the barman. "I think that calls for a schnapps on the house!" He opened the freezer and whipped out a bottle of a colourless hazelnut liqueur and four small shot glasses, which he lined up on the bar. The bars often handed out free schnapps to their well-known customers, which meant that by the end of each evening in the Yumbo Centre, Alan and George had usually consumed about ten different types of alcoholic drink. This–and their penchant for strong marijuana–went some way towards explaining why the night porter always seemed slightly apprehensive when he let them into the hotel at four in the morning. The sight of them pressed up against the plate glass of the front door, gurning and laughing, hair messed up, clothes in disarray–clearly struck fear into his heart. The poor guy probably thought he'd woken up in an asylum. The barman raised his glass.

"Salute! To finding true love."

"To finding true love!" The drinks were dispatched and there were gasps all round.

"Okay then, lads, I'm going to love you and leave you," said George, producing a white handkerchief and wiping his mouth. Alan looked disappointed.

"Aren't you coming to see the strip show at the Block?"

"Well–it was a bit of a disappointment last time, wasn't it?"

"Peter said the guy was off his eggs. He says the one they've got tonight is much better." George finished his beer off and put the glass down on the bar.

"Peter always says the guy they've got tonight is better than the last one, and it's always a disappointment. No, I can do without it. I'll see you later." He kissed them all goodnight and headed briskly for the door.

*

GEORGE had no idea where he would find the boy who had been giving Alan the eye, so he decided to begin by looking downstairs around the square. The pubs and cafés were much quieter now because most of the action was shifting upstairs. He could see that across at Hummel Hummel there were only a few stragglers hanging around, and the waiters had started stacking up the plastic chairs that had been so carefully laid out in front of the bar only hours earlier. He was feeling quite tired and could have gone to bed, but felt in his heart that the night still had something in store for him, and he didn't want to go back to the hotel just yet. The music was pumping out in Na Und and the dance floor was packed, but as far as George could make out the boy wasn't there. He carried on walking, past Construction. Dozens of guys were standing around drinking lager out of bottles. They all appeared to be in their forties, heavy-set and with shaved heads, wearing things like checked shirts, overalls, jeans and leather trousers. It was a toned-down facsimile of S&M-type bars George had been to over the years, in cities such as Cologne and Berlin. He doubted very much that the young man would be in there–it didn't seem to suit his style somehow. There were bars on the first floor on this side of the plaza too–so George decided to pop upstairs and have a quick look. He reached the top of the stairs and could see that things were already pretty raucous. There was loud music, shouting, and the sound of bottles rolling underfoot. He picked his way apprehensively through the crowd. It was hotter here because of the crush of bodies, and faces shrieked and leered as they moved through his field of vision, while his nostrils were assailed by smells of sweat, poppers, dry ice and marijuana smoke. In front of one of the bars people were standing in a circle clapping their hands and watching, as two slim young men dressed as cowboys stood face to face, gyrating to the music, arms outstretched, rubbing their bodies against each other. Each wore twin holsters and had his ten gallon hat pushed to the back of his head. George squeezed through and found himself outside a small fast food restaurant called Monroe's that stayed open more or less until dawn. Sitting at a table by himself, near the balcony which looked out over the plaza, was the lad who had come into Hollandaise. The waitress had just put a huge plate of chips in front of him, and he was in the process of covering them with tomato sauce. George smiled. How could a guy eat that rubbish and stay so thin? Probably because the bugger would dance until dawn, and then spend the whole day in bed having sex. The joys of youth.

Terry loved the chips at Monroe's, but he wasn't particularly hungry. He had come here mainly to think things through, to try to get his mind and emotions into some kind of order. Suddenly coming across Alan Reid like that in a gay bar here in Gran Canaria had been a big shock. Terry had experienced a surge of adrenaline, that sensation of tightness and butterflies in the stomach that were brought on by exposure to an object of desire. But nearly a decade had passed since he'd seen Alan–which was why he was so surprised by how powerful those feelings still were. Surely he had left all that behind a long time ago! Now, part of him was thrilled at the possibility that the fantasies he'd built around this man might actually become reality–but there was also a huge fear that someone whom he had admired for so long from afar could suddenly be within reach. He felt the paralysis of the voyeur who is discovered hiding in the bushes, and invited by the people he's been watching to join in. As he squeezed ketchup and mayonnaise onto his chips and ate the first forkful, he was so engrossed in his thoughts that he failed to see the figure approaching the table.

"Mind if I join you?" George Hope stood over the lad, smiling. Terry chewed quickly, looking down then up, not wanting to speak with his mouth full. He wiped his lips with a paper napkin.

"Not at all." George picked up the menu.

"What's the food like here–any good?" Terry was dumbfounded by the progression of events. First this apparition from the past had confronted him and now, when he was trying to re-group, Alan's friend had hunted him down for some reason. But the guy was pretty good-looking, so he pulled himself together and turned on the charm.

"The food's fine: just what you need after you've spent the night filling yourself with beer." George looked down.

"A portion of chips–how very British." Terry laughed.

"I know, the woman here keeps telling me I'm going to put on weight. better help me eat them." He handed George a plastic fork.

"You were in Hollandaise earlier, weren't you? I think I know your friend. Is his name Alan Reid?" George skewered a couple of chips and dipped them in the pink streaky glob of mixed-up ketchup and mayonnaise. He vastly preferred chips without such adornments, but was actually quite hungry by this time and was therefore grateful for food of any kind.

"It is indeed."

"I went out with his daughter when we were at school."

"Jane? Oh, well you'll be pleased then to hear that she's married with children now. Lives down in London. But why didn't you come and say hello?" Terry looked over the edge of the balcony into the square below. What could he tell this man–that he'd fancied Alan for years, and that one of the main reasons he had carried on going out with Jane was the crush he had on her father? That seeing the guy he used to fantasize about every night for years had knocked him for six? Of course he couldn't.

"I was just a bit shocked to see him in a gay bar. I mean, nobody back home knows about me, and I thought it might be embarrassing. Of course it doesn't mean that you're actually gay if you're in a gay bar but... is he?"

"Well the official version, the version he'd tell you, is that he's bisexual–although he's always really been gay as far as I know. But he still likes to hold on to the idea that he isn't. In fact, if he'd seen you he might have been a bit concerned too that word would get out that he'd been hanging around with a bunch of queens in Playa Del Ingles."

"There's no danger of that," said Terry. "I wouldn't tell anybody– because if I did, I'd have to explain what I was doing there." George patted his pockets. He had seen the way Terry looked at Alan in Hollandaise, and the way he had bolted out of the door, and he felt sure that there was more behind the lad's reaction to his friend than he was letting on. He pulled out the magic glasses case.

"Mind if I smoke?"

"Not at all, but if you're going to, can I scrounge one off you? I think I've left mine in one of the bars."

"I wasn't thinking about cigarettes," said George roguishly, carefully removing the last joint of the evening. "Although I have some of those too if you really want one." Terry was clearly quite taken aback. George spotted him staring. "It does wonders for my arthritic bones," he explained. Then he shook his head. "You youngsters think this stuff is the unique preserve of people your own age but let me tell you, I have friends in their sixties who think nothing of taking ecstasy and cocaine."

"You're preaching to the converted," said Terry. "I know quite a few older guys who go clubbing in Manchester, and they love it. But all that gurning and sweating and waving their arms in the air–it seems a bit too much like hard work to me."

"Are you more of a pipe and slippers man, then? Is that why you go for old fogies?" Terry looked thoughtful–taking George's question seriously even though it had been meant as a throwaway bit of banter.

"No it's not," he said eventually. "I'm not sure why I go for older people, to be honest. It could be something about being attracted to character–you know, things like warts and wrinkles. I find young bodies nice enough to look at, but there's no sexual interest there, because they seem too perfect. The passing years add something, a special quality. And I just feel more comfortable around older people. Don't get me wrong, I've got plenty in common with people my own age as well."

"You're a very pleasant boy," said George, handing over the joint. "It's genuine guys like you who give hope to old farts like me, but there aren't enough of you around. Far too many youngsters out there are just on the make for whatever they can get."

"That irritates me a lot. I've lost count of the number of times I've been asked if I'm on the game. I've got nothing against rent boys as it happens–but it's this assumption that money is bound to be involved that pisses me off." George laughed.

"Take it as a compliment–they obviously think you're too young and gorgeous to be genuinely interested in ancient relics." Terry took in another large lungful of marijuana smoke and coughed.

"There should be some sort of health warning on that tin of

yours. What kind of weed is this?" George had closed his eyes and was breathing slowly, letting it wash over him.

"Just a little something my Dutch boys got hold of for me."

"Dutch, eh? Makes sense. They certainly know what they're doing when it comes to dope." Terry handed the joint back–his eyes already bloodshot. And remembered going round to the house to see Jane, and finding her not there. Her father Alan answering the door, telling him she'd gone shopping with her mum. Saying, while you're here, can you just help me get something down from the loft? And Terry following this man up the stairs, fascinated by the contours visible through the thin, shiny material of his shirt, which gave hints about the shape of the body underneath. He was intensely aware, as all young people are, of the slightly acrid smell of an older man, whose tissues have been marinading for years in those mysterious juices squeezed from some dark corner of the male body. Excited by the slow, confident movements. Thrilled to be helping him moving the stuff around in the hot, confined attic space. Feeling slightly restless. Going home afterwards and having a bath and playing with himself.

"So you went out with Alan's daughter for a few years," George was shaking his head. "Fancy bumping into you here... wait until I tell him."

"How do you know each other?"

"We met back in the fifties, during our national service. A bit before your time."

"Are you and he lovers?"

"Good heavens no! We've played around a few times, but nothing more than that. We're like family really. I knew his wife, and I'm Jane's godfather–but even though we've been through so much together I sometimes think he's a bit embarrassed by it all, by the fact that I'm gay and I don't conceal it. He's the opposite. I wouldn't say he's lived his life in denial but there are definitely big aspects of it that he's had to keep in the background."

"Must have been difficult."

George looked across the tables at a seven foot high drag queen, dressed in a blue sequinned dress and with huge glittering gold platform boots on, all lipstick, eyelashes and black beehive wig, shoving a hot dog into her mouth. Next to her was a macho-looking, dark-haired young man who was shouting furiously in Spanish, while she kept eating and completely ignored him. It was a somewhat unconventional domestic scene.

"Perhaps, yes. I've often wondered how he's kept it together–but then again sometimes I've envied him because he's had an escape from this strange world of ours. He's been able to walk away from it, to go back to his wife and family while I've had to go on flying the flag, searching for that particular bar in a certain city, or that isolated spot known to be frequented by people like us. But I do find it ironic though that despite everything, despite the fact that he managed to create an almost completely straight life for himself, the way things worked out, his homosexuality claimed him back in the end. You can't change what you are."

Young Terry, head spinning from the genetically modified dope and the night's strange developments, pondered the implications of this statement, as the scenes around them became increasingly chaotic. There was a sudden shout as the drag queen poured a large paper cup full of Coca Cola all over her companion, laughing as she did so. One of the macho guy's hands flew up and delivered a sharp slap across her face. Hardly flinching, and in fact while still moving in time with the pumping music, she quickly raised one of her knees into the man's groin. He gasped and folded over, slumping to the ground with his face puckered in agony. The drag queen dropped her empty cup on him and its plastic lid popped off, scattering ice cubes about as she turned on her heels and flounced away.

"Looks like things are going to get a bit rowdy up here," George said. "Better head off." They looked at one another–and despite the shouts and the smoke and the ear-splittingly loud samba music, the paper plate smeared with tomato sauce and mayonnaise, the full ash tray, the stained table cloth and the scrunched-up paper napkins, something quiet and delicate passed across the table. George, who had decades of experience dealing with this kind of thing, took the initiative. He smiled, and the smile was returned.

"What are your plans now?"

"I was just going to go back." Terry looked at his watch, saw that it was two forty-five, and laughed. "Get an early night for once. But I suppose when you're on holiday in Playa Del Ingles, that's a bit like being in the desert and praying for rain." George maintained eye contact.

"I was thinking about turning in too–which hotel are you at?" Terry was picking at the remains of the food.

"I'm staying with some friends–a straight couple I've known since university. You'd be welcome to come back though. Rob's a stripper at one of the bars, so they're pretty gay-friendly–and they don't mind me taking people back at all." George raised his eyebrows.

"Where does your friend work?"

"The Block–why, do you know it?"

"Know it? We're practically shareholders. Alan will be in there anytime now."

"Well, Rob's doing his show tonight and tomorrow. He's on two nights in a row because the usual guy is ill. Your friend won't be disappointed–Rob's got the biggest cock on the island, possibly one of the biggest cocks ever, as far as we know."

"With a bit of luck it might cheer Alan up. Now where is this flat?"

"It's not a flat. They live in a villa not too far away, on the hillside overlooking Maspalomas. Rob's parents are pretty well-off."

"They must be delighted with their son's career." Terry sniggered.

"He's one of the most intelligent people I know. Studied philosophy and got a first. The university asked him to stay on to do a doctorate, but he's always wanted to be a writer. The stripping is just a sideline."

"Doesn't it bother him that he's probably cleverer than the entire audience put together?"

"I don't think so. He says that after years of intellectual sparring, of constantly having to prove himself academically, he actually likes the dumb adulation." George shrugged.

"I suppose if God's given you a big brain and a big cock, it's up to you to choose which one you're going to use to change the world."

"You should be a philosopher."

"Never mind that. Listen, we can go back to my hotel if you like. It's just round the corner. Alan and I have separate rooms so it's no problem."

"Yeah why not?" Terry suddenly adopted a coquettish look. "I can always get a taxi back later, if you kick me out."

"Seems unlikely at this point."

George led the younger man up the staircase next to Monroe's and then at street level turned in the direction of the hotel. Just as they stepped onto the pavement, he spotted Mark walking past, heading back down into the Yumbo Centre. He had changed his clothes and looked even more handsome than before. Their eyes met and Mark looked quickly from George to Terry and back again, understanding the situation, nodding in appreciation, giving him a discreet but knowing smile. There was no malice in his expression, but George felt slightly guilty, as if he had been caught doing something wrong. This was strange, because Mark had blown him out earlier, and there was therefore no reason why George should feel at all bad about going home with Terry. But he liked Mark and had no desire to burn his bridges. It was all a bit of a mess, really, but he was drunk and stoned and going home with one of the most handsome young men he'd seen that night, so it was hardly the time to sort it out. Besides, he was bound to see Mark again in the coming days.

*

WHEN Alan returned to the Block it was so packed that he could hardly get inside. It was also much hotter, on account of the number of bodies and the powerful spotlights that were now shining onto the cage in the corner. As he eased himself through the crowd on his way to the bar, Alan felt the heat of one of the bright beams on his neck. He also noticed that the staff had shed their carnival gear, and were now decked out in shorts and T-shirts. The change of clothes was a good idea–Alan could already feel a trickle of sweat down his back. There was a fidgety, expectant atmosphere and he sensed that the stripper was about to come on, so he quickly ordered a beer and turned around to watch the show. It was such a tiny place that he was actually less then five feet from the cage. The music was turned off, and there was shouting and clapping as a broad-shouldered young man emerged from the dark room and swaggered through the crowd with an exaggerated, bullish gait–then hopped onto the podium and squeezed between the bars in one smooth movement. Someone behind the bar pushed a button and the room was filled with the first raunchy bars of Etta James singing "I Just Want to be Loved By You". He was an athletic, big-boned fellow–and he was wearing a policeman's uniform. Last night's stripper had been dressed in something similar, and had stretched out the process of disrobing to ridiculous levels. He had eventually got down to a little thong, which he kept on until the very end of the act. He needn't have bothered removing it. Alan had felt cheated by the whole display–and could tell from the unimpressed sighs all round that his fellow punters felt the same way. Tonight, though, it was a different story. The music had only been playing for about a minute, and this guy was already stripped down to his pants, gyrating his hips, rubbing himself all over the bars at the front of the cage, reaching out and pulling people's hands towards his body.

Alan had enjoyed both male and female strippers in his time and he had to admit that even though these days he preferred going to bed with a man, he still found female bodies ultimately more erotic in this kind of situation. There was something more extravagant about their shapes–more capacity for pendulous, lascivious movement. Men's bodies could be powerful, but they somehow lacked the grandeur. Except, as young Terry would have argued had he been there to discuss the subject, in the case of older men–whose rounded paunches seemed to have the same kind of appeal to him as a pair of woman's breasts could have to a heterosexual male. The stripper now removed his pants, and instantly the attention of the entire bar shifted to one thing. And what a thing it was! The tempo of the music had changed and the young man, who seemed possessed by the rhythm, squeezed out from behind the bars and jumped down among the audience–which moved back, intimidated. But there was no escape. He walked up to the nearest punters, grabbed their hands and placed them on his cock, which seemed rather improbably to be getting even bigger. Alan's eyes were locked in place–it was as if the traditional relationship between the snake and the charmer had been reversed, and the serpent was now the one with the capability of putting the man under its primeval spell. Suddenly the fellow standing in front of Alan, a nervous, puppet-faced man, bolted off to the toilet, leaving him in the front line. Attracted by the movement, the stripper reached over and plucked Alan from his position at the bar. Another man was already holding the lad's dick, and he motioned for Alan to put his hands on it too. Alan was rather shocked to see that even with four pairs of hands grasping it (he was unable to get his fingers all the way around), the bulbous end was still poking out for all to see. But eroticism was strangely absent from the moment. The thing was so big and pumped up that it seemed to have a rubbery, artificial quality–an effect accentuated by the dark, oily sheen of the skin. It was like something that should be exhibited in a glass case in a museum, and he doubted whether it could actually be used for any sexual purpose, without causing serious injury to those involved. Nevertheless, Alan could see that those around him were drooling at the sight of it. There was a sort of tribal frenzy about the crowd and he felt suddenly uneasy. He disengaged himself from the knot of bodies and pushed his way through to the door. Outside, back in the fresh air, he felt enormous relief. He slowed his pace and looked around. The market stalls in the plaza were mostly closed up now. As he walked past one, Alan saw an old gypsy woman sweeping with a broom around the back. A small wrinkle-faced man, presumably her husband, was cleaning out a popcorn machine. He stopped and smiled, and Alan smiled back, grateful for the civility of it after the strangely bestial scene in the bar.

The people who ran the Sky Rider had also packed up for the

evening. All the lights had been turned off, and the cage had been hoisted about twenty feet into the air and covered with a tarpaulin. It rocked gently back and forth in the soft night wind. At Na Und they were playing only slow tunes now, and there was the distinct feeling that the evening was coming to an end. There were a few couples left on the dance floor, clasped tightly together, oblivious to everything but the music and the feel of their partners' bodies. Among them Alan spotted Mark in the arms of a tall and very smartly dressed older man, with a magnificent mane of white swept-back hair and a bushy moustache. Alan smiled–he was pleased that the lad had found someone else and hoped his rendezvous would be more successful this time. There was no sign of George and he saw no one else he knew. A couple of people looked his way but they seemed half cut, and weren't his type anyway. He drifted past and climbed up the stairs to the first floor. The place was heaving, and he had no desire to fight his way through the crowd, so he decided to go back down, walk across the plaza and check out the bars upstairs on the other side. It was a little less busy over there, but the music was very loud. He made his way past several places, where the average age looked to be about eighteen. The clientele was what George called the tight T-shirt brigade. As Alan moved along someone shouted out in a waspish voice–obviously hoping that he would hear.

"I can't believe they've started letting OAPS in here." Alan allowed himself a bitter smile. A few years ago he would have been really put off by a comment like that–but not any more. The person who had said it was obviously too shallow to see that he too would be older one day, and could potentially find himself in a similar situation. Alan ducked into a leather bar further along the corridor and bought himself a beer. As his eyes adjusted to the dim light, he saw that at the far end a big sheet of military camouflage webbing had been hung up. There were indistinct signs of movement behind the membrane, which obviously concealed the entrance to the dark room. He sidled over and scrambled through the slit. In front of him he could see a corridor lined with cabin doors. He moved forward, and through an open door made out a man lying in a sling, partially clothed in something made out of black plastic and bits of metal, surrounded by shadowy figures who were all working on different parts of the suspended body. Alan heard slapping sounds coming from another cubicle. He walked to the end of the corridor and turned the corner, to see that the labyrinth opened out into a larger room, with another sling in the corner and what looked like an old tin bath in the middle. A naked man was lying in the bath, pleading for someone to urinate on him. Alan needed the toilet quite badly and for a moment actually considered doing what this person wanted him to do, but then he stopped himself. It was a line he was not prepared to cross–not tonight at any rate. And anyway, what was he doing in the midst of such depravity? This was not the way he had expected things to turn out. What would his wife have made of it? Was she watching him now? He hoped not. Everything up to the point when he went to the strip show could be explained, was within acceptable parameters, but now he was just scraping the barrel, mooching around on his own, hoping that one last thrill would be offered up. It was getting late and there was an urgency about the way in which people were prowling, desperately trying to find someone suitable before closing time. Several men made a grab at Alan as he made his way down the darkened passage, but he gently removed their hands and continued on his way. As he moved back towards the light he glimpsed his reflection in a mirror attached to the wall. He stopped and looked more closely in the dim light, worried that perhaps the things he had been exposed to had somehow etched themselves upon him–but there was no sign of that. It was the same face he had known all these years. There was a certain tiredness about the features–a jaded quality brought on no doubt by the excesses of the holiday; and perhaps a hint of loneliness in the eyes. He turned away and headed back into the bar, where he placed his empty bottle on a table on his way out. Reaching street level he looked up and saw the moon high in the sky, shining down with a harsh blue-white light. What had he achieved tonight? He had rather ignobly snatched someone from under his best friend George's nose, only to squander the opportunity. He'd made a fool of himself by flirting with another young man in front of his boyfriend–although of course he was delighted that his interest in young Steve was reciprocated. It was a false dawn, though, and he felt certain that nothing would come of it. The evening's shenanigans seemed at that moment to be rather pathetic, nothing more than a futile and inconsequential jig around the maypole. But perhaps he was being a bit harsh–after all, no one seemed to have been hurt by his actions. All the other men he had been involved with that night, young Steve and his older friend Frank; Mark; probably George too, had gone home with someone else. They would be able to reach out during the night and feel that there was another human being there. But what would Alan have to console himself? The knowledge that he had touched what was surely one of the largest penises ever? So what? It had been nothing more than a mirage. If he had gone with George instead of going to the strip show, perhaps he would have met the young chap that his friend had gone off looking for–and then, well... who knew what? Forty years of married life had left him peculiarly unprepared for all this. He wondered if his ineptitude was simply down to the fact that he had been out of the courtship game for so long, or whether things were always this difficult in the gay world. But he couldn't really blame his environment, he'd had his share of the chances. Maybe–and this was the most galling thing to have to admit–his problems were all down to his own personality. On the way to Hollandaise, George had affectionately referred to him as a 'complex case', and at that moment Alan could see exactly what his friend had been getting at. But this was all academic. He was back at the hotel now and at the reception desk the night porter was doing the books for the previous day, while listening to some salsa music on a small transistor radio. He smiled broadly as he saw Alan approaching, and said good night as he handed over the key. Alan took the lift to the third floor and then walked along the corridor to his room, his steel heels clicking on the tiles. George–who had the room next to Alan's–heard the footsteps and knew that his friend was safely home, but he didn't dwell on it too much because he had other more pressing matters to attend to. Alan entered his room, turned on the large ceiling fan and opened the window, stripped off and went into the bathroom to brush his teeth. Within minutes he was under the sheets and sound asleep.

PART TWO – A NEW DAY

ALAN HAD NOT turned in until after three in the morning, but he was awake at eight thirty. Even though the thick curtains kept out most of the bright Canarian sunshine, something about the ambience of the room told him that it was already hot outside. He pulled back the heavy fabric in front of the windows and was shocked by the intensity of the light. He stepped back, screwed up his eyes and moaned like an old vampire about to disappear in a puff of smoke. After a few seconds he slid the balcony door wide open and walked outside, to check whether the underpants he had washed the night before had dried. They were still slightly damp–but would be nice and dry in time for him to put on a fresh pair before going out tonight. No one was lying on the loungers around the pool as yet, although a few towels had already been placed on the ones in the best positions. Alan looked up from the pool towards the balconies opposite his room, and saw a little old man a couple of floors up, banging one of his sandals against the balcony railing–presumably to get the sand out. The man finished what he was doing and then looked up and saw Alan watching him. He quickly glanced right and left to make sure no one else was watching, then pulled up the towel that was wrapped around his waist, flashing his cock in Alan's direction. Alan smiled and waved across. The man rubbed himself a few times, blew Alan a kiss and dropped the towel back down. No sooner had he done so than a short, fat woman with the face of an angry gibbon waddled onto the balcony, sat down at the table, and lit a cigarette. He must have heard her coming. The stranger–whom Alan and George had nicknamed Balcony Man–flashed himself at them whenever he got the chance. He was German, and they often saw him at dinner with his wife. Of course on those occasions he ignored them, but whenever he saw either of them out on their balcony, he would put on a little show—as long as there was nobody else around. Alan shook his head. The guy was sailing very close to the wind—but even though he was seventy if he was a day, there was something quite sexy about his impromptu bouts of exhibitionism, and at the end of the day what he had was definitely worth showing off.

Alan had a routine that he followed each morning. He put some suntan oil on his nose, his ears and the back of his neck before breakfast, so that it would have a good chance to soak in before he started the long walk to the beach. He and George had agreed that if one of them had company for the night, they would leave the red 'do not disturb' sign on their door, so that the other would know not to knock before going down to breakfast. As Alan left his room he saw that the sign was there, confirming his suspicion that he had been the only one left on the shelf last night. He felt much more relaxed about it now than he had before he went to bed. He didn't particularly envy George, who would have to make conversation with a stranger, while dealing with a hangover and going about his ablutions. It had taken Alan a long time to get used to the quietness of the mornings after Marge had died and in some ways he didn't really want anyone else to invade it. After breakfast he went back to his room to brush his teeth and pick up his rucksack, noticing that George was still in 'do not disturb' mode. He stopped at one of the supermarkets on the Avenida Tirajana to buy water, cigarettes, some fruit and a newspaper—then continued on foot straight down towards the Riu Palace, which he reached about ten minutes later. The hotel overlooked the sand dunes and the beaches of Maspalomas, and had panoramic views all the way across to the lighthouse and the hotels on the island's southernmost tip, probably about a mile and a half away. In a moment Alan would continue his journey by clambering through a gap in the iron fence and picking his way down a rocky incline to the dunes below—a route that was taken by hundreds of people who walked from Playa Del Ingles to the gay beach every day. Before setting out across the dunes Alan liked to stop for a few minutes and look over the railings, taking in a view that always amazed him even though he had seen it umpteen times.

It looked like a bungling deity had picked up a chunk of the Sahara desert and dropped it onto the island by accident, while trying to carry it across the Atlantic towards America. Huge, undulating banks of golden sand, shaped by the winds that whipped across this most exposed part of the island, stretched into the distance. Because they were moulded by the same wind all the hillocks, which were roughly crescent-shaped, pointed in the same direction. Seen from this angle the vast network of canyons and peaks had an incredible, almost geometric orderliness about them–but there was also an organic quality, like the curves of a large meandering river or the contours of the human body. The inclines that were downwind were shallow and easy to climb up, those that faced the wind were much more precipitous, and people liked to throw themselves off, knowing that further down their fall would be broken by tons of soft sand. Because of the wind the dunes continued to move day and night, their shapes and formation slowly changing inch by inch as puffs of sand were blown off their pointed tops. Alan liked the fact that each time he visited the island and looked across to Maspalomas, although the overall impression was similar, he was actually looking at a completely different landscape. But the shifting of the dunes, like the flow of a glacier, was completely indiscernible to the naked eye.

Over to the west vegetation had taken hold–and the massive banks of sand had given way to a wild landscape of bushes, trees and shrubs, like a desert oasis. Here the dunes were anchored by the plants' roots and no longer shifted, becoming instead a complex labyrinth of woody areas, clearings, hills and hollows. Running through the middle of all this like a spine was the flat bed of a dried-out river, a vast stretch of cracked and desiccated mud that crunched underfoot. This harsh landscape was broken by the occasional island of trees, in which people often set up camp for the day, laying out their towels, putting up their parasols, and keeping their bags of provisions cool by hiding them in the shade of the trees. And in the distance towering above it all was the lighthouse of Maspalomas–a useful point of reference for anyone who became lost in the dunes. Alan climbed through the fence and edged his way down to the sandy plain, then padded off towards the vegetation. Within minutes he was standing in a small clearing that was a particular favourite of his. It was bounded on all sides by arid hillocks covered with bushes and shrubs, and hence sheltered from the wind, but he could clearly hear the sound of the waves breaking on the beach a quarter of a mile away, as well as the song of wagtails and blackbirds, and the scratching of lizards in the undergrowth. Even the whisper of a small black beetle moving across the sand near one of his feet was audible. This was the best time of the day, before droves of people started clumping around and scaring off the birds and animals. The magic would return later on, after six o'clock in the afternoon, when most of them had gone back to Playa del Ingles for their fix of beer or coffee and cakes, and the dunes would be bathed in the golden light of the early evening. Alan looked around at the bushes, marvelling at the way the long spikes on their branches seemed to form complex three-dimensional geometric shapes, like the models used by science teachers to show their pupils the structure of molecules. The warm sand under foot deadened sound, increasing the sense of being cut off from the normal world. A gentle wind whispered through the dried-out leaves of a huge palm tree nearby, which creaked as it was eased back and forth by the currents of air. He heard the faint buzz of a plane high overhead and looked up, shading his eyes, to see sunlight glinting off metal–perhaps the fuselage or wings–and several pinpoints of colour tumbling down towards the island. Skydivers often did their jumps at this time of the morning when the air was cooler and there were fewer convection currents. In a minute or two he might even hear the flutter of the parachute silk close at hand as one of them tried to land in an open spot where there were fewer trees. On one occasion a handsome young guy had landed nearby, rolled up his parachute, stripped off and had speedy sex with Alan in a bush. Ten minutes later, when someone in a Jeep had come to pick him up, he was already back in his gear and ready to go. Opportunities presented themselves in the most unusual ways.

Alan always felt at this time of day that the landscape belonged to him. He would wander around naked (for nudism was permitted throughout the entire area), checking out various landmarks. If he had been a dog, he would probably have cocked his leg here and there, marking his territory. He and George even had names for bits of the dunes that had a special significance. One of them, which he had walked past a few minutes ago, held a particularly strong and sinister resonance. It was a huge old palm tree, its main trunk incredibly stout and split half way up into three separate trunks, from which the spiky leaves sprouted. It looked like a massive trident, protruding ominously from the flat, cracked earth. For this reason, and because of the dark atmosphere around it, they called the tree the Devil's Palm. That and other landmarks gave Alan and George a good frame of reference for discussing goings-on within the dunes, or arranging to meet up. But they never waited for each other too near the Devil's Palm, because they both felt the strange vibrations generated by the old tree. Alan had now done the rounds and people were starting to spring up here and there, some settling down to sunbathe, others passing through on their way to the beach–some just here to see if they could get a bit of sex before rejoining their families for the day. He wondered whether he should take the quickest route to the gay beach, straight across the dried-out river bed–passing near the large square that the boules players had marked out so they could play naked each day–or whether he should walk towards the Maspalomas lighthouse, which he could see poking up behind a hill nearby, and do a bit of a dog-leg detour through what he and George called the Last Chance Saloon: a clearing in the middle of some dense bushes in which a few men could usually be found loitering. After a few seconds of thought, he decided to have a quick look in the Last Chance Saloon–after all, what harm could it do?

*

TERRY had arrived in the dunes about twenty minutes earlier. He'd left George's room at about the time that morning when Balcony Man was flashing his wares at Alan across the hotel pool. George was out for the count so the younger man decided to slip away without waking him up. He obviously needed his sleep and besides, Terry didn't want to hang around because he had to be back at the villa in time to be picked up by Alex and Dieter, who came in the car to get him every morning on their way from Puerto Mogan to the beach. He had woken up very early, before six o'clock, but was unable to go back to sleep because of a rather vivid and troubling dream. In it he was in a swimming pool changing room, drying himself and preparing to get dressed after his swim, when a handsome grey-haired man came in and started to undress. It wasn't a place he recognised and yet at the same time it felt familiar, perhaps because it was one of those composite locations generated by the subconscious during dreams, incorporating the characteristics of many of the swimming baths he had visited throughout his life. There was something dirty and disheveled about it, as if it had been built in Victorian times and now needed a spot of renovation. He noticed cracks in the floor tiles, and the white paint on the walls was blistered in many places and covered in large, rust-coloured stains. Heavily-cladded pipes, probably connected to an ancient rumbling boiler somewhere in the building, snaked around the walls just below the ceiling. There were battered lockers and a couple of long wooden benches, the varnish almost rubbed away by generations of bathers sitting down to dry their feet and put their shoes and socks on. Between the benches was a metal frame with rows of clothes hooks on it, like the ones in school cloakrooms. Terry watched furtively through the items of clothing that were hanging from the brass pegs while the man took his clothes off. He could see stout shoulders and powerful legs; the man's rounded belly and a scattering of white hair on his suntanned chest. The guy turned away as he was about to pull down his pants, almost as if he suspected that he was being watched–and Terry got a good look at his chunky, well-shaped bottom. The older man slipped on a pair of bright red Speedo-style swimming trunks, had a shower and then walked through the plastic curtain that separated the changing room from the swimming pool area itself. He walked away slowly, looking back at Terry with a slight swagger, almost like a come-on, but too ambiguous to say for certain whether or not there was anything there. As Terry watched him disappear, the changing room melted into something resembling a forest clearing, the clothes rack with its row of pegs transformed into a hedgerow, the lockers and pipes above them metamorphosed into indistinct vegetation–a tangle of bushes and shrubs, dark and difficult to make out on the periphery of his vision.

Terry walked around to the other side of the hedgerow, where he saw that the older man's clothes were hanging from a branch. He looked around to make sure that no one else was there and then–feeling ashamed but unable to stop himself–moved forward and started to rummage among the clothes, quickly finding the man's navy blue Y-front underpants. He turned them inside out and then pushed the crutch to his nose, sniffing strongly and savouring the smell impregnated into the fabric, closing his eyes as he felt himself getting hard. He couldn't say how long he stayed like that, clutching the pants to his face, oblivious to everything except that indescribable smell, but when he re-opened his eyes the dimness of the clearing was once again the bright neon light of the changing room, and standing around him, where the trees and shrubs had been, were all the people he knew. In the front row he could see his ex-girlfriend and her family, his own parents, his friends and colleagues, his former teachers–all staring in disgust, utterly judgmental. He woke up with a start, drenched in sweat, feeling his heart beating in his chest. Had he cried out? George was breathing rhythmically next to him, undisturbed, so he suspected not. He went quietly to the bathroom and had a pee, looking at himself in the mirror as he had a drink of water. He smiled at his reflection as he screwed the plastic top back onto the bottle, relieved that nothing had really changed at all. There was no need to feel ashamed, it had just been a dream–but that message from the unconscious had lodged itself in his mind like a splinter, and when he lay back down and tried to get back to sleep, cool and comfortable as the dawn began to infiltrate the room, he found himself unable to drift off. For an hour and a half he stayed like that, his thoughts free-wheeling as the light coming through the gaps in the curtains became gradually stronger–but eventually he decided to give up on sleep and head back to the villa. As he walked along the open-air corridor from George's room to reception, he saw hotel staff arriving at the rear entrance, chucking away their cigarette butts and making good-humoured comments to one another in Spanish. The Canarian holiday machine was cranking itself up for another day. He slipped out of the entrance and crossed the Avenida Tirajana, delighted by how quiet it was, experiencing that queer elation often felt by people as they make their way back home after a night spent in someone else's bed. All was silent at the villa and the door to Rob and Helen's room was closed so he stripped off, showered, and went to the kitchen for coffee, orange juice and a bowl of cereal. Alex and Dieter turned up soon afterwards and on the way down to Maspalomas, as they drove through the hinterland of holiday bungalows, hotels and whitewashed apartment blocks to the lighthouse at Faro, Terry told them everything that had happened the night before. He described how George had followed him to Monroe's, and explained how during their conversation had confirmed that the man they'd seen at Hollandaise was indeed Alan Reid. Terry also explained how he knew Alan–about how as a teenaged boy he had gone out with Alan's daughter Jane for a few years, during which time he had fallen in love with her dad. He also confessed to staying over at George's hotel. Now ensconced in their favourite spot in the dunes, Alex laughed as he stood on a spread-out rainbow-coloured beach towel with the words "Fort Lauderdale, USA" woven into it, and rubbed some sun cream into his lover's back.

"You certainly like to make life complicated for yourself, young man."

Terry was sitting on his own towel with his legs stretched out, propped up on one arm, gazing through his wrap-around Ray Ban sunglasses at the expanse of arid terrain. It was already pretty hot. A couple of naked men were loitering in an area of bushes and trees not too far away which the Germans called the Hauptbahnhof, or Central Station–because of the large number of people who passed through it looking for sex.

"I don't set out to," Terry replied a trifle defensively. "It just seems to go that way."

"So what are you going to do next?" Dieter spoke as he stretched out on the ground, face-down.

"I'm not sure. I mean, on the one hand I really want to see Alan, but on the other, I don't know... the prospect fills me with dread somehow." Alex laughed.

"That doesn't sound like the fearless young Englishman I know."

"Maybe, but this is an exceptional situation. Something that I could never have bargained for."

"And so much the better for that," said Alex. "I've found in life that these are always the most interesting situations. Perhaps it's just the kind of shake-up you need." Terry suddenly stood up and leaned forward, staring intently at the bushes of the Hauptbahnhof.

"Speak of the devil," he hissed. "There he is." Dieter flipped over and sat up, following the direction in which Terry was pointing.

"Very nice," he said appreciatively. "Not bad at all." Alex gave him a light slap.

"Hey, stop ogling." He joined the others in looking across at Alan. "So, here is our man–off looking for some early morning mischief. And who can blame him?" Dieter nudged Terry.

"Go on then," he said. "Now's your chance. You'd better hurry though, in case someone else gets to him first." Terry bent down to his rucksack, rummaged around and brought out his hat. There was a jumpy, nervous quality to his actions. He clearly wasn't keen to follow Alan but he also didn't want to appear cowardly in the face of their challenge.

"Are you sure?" His question was directed almost more to himself than his friends.

"Come on," urged Alex, "get in there! What is it you English say? Who dares wins." Terry's demeanour was more that of the condemned man than the conquering hero. He sighed.

"Right then–wish me luck."

The others clapped their hands and shouted encouraging remarks behind him as he padded across the sand in his flip-flops towards the bushes, wondering what on earth he was going to do when he got there. He could hear his heart beating in his ears. What would he say? Would Alan even know who he was? The area in which all the mischief took place was a clearing in the middle of some particularly dense bushes and trees–which could only be entered from this direction through a tight little opening in the vegetation, and it was hard to get through without scratching your legs and arms on the thorny branches. Terry decided to go around the back where it wasn't quite so overgrown, and where he would be able to get an idea of what was happening before going in. He made his way around the trees, passing a few people lying in the sun, who all gave him the once-over as he went by, checking out this handsome new arrival. Like many homosexuals who'd visited Gran Canaria a few times, Terry had intimate knowledge of the network of tracks that ran through the bushes. Just up ahead a tree had fallen over, so that its trunk was at a forty-five degree angle to the ground, forming a natural barrier between the expanse of the dunes and the clearing at the centre of the Hauptbahnhof. Terry clambered through, into a position where all that lay between him and the clearing were some chest-high shrubs, a bit like gorse bushes, that he could easily get through if he wanted to. He could now see what was going on without necessarily being visible to those who were inside. He got there just in time to see Alan Reid advancing towards a young-looking guy who was playing with himself under a tree, slowing moving his hand up and down what looked like a long, thick cock. Terry turned on his heels and walked quickly back out into the open. Head down, feeling for some reason humiliated, he strode past the people who'd seen him coming in, avoiding eye contact with them. Within minutes he was back at the place where he and his friends had settled for the morning–but they were nowhere to be seen. They'd probably gone off for a walk, to see if any of their other pals had arrived in the dunes. Terry flopped down onto his towel moodily and lit a cigarette, thinking that his date with destiny would have to wait.

*

BACK at the Hauptbahnhof, Alan was having second thoughts. The stranger had looked slim and appealing from a distance, but up close things were not all they had seemed. He cursed himself for having left the hotel room without first washing his sunglasses–the lenses of which had become so streaked with suntan oil and sweat in the previous few days that he could no longer see particularly clearly through them. Now, only a few feet away, Alan saw that what had appeared to be juicy pectoral muscles were in fact tired and sagging tits, and the tanned and smooth skin was in reality leathery and loose, covered in liver spots and moles. The guy was wearing a baseball cap and big mirrored aviator-style sunglasses, which had also made him appear younger than he obviously was, but the hair sticking out from under the hat was grey, and the skin around the neck was wrinkled and falling in little folds.

"Christ," said Alan under his breath. "The bugger's older than I am." The stranger turned and headed deeper into the bushes, motioning for him to follow. Despite his sense of revulsion Alan felt a mysterious compulsion to go on. The branches and thorns scratched his arms and legs as he inched his way through to a shady clearing a few feet ahead, where the stranger was waiting for him, leaning against the trunk of a dead tree and sniffing hard on a bottle of poppers. As Alan emerged, he noted with distaste the used condoms lying around, the small foil sachets that had once contained them, the crushed beer cans, the empty cigarette packets, the plastic water bottles and the wads of desiccated tissue that people had discarded after wiping their private parts. How appalling, he thought, that those who had sex here didn't have the decency to take their rubbish away with them when they finished. The heat was stifling and the place stank of urine. There were toxic little bowers like this scattered throughout the dunes, gradually killing the trees and bushes in the vicinity and driving away the wildlife. No wonder the Canarian authorities wanted to turn the whole area into one of those protected nature reserves where people weren't allowed to go. Alan laid down his rucksack in the cleanest spot he could find, then took off his hat and placed it on top. The stranger slipped the poppers bottle into a small bum-bag clipped around his waist, the only thing he was wearing apart from the hat and the shades, and came forward to give Alan a kiss. As he moved closer Alan caught a fleeting glimpse of his own reflection in the lenses of the guy's sunglasses. His face—distorted by the convex mirrors—appeared bloated and ugly, the skin pallid in the harsh light of the clearing. But his expression was the most shocking thing of all. The smile he'd tried to muster had become a grotesque rictus, because of the disgust and apprehension he felt about the whole scene. It was the final straw. With the stranger nearly upon him, Alan quickly turned and picked up his bag and hat.

"I'm sorry," he muttered. "I can't do this." The man backed off and held up his hand, nodding to show that it was no problem. This kind of thing had probably happened to him before. He said something in a foreign language, which Alan guessed was either German or Dutch, and moved back to the tree trunk, where he pulled out his cigarettes and lit one. Alan said goodbye and pushed his way back through the bushes, hearing twigs snap, feeling them scratching his skin but not caring because he wanted so much to be back in the fresh air and sunlight. Out in the open he took off his rucksack, removed a large bottle of water from it and took a mouthful, swooshing it around and then spitting it into the sand. He drank properly, feeling the cool liquid moving down into his stomach, then put the bottle back into the bag, zipped it up and bent down to rub his legs, clearing off the bits of twigs and other vegetation that had become stuck to them as he made his way through the shrubbery. Alan then took off his glasses and wiped his face and forehead with a handkerchief—which he then used to clean the lenses of his glasses before putting them on. Satisfied that he was in good shape once again, he slid the rucksack back onto his back, looked behind to see if he'd left anything lying on the ground, then turned and headed out towards the open expanse of sand beyond the trees.

*

TERRY first met Alan Reid at the eighteenth birthday party thrown for Miranda, the sister of the girl he was going out with at the time. Like many well-raised adolescent boys, he was pretty awkward about the whole business of what his dad called 'courting'. On top of that, he'd only been seeing Jane for a month or so, and was therefore nervous about the party because he felt he would–as the new boyfriend–be subject to her parents' scrutiny. The apprehension made him feel slightly clammy as he sat in his father's car on the way to the bash, wearing a jacket and tie for the first time in years and clutching a carrier bag that dangled between his knees, which contained a box of sugared almonds and a bottle of wine. He felt more like a condemned man on his way the scaffold, or a soldier about to go over the top, than someone who was out to have a good time. No wonder so many of Jane's friends went out with sixth formers, who were more confident and less spotty, and who had overcome challenges that seemed insurmountable to Terry, like getting into nightclubs and driving. As they turned into the street where Jane lived, Terry's father smiled and reached across, putting his son's thigh with a closed fist–a sort of macho expression of paternal support.

"Relax. Have a few drinks but don't get too pissed, or you'll make an idiot of yourself."

"Thanks," said Terry, so preoccupied with his thoughts that he barely registered this dubious gobbet of wisdom. As he got out of the car he could see the shapes of people in the hallway, and hear the sounds of loud voices inside the house. It was a warm day and he felt terribly overdressed as he advanced up the path. In the hall a man and a woman were discussing a touring production of A Midsummer Night's Dream that had come to the local theatre recently. Somewhere, music was playing. The man noticed the new arrival and broke off.

"Welcome!" he shouted, grabbing Terry's hand and waggling it about.

"Hi," said Terry rather meekly. "I'm a friend of Jane's."

"I'm her uncle–pleased to meet you. They're all out in the garden. Just go through the kitchen, and help yourself to a drink."

Terry walked along the hallway towards the back of the house, past the lounge and what he presumed was the dining room, in which presents were piled, still wrapped, on a highly-polished mahogany table. Moments later he came to the kitchen, one side of which had been knocked through into a large conservatory that led out into the garden. Seconds later Jane–who was standing next to the sink with her back to the door, stirring fruit punch in a cut glass bowl–would turn around and see him, put down the ladle and come forward to give him a hug, blowing away any anxiety he had about coming here. But for now Terry stood blinking in the doorway, filled with doubt–and it was at this point that he spied a man in the conservatory topping up drinks for some women, standing in the shadow of a vine which grew up one of the walls, and covered half of the ceiling. They were all engrossed in an anecdote he was telling as he carefully poured the Champagne. The scene reminded Terry of paintings he'd seen in churches and museums, in which groups of people were pictured in a huddle, gazing in wonderment at a baby or an angel or something with religious significance. The man concluded his story with a wink and a slightly lascivious flick of the tongue, and they all laughed. He was tall and robust with legs that seemed on the verge of bursting out of the cream-coloured corduroy trousers he was wearing. His checked cotton shirt was wide open at the neck, so that a fair amount of grey chest hair was visible. Terry's eyes followed the curve of the fabric over the man's slight paunch, lingered for an instant on his crotch and then moved back up to the face and the mop of grey hair that sprouted from the top of his head. He wore thick-framed glasses that made him look vaguely academic, but also a bit like a comedian–an impression accentuated by the queer stance he'd adopted, with one of his hands on his hips, and the other holding out the half-empty bottle as if it was a bomb that was about to go off.

When it happened, this first sighting of Alan Reid didn't strike a chord with Terry. At sixteen, he hadn't started to acknowledge consciously the fact that he was interested in older men, and he was still therefore living the life of the typical heterosexual adolescent boy. And as with most infatuations, there were no warning signs– no indications at all that here was someone who could spark an obsession. Alan was just a guy standing talking to some women at a party. When Terry looked back on that moment years later and tried to recall it in detail, he would swear that there'd been a minuscule pause when he caught sight of Alan–but that was probably his imagination trying retrospectively to imbue the moment with some sort of significance. It was far more likely that everything–the party conversations, the music, the laughter–continued as before. Jane introduced them to one another later that afternoon in the garden, when things were calming down and many of the guests had left, and they chatted about cars and football. It was all so normal–and yet in the two and a half years that followed, Terry's crush would grow so much that it was really a miracle that he hadn't done something idiotic before he went off to university, and his relationship with Jane drifted gradually to its natural conclusion. The last time he saw Alan before their surprise meeting in Gran Canaria a decade later, was when Mr and Mrs Reid took him and Jane out for dinner a few weeks after they finished their A Levels–and Terry's desire for the older man was at the peak of its intensity.

"Do you know where this restaurant is?" Jane pouted her lips as she sat in the passenger seat, staring intently at her reflection in a compact mirror, worried about a small spot an her chin. Terry– freshly unshackled from his L-plates–was driving them to meet her parents in his aunt's old Morris Minor.

"Of course," he said. "I've driven past it dozens of times. There's a big Post Office on the corner. We can park around the back." Jane finished what she was doing and put the compact back into her bag. Terry risked taking his eyes of the road for a fraction of a second, just to see her sitting there the passenger seat. She'd put on her most glamorous dress: an off-the-shoulder number made out of a silky oriental fabric that her sister Miranda had sent back home during a trip to Thailand. It was short and black, with red dragon shapes embroidered into it that matched her lipstick.

"You look amazing," he said quietly. "Way too good for me. Am I smart enough?" At this moment he really felt love for her despite the fixation he'd developed on her father. It was an odd incidence of doublethink, something deeper that could maybe be called doublefeel–the kind of emotional web that humans often weave around themselves. Jane smiled.

"Bringing along a jacket was certainly a good idea–and I suppose I should be grateful that you're not wearing those bloody white baseball boots." He looked wounded.

"Cheers."

"But then again, mother loves you so much you could wear whatever you liked and you'd still be the blue-eyed boy. I don't know why she doesn't just ditch dad and go out with you herself. Have you ever considered becoming a toy boy?" This was said in a jocular enough fashion, but there was an underlying seriousness–even an edge of jealousy–about it. Jane's mum made no secret of the fact that she was keen on Terry. He kept his eyes on the road.

"The only reason she likes me is because she thinks Miranda's boyfriend is a drug dealer." Jane laughed.

"Miranda's boyfriend IS a drug dealer, but that doesn't explain why mum always gets so excited when you're coming around. It's like that film, The Graduate–even dad's noticed." In reality, Terry was partly to blame for what had happened. As he'd fallen more deeply in love with Jane's dad, he had tried externally to compensate for those emotions, to cover his tracks as it were, by paying more attention to her mother, who had started to flirt with him in return. It was awfully complicated but from Terry's point of view it was much better than if the truth were to come out—so he'd allowed it to develop, even encouraged it.

"I think you're doing your mother a great disservice. She's only trying to be friendly, and I appreciate it very much." Jane seemed satisfied by this.

"Yeah," she said. "I suppose I should be grateful that the two of you get on at all."

The restaurant was on a busy road with double yellow lines up either side, so Terry continued on a bit and then turned into an alley around the back, where there was a small car park used during the day by a firm of solicitors with offices further down the street. They didn't seem to mind people parking there at night and at the weekend. Jane's dad was reversing his car into a space as they turned the corner. Terry tucked the Morris in nearby, jumped out and went quickly around the car to open the door on the passenger side. Jane emerged, beaming, radiant—a teenage dream.

"Such a gent," she said. Alan Reid walked towards his daughter to give her a kiss.

"Bloody crawler, if you ask me."

"Listen to him," said Mrs Reid, following behind her husband. "I'd give my back teeth for a man who did that kind of thing for me." Terry held up his hand.

"Actually folks, sorry to disappoint—but I only did it because the door mechanism is broken and it can't be opened from the inside." Jane shook her head.

"I should have known."

"That's not safe," said Alan, opening his arms and ushering them all away from the cars towards the restaurant. "You should get it fixed straight away." Terry had in fact driven just that afternoon to a garage on the other side of the city which specialised in older cars, to pick up the replacement parts.

"Dad and I are going to do it next weekend," he said.

"Well if you can't, I'm sure my friend George will have a look at it for you. He's very good at things like that." Jane smirked.

"Yes," she said sarcastically. "Uncle George loves getting his tools out."

"That's quite enough of that, young lady," said Alan. He patted Terry's shoulder. "Anyway, you're leaving the car here tonight, aren't you?"

"I hadn't really thought about it."

"Why not? You can have a few drinks and Marjorie will drive us home. I'll give you a lift back tomorrow so you can pick up your car." Mrs Reid chipped in.

"Yes, do come back with us. I've made the spare room up specially for you." Terry remembered an incident six months previously when he'd stayed there after a party, and during the night had gone to the loo–only to find Alan on the landing, half drunk and wearing only his underpants, heading hack from the toilet to his bedroom. The young lad had stood there paralysed, as Alan tottered past with a drunken leer on his face and mumbled some sort of apology. The recollection was shattered by Alan's voice, so quiet it was almost a whisper, close to his ear.

"And no sneaky bed-hopping in the middle of the night, understand?" Terry felt his face colouring–it was almost as if the older man had read his mind. He looked helplessly at Mrs Reid. Luckily, Jane came to the rescue.

"Chance would be a fine thing," she huffed, rolling her eyes. "How embarrassing! Mum, has he been drinking already?" They all laughed, including Terry, whose awkwardness subsided. Jane's family spoke much more freely to one another than Terry's, and it always took him a bit of time to get used to the rough and tumble of it, coming as he did from a home in which keeping the lid on things was the norm. Jane tightened her grip on his arm.

"Ignore them, they're bonkers."

"What was that?"

"Nothing, father dear. Just saying how marvellous you are."

As they approached the door of the restaurant, Terry saw that it was a classy place. The whitewashed façade was illuminated with spotlights at ground level, which were concealed between big pots of well-kept shrubs and greenery. Beautiful hanging baskets were suspended from brackets attached to the wall. The lighting inside was dim, but Terry could see through the leaded windows that many of the tables were full. He looked at the menu, which was inside a glass-fronted box on the wall next to the door. Everything was written in Italian, but it was pretty easy to recognize what the dishes were. Terry stood back so that Alan could go in first, then held the door open for the two women, eventually bringing up the rear, greeted by a pleasant warm waft of air which brought with it smells of garlic and grilled meat, herbs and coffee. They were taken to a table at the back of the restaurant, next to a patio window that looked out onto a walled garden about fifteen feet square, with an illuminated fish pond in the middle. After they'd ordered and Alan had filled their glasses with wine, Mrs Reid leaned towards Terry conspiratorially, the flame of the candle on the table reflected in the pupils of her eyes.

"There's something I've been meaning to talk to you about," she began. "I know you've both got summer jobs, but Jane and I want to go to London together before she goes away to university. We just want to do a bit of shopping, maybe see a show or two–girls' stuff, really, the kind of thing that bores my husband rigid. But if he feels that he's being left out, he'll sulk terribly–and this is where you can help. Alan has been going on for years about how he wants to go to the Lake District. What would you say about accompanying him for a few days walking, while we go off to London for the weekend?" Terry had glanced a few times at Alan while Mrs Reid was talking, and noticed that he was looking across the table rather severely over the top of his glasses, shaking his head slowly back and forth. He clearly didn't approve of his wife's plan–which was a shame because the idea of being alone with Alan, perhaps spending the night in a tent amid the high peaks, the older man's body inches from his own, appealed enormously to Terry. It would probably be the basis for some sort of fantasy later when he was alone in bed. But for now the one thing he definitely didn't want to do was incur the wrath of Mr Reid, who looked majestic in the candle light with his shining face, his grey hair and his metal-framed glasses perched on the end of his nose.

"Um, well, obviously I love the Lakes, but I'm not sure I'm going to be able to manage it, because I'm doing this job up until a few days before I go off to college, and I need that time to get myself sorted out." Alan sat back and grinned, slipping Terry a triumphant wink that made his heart leap. Mrs Reid looked disappointed.

"Oh that's a shame."

"Never mind dear," said Alan. "You and Jane can still go away for the weekend. I am capable of looking after myself you know, despite what you might think."

"I know. I just thought that it might be nice for you two to do something like that–a bit of male bonding. And you always said that your holiday in the Lakes with George was one of the best you ever had."

"Yes, but that was a long time ago when I was young. Sleeping in a tent was no problem. Nowadays I need a bit of luxury for these old bones."

"In that case why don't you stay in a hotel or a bed and breakfast? You don't have to go camping." Alan changed tack.

"It makes no difference anyway, because Terry can't come–but it's something we could always bear in mind for another time, eh Terry?" Later, after they'd eaten pudding, Terry was in the toilet when Alan came in, walked straight to the urinal and stood next to the young man, unzipped his fly and pulled out his cock. Terry didn't dare look directly at it but out of the corner of his eye he was able to get a sense of something pale pink and pretty substantial. Alan spoke quietly, almost to himself, as he began to pee.

"Bloody women. Take over your life if you let them." Terry smiled weakly, noticing Alan glance at his cock, which had shrivelled almost to nothing because of a sudden surge of adrenaline. Several long seconds later he managed to find his voice.

"I know what you mean."

"You've got to love them, though, eh?" Alan finished his piss, zipped up and turned to the wash basin–where he ran his fingers under the tap for a few seconds, grabbed a paper towel to wipe them dry and then headed back out into the restaurant. Terry was so unsettled that he couldn't remember whether he'd actually used the toilet or not. He buttoned up his fly and went outside. Back at the table, the conversation continued as before. If either of the women thought it was weird that Alan had followed Terry to the loo, they didn't show it. Jane's mum was expressing concerns about Miranda's wayward boyfriend–something she often did.

"I mean he says he's going to be a writer, but I've never seen him put pen to paper in all the time we've known him." She turned to her husband. "Have you, darling?" Alan dropped a cube of brown sugar into his coffee and then slowly stirred the black liquid, a grave and pensive look on his face.

"I've read some of his stuff," Jane piped up. "It's... different."

"Yeah," said Terry. "And he's talking about doing some work experience on the local paper as well." Mrs Reid's eyes flashed.

"Paid employment? The mind boggles." Alan shrugged.

"He's a nice enough lad. I think he just needs to find his feet, that's all. You know how kids are these days–they're not like we were at that age. They have different ideas." The conversation continued that way for the rest of the evening, delving into this or that area of family life or local gossip, light debate, a few anecdotes–what's commonly described as 'putting the world to rights'. It was a pleasant evening, and Terry contributed as much as the others, eager to show that he could hold his own in such a situation, keen to impress Jane, her mum and of course Alan. It wasn't until later when they had all gone to bed and he found himself alone in the Reid's spare bedroom that he was able to devote some time to considering what was going on between himself and Alan. The incident in the toilet had lasted less than two minutes, but it was one that would perplex Terry for years to come. Why had Alan turned up like that? He'd sauntered in quite casually, without displaying the sort of body language that people usually did when they were really desperate for the loo. There were no 'oohs' or or other expressions of relief when he started to pee. It therefore seemed logical to assume that he could easily have waited for a couple of minutes, until Terry returned to the table–which suggested that he'd done it on purpose, deliberately to make contact with the boy while he was there. But if Terry allowed himself to accept that, then the situation became even more enigmatic. What had Alan been trying to say? The way he'd talked about women had been almost apologetic–as if he was making an excuse for something. Maybe Alan suspected that Terry had feelings for him, and had come in just to test the water, to see how the young man would respond. If that was the case, Terry could hardly have handled the situation more badly, standing there tongue-tied and white as a sheet. It was a reaction that had not only betrayed his true feelings, but also robbed him of the chance to say something about it, to make some kind of an excuse.

Terry of course knew by now that he was in love with Alan, and he had the good sense to recognize that his emotions could colour his interpretation of events–perhaps imbue them with more significance than they actually possessed. But he was also convinced that there was more behind it all than just wishful thinking. What had happened in the restaurant was a classic example of this, as was the earlier incident when Terry was staying at Jane's and they met on the landing. On the face of it, it seemed innocent enough: a guy on his way to the toilet in the middle of the night bumps into his girlfriend's dad, who just happens to have been a few moments earlier. But Terry had believed strongly at the time that Alan hadn't been making his way back to bed when they met. For one thing, the boy had been lying awake for a while and he hadn't heard the toilet flush or the bathroom taps being run–or indeed any of the usual tell-tale sounds that suggested someone had been to the loo in the dead of night. Terry suspected that the older man had been hanging around out there on the landing for a while, loitering with some sort of intention–and his demeanour, slightly apologetic, slightly ashamed, seemed to give credence to this theory.

The reality was that many things had happened between Alan and Terry during the few years in which the young man went out with Jane that were just as open to interpretation. Terry had on occasion felt like a water diviner whose rods had suddenly crossed over as he walked across the landscape. These incidents and the suggestion that they contained had served to inflame his obsession with Alan, to make his passion even stronger. But was it fool's gold, or the real thing? In future years, he would chat men up on the basis of nothing more than a friendly glance, which was on the face of it far less of an indication that they might be receptive to his advances. But by then he was more experienced, more confident–and there was less at stake. In truth, as the years went by, he was quite happy to leave behind that lovesick teenager and those awkward, ambiguous moments–confident that he would never have to deal with that particular situation again, that it was something he could forget for good.

*

CLOSER to the beach, Alan could see that during the heavy rain of the previous couple of days some of the depressions between the dunes had become flooded with water, creating a series of small lakes that roughly followed the coastline. People stood at the tops of the sandbanks looking down at the water and scratching their heads. The weather had been pretty bad–and this part of the island always felt the full force of it. When he reached the beach Alan could see the tracks left by huge tyres, evidence that the mechanical diggers had been out early this morning, flattening the sand so that the sun loungers and parasols could be laid out. He looked up and down the beach, to see if there was much evidence that the storms had changed its shape–but it looked more or less the same as it had done two days ago, when he and George were last here. A couple of years before they'd been caught in the worst winter weather seen by the island in a decade. The storms had been so bad for three days that even in the middle of Playa Del Ingles it was almost impossible to go outside. The Avenida Tirajana became a river, and the wind made awful moaning sounds as it blew through the corridors of the hotel. George stayed in his room drinking brandy and playing backgammon with a Moroccan boy he had picked up at the bus station in Las Palmas. The hotel lobby was packed with disgruntled visitors, refugees from the beach with their tracksuit bottoms and their ill-fitting jumpers, sitting around coughing and complaining. Occasionally one of them would lift up the net curtains, to see if there was any sign of a break in the clouds. The hotel did its best to cheer them up, with bingo, cocktails and cookery demonstrations, but it was really no good. Some even talked about trying to book a flight home. Alan sat quietly in reception; reading his book and watching as the staff used towels to try to stop the water pouring through the front doors. At one stage the manager of the hotel, a feisty young woman who always wore a black suit and high heels, charged outside and stared up at the sky, glancing at her watch as if trying to tell the gods that enough was enough, it was time to stop the onslaught. When the skies finally cleared and Alan and George made it back down to the beach, they found that huge stretches of it had been blown away, leaving jagged sections of bedrock exposed. Hundreds of thousands of tonnes of sand had vanished–presumably into the sea. It would take the municipal authorities six months to push enough sand back onto the beach with mechanical diggers to return it to anything like its original shape. Several of the big hotels on the promenade at Maspalomas suffered so much damage that they were forced to close for a year.

This morning though, there was just blue sky and a gentle breeze to take the edge off the heat of the sun. When it was really windy the lads that ran the place, who all wore shirts with the word 'Hamacas' printed on the back, would surround the loungers with a huge windbreaker made out of fine netting. But even with that in place, the sand would be whipped through the gaps and stick to the sun cream on your body, creating a strange, scaly layer like lizard skin. There would be sand everywhere: in your pants, your eyes, even in your teeth. The only thing to do on those occasions was retire to the dunes and hope that the hillocks and vegetation would protect you from the worst of it. Alan decided to have a quick dip before he settled down for the day. He found a couple of loungers that didn't look too dilapidated and stripped off. He placed his shoes neatly underneath the lounger he'd chosen for himself, spread his beach towel on top of it, and took out the small wooden brush that he and George used for cleaning the sand off their feet. He then put his clothes and rucksack onto George's lounger so that other people could see that it had been reserved.

Down at the water's edge he turned to look inland, feeling the sun on his back and the cold Atlantic lapping around his ankles. In the foreground was the beach, with a seemingly endless stream of people tramping along the sand in both directions, in all their variety. Whenever the sun shone they came in their thousands, irrepressible as the waves. It was like Lowry by the sea with the colour control turned all the way up: small figures swarming about, dwarfed by the scale of the scene. Most wore shorts or at least swimming costumes, but this too was a nudist area so there was a fair amount of bare flesh. There were young people, families, children with buckets and spades and beach balls, dogs, people dressed quite formally looking as if they had decided at the last moment to come to the beach instead of the office. There were older people, stick-thin and bent over, fighting their way over the sand against the odds, and fat jolly men with moustaches and bellies hanging over tight swimming trunks, their rotund wives bursting out of their bikinis. Alan had once seen a huge woman naked from the waist up; lumbering down the beach, trying to pick up her hat which had been blown off by the wind. Each time she got to it and went through the improbable motions of bending her huge body to pick it up, a playful little gust would send it just out of reach. Alan had stood a discrete distance away, laughing quietly as she muttered curses in German.

Further back he could see the gay beach itself, a block of neatly-arranged orange sun loungers, about two hundred of them, covered with all manner of sheets, towels, bags, bodies, newspapers, bottles of sun tan oil, all the beach paraphernalia that people carried here day after day. Between the loungers, orange and blue parasols were planted in the sand, most tilted back so as not to block out the sun. To the left of the rows of loungers, from Alan's vantage point at the water's edge, was a fairly flat, open area of beach which he and George had nicknamed the Pasture. It was densely populated with men: some standing together in groups, many lying down, others sitting chatting, some concealed within brightly-coloured nylon windbreakers like tents cut in half, some lying on their bellies waiting for a helpful stranger to come and rub some oil in, some sitting with their headphones on staring into the distance, some constantly looking around, sizing-up their fellow sun-worshippers and trying to read, but apparently unable to complete a whole page without being distracted by someone walking past.

Towards the back of the loungers was a white pre-fabricated kiosk, cuboid in shape, and surrounded by wooden decking that was covered in peeling green paint. A rainbow flag attached to a pole on the top fluttered in the breeze. Above the counter were emblazoned the words 'Kiosco Beach Maspalomas Number 7'. There had been a similar kiosk at the back of the Pasture, 'Kiosco Beach Maspalomas Number 6', but it had been uprooted by the storms two years ago, and was found lying on its side a few hundred metres away, near the bushes that people on the beach used as a toilet. It had been so badly damaged that the authorities never bothered to put it back in place. Number 7 was run by a chubby, good-humoured lesbian–whose force of character was such that people walked miles just to have a beer there. She spent the days sending up the beach queens, and playing the disco and house music they adored at huge volumes. At this time of the morning the sound was low and pulsing, because early on she was always hung over and a little subdued. There were just a few people sitting around on the tall bar stools attached to the decking, having a coffee or perhaps an early beer, and eyeing up the talent. Behind the kiosk he could see the dried-out river bed through which he had just walked, curving its way through the mounds of sand back towards the dunes, and in the distance the high peaks of the island's mountains, their ridges running parallel to the beach upon which he was standing. The highest point, the notched peak of Mount Roque Nublo, stood at the centre of it all. The shadows of clouds slid over the surfaces of the mountains, engulfing patches of the uneven, biscuit-brown and moss-green surfaces, and changing their colours to darker shades of blue and black. On most days these clouds hovered menacingly around the peaks, but they could also spread southwards over the swimming pools, dunes and beaches of Playa Del Ingles and Maspalomas, blocking out the sun and leaving people scattered and restless, deflated by the prospect of having to return early to their hotels and holiday villas.

Alan turned back towards the sea and stood just at the point where the water was getting as far up the beach as it could, his feet wide apart and his arms stretched out in either direction. There was nothing between him and the horizon except miles and miles of calm sea. He took deep breaths, feeling the warmth of the sun as the wind created tingling sensations on his skin. He knew of few places where he could feel such harmony with existence–such purity. He walked slowly forward into the cold water, enjoying the shock as the waves engulfed his body, coyly turning himself to one side each time one crashed into him. A yellow flag was flying in the distance, which meant that the water was safe enough if you were a decent swimmer. He wouldn't come in this far if it was red–people had died disregarding the warnings on this stretch of coast. When you looked at the satellite photos of the island that you could buy from the souvenir shops, which made the mountains look like the gnarled skin on an old Norwegian fisherman's face, it was easy to see why. The whole beach system around Playa Del Ingles and Maspalomas was a salient jutting out into the ocean–so that when you went for a swim you were actually exposed to the full force of the Atlantic currents. Soon he was up to his neck–just one of many heads bobbing up and down like seals in the swell. He turned to look back at the crowded beach, stretching his leg down to make sure he could still touch the sand. Getting out of the water was always slightly harder than going in–because after it broke each wave slid back down the beach, sucking sand, stones, feet and legs with it. Alan pushed forward, feeling the currents dragging him back. Finally, after his legs had taken a battering in the surf, he was free. He returned to the loungers, picked up his sunglasses and put them back on. He then lay down and started rubbing sun cream into his body. Alan usually liked to read a thriller or a murder mystery while he was sunning himself, but this time he'd fancied a change and had asked George to lend him something. George gave him a book he had just finished, about a gay soldier who'd lived in ancient Greece. At the beginning of the book the soldier, whose name was Gordas, was a member of the Sacred Band of Thebes, the legendary army belonging to that city. Pelopidas, the enlightened general in charge of the Sacred Band, encouraged his men to have homosexual affairs, because he realised that their performance in battle might be enhanced if they were fighting to protect one another as well as the city. The ethos was that each soldier would not want to appear cowardly in front of his lover–with whom he fought side by side on the field of battle. Alan hadn't read much gay literature, but the idea of this book appealed to him because these were men of courage, who were not in the slightest bit limp-wristed. The other thing that he liked was the fact that in the Sacred Band, love affairs were encouraged between older and younger men–the theory being that the strength and zeal of youth would blend harmoniously with the experience and wisdom of age. Alan was about half way through the book, and the Sacred Band–which had been riding high for nearly four decades–had just been beaten to a pulp by Philip of Macedon and his son Alexander, at the Battle of Chaeronea. Out of three hundred soldiers, only a handful of the Sacred Band survived, and Gordas was among them. But Philip of Macedon was so impressed by the way they had fought, he said that any Theban who was willing to swear allegiance to him could join his own troops. Not knowing what had happened to his younger lover in the battle, Gordas decided to accept the offer. Philip, who was obsessed with his future, as his son Alexander would also be, decided after the battle to march to Phocis in order to consult the Delphic Oracle. Alan opened the book and the boarding card from his flight to Gran Canaria–which he was using as a bookmark–fell onto the lounger between his legs. He noticed that the suntan oil on his fingers had left greasy smudges on the pages of the book. George wouldn't mind, though–once he had read a book he didn't care what happened to it. Alan tucked the bookmark into the back pages and began to read.

*

THE soldiers had continued their march from the plain of Chaeronea for many hours, and now with the descent of darkness Philip and his generals decided that it was time for the men to rest. They first set up camp, and then lit fires and began preparing the evening meal. Gordas had been chosen to accompany Alexander and his closest comrades. He had spent the day marching with a heavy heart. It mattered little that he knew none of the soldiers around him. He had no desire to speak to them–most of those whose company he longed for had all died in the slaughter at Chaeronea. More than anything in the world, he wanted to lie once more with his lover Deridas in the garrison at the Theban Cadmeia, sharing the tenderness that he knew would have exorcised some of the horrors of that most bloody battle. But what had become of Deridas? For many hours their phalanx had held its formation despite the Macedonian onslaught, and they had fought together, side by side, one fending off attacks on the other, then receiving the same protection from his comrade. In their form of battle staying together and making sure that the line remained unbroken were the most important priorities–and protecting a lover from the blows of a vicious enemy was the sweetest pleasure that battle could bring. Deridas was a young man but he was already a strong warrior, and he had fought bravely. But then, in a sudden and ferocious attack, Philip's son Alexander and his forces had broken through the Theban line. In the confusion that followed, with the Sacred Band outflanked and attacked from both the front and the rear, Deridas had disappeared. Gordas could not stop and look for him because his priority was to try to re-group with any other members of the Sacred Band he could find, and mount some kind of defence. Then his recollections became unclear. Perhaps he had been struck on the head, but the next thing he remembered was being lined up in front of Philip, the Macedonian king–and that great leader's words of praise for the Sacred Band and the way its members had fought. Then came Philip's pledge to the survivors: join me and be honoured, or join your comrades in death. Some chose death–but Gordas had not seen his lover slain, and therefore, hoping that Deridas had somehow survived and that they could be re-united, had decided to accept this new leader. If he discovered later that his lover had died, he could perhaps use his position within the Macedonian ranks to avenge his death. Now, though, sitting among strangers, feeling the chill that descended on the arid landscape at night, he wondered if he had made the right choice. It would certainly have ended his torment to accept Philip's blade, but as long as there was a possibility that Deridas still breathed, Gordas had to go on–no matter how hard it was to do so. His thoughts were interrupted by a shout from one of the young Macedonians.

"Oy, Theban. We've been discussing which one of us will get the pleasure of your company in our tent tonight. We're keen to experience first-hand the skills that have made the Sacred Band so famous." There was laughter from those sitting nearby. Gordas was a stout, handsome warrior, and the Macedonians–their blood high from the victory–had indeed been watching him as they marched throughout the day. But no matter how dangerous these fighters were, Gordas resented the way they had been looking at him as if he was a piece of meat at the market. He smiled as he spoke, but those who looked on him saw in the firelight a mask of hatred.

"I'd be glad to show any of you my skills. Especially those involving my sword." There were hoots from Alexander's henchmen.

"It seems," ventured one, "that several hours without the company of his younger lover have left him a little hot-tempered." Gordas moved his hand down towards the small stabbing-sword at his waist.

"In Thebes when young donkeys bray too loudly," he hissed, "we cool their tempers with a swift castration." There were sniggers. The vociferous young soldier was not deterred by what Gordas had said.

"And in Macedonia, we whip old donkeys when they become too stubborn." Gordas remained still as he spoke.

"You should take care that you don't get bitten or kicked." A slim, dark figure emerged from the shadows cast by one of the tents nearby.

"Gentlemen," said a voice with a peculiar clarity, as if the reed of a wind instrument was lodged in the throat of the speaker. "I think we should extend towards our new comrade a little more courtesy." The consonants at the beginning of the last two words were given a shocking emphasis. Gordas watched as a short young man, whose body looked almost too frail to carry the large head, moved slowly towards the fire and stood over the young soldiers. Their demeanour immediately became more subdued. Alexander had arrived. "Theban," he said, "I must apologize. My colleagues haven't seen their women for a few days–and sometimes their exuberance somewhat outweighs their good sense." He turned hack to his own men. "Warriors," he said, "you have much to learn from this Theban, who stood alone against us after his phalanx had collapsed around him, but still survived. His lessons will indeed take us further in the field of battle. So clear a space for him at the fire. Tonight he will drink my wine, and learn how hospitable we can be to those who have earned our respect." Several of the young soldiers relinquished their positions near the fire and moved into the semi-darkness. Quiet conversations began, and a flask of wine was passed around. Gordas stayed where he was, feeling the weight of his hand on his knife.

Alexander stood watching him, evidently expecting him to stand up and join the others. A large part of the older man wanted to defy this young pretender in front of his band of upstarts, but he knew that a man like Alexander would not allow that to happen. Gordas also knew that he had no chance of escape, and if he were slain here he would never find out what became of Deridas.

"I am honoured to be asked to drink with you," he said, standing up.

*

A SHADOW passed over Alan, and he squinted up to see George standing with the sun at his shoulder.

"Morning dear. I see you got loungers in a prime position. Fancy a beer?" Alan laid the book aside.

"Why hello there, stranger! I thought perhaps I might have lost you for good this time."

"Yes, well, all these late nights do catch up in the end. I fancied a lie-in. Now it's time for the hair of the dog. What about you?"

"Oh. Last night? Nothing dramatic." Alan thought for a second about the stripper and about the man in the bath, but here in the blazing sunshine it seemed like something that had happened in another life. George was already walking off in the direction of Kiosk Number 7. Alan stood up, pulled on a pair of shorts, grabbed his wallet, and followed his friend. When they reached the small structure the decking, covered with a dusting of fine sand, felt hot and rough under foot. As expected, they received a huge welcome from the fat lesbian, who laughed and kissed them both. George ordered a couple of beers and a toasted ham and cheese baguette for himself. The woman poured the beers and then removed the sandwich from the fridge. Spanish dance music was playing; George shook his hips and slid his feet across the decking in time to the beat as he waited. Before she unwrapped the baguette, the woman held it in front of her crotch, stroking it suggestively in his direction. George and several other punters laughed. She then placed the sandwich in a stainless steel mini-grill in the corner of the kiosk. Alan sat on one of the tall stools and looked out to sea as a plane buzzed overhead, following the line of the beach towards the lighthouse at Maspalomas, trailing a banner advertising a German drinking den not far from their hotel called Horst's Bierkeller. George brought the food and drink over and sat opposite him. He squeezed mustard and tomato sauce out of small sachets onto his sandwich and took a bite. He sighed.

"Beer and baguettes–the breakfast of champions."

"So where did you end up last night?"

"I met a lad who says he knows you, that he went out with your daughter when he was at school. He was staring at you in Hollandaise. Did you see him? Very handsome boy." Alan watched his friend eating.

"Sounds nice. Did you get him into bed?" George caressed the condensation on the side of the big plastic cup containing the beer, saying nothing.

"So that's a yes then." Alan yawned. "How was it? This is the latest you've ever got down here, so it must have been good." George looked smug.

"Lovely, yes." He paused, his expression changing slightly. "I do wish he hadn't buggered off while I was still asleep, though." Alan pointed accusingly.

"Cradle snatcher!"

"He's not at school any more–he's in his twenties for goodness sake."

"I'm only kidding. What's his name?"

"Terry Fowler." Alan sipped his beer.

"Yes I remember him. Pleasant enough lad–but at the end of the day he was just another spotty schoolboy chasing after one of my daughters. Very well mannered, though, if I remember rightly. Will we be seeing him later?"

"He said he'd be coming down–but I think he's a little bit shy about speaking to you."

"Does anyone back home know that he's gay?"

"I don't think so."

"Oh dear, that old chestnut." George scrunched up the foil that his sandwich had been wrapped in, and threw it into the bin near their table. He clapped his hands to remove the crumbs that were stuck to them.

"Well, you spent most of your life in the closet, married with children and all that, while I lived the life of what they used to call in more conservatives times a confirmed bachelor. I'm not sure who ended up better off. When I really think about it, I'd have to say I reckon you did. The gay world was always there for you to dip into if you fancied it–but then you always had your family life to fall back on. You had your cake and you ate it too." Alan shrugged.

"You know I never put it about when Marge was alive. You and I had our moments, but you could hardly say I planned it. I was just trying to make the best out of life, like anyone else."

"You and me both. I'd somehow expected things to be a little bit more clear-cut by this stage, but it hasn't really worked out that way."

"I thought you loved the bachelor lifestyle." George thought carefully. After several disasters and false starts, his one and only long-term relationship had lasted four years–and had been one of the happiest times of his life. But it had all fallen apart in the end, leaving him wondering what exactly it had been for. And then there was the curious business of the man sitting opposite him, looking with his old-fashioned shades and his white, swept-back hair like some kind of over-the-hill matinee idol–who he fell for the very first time they met, and who, even though he couldn't allow himself to be the lover George needed, had nonetheless never quite let him go.

"I'm not sure about the bachelor lifestyle," said George. "It's something you grow into because that's all there is. But it does have its advantages. And yes, I have had a lot of fun. I've done things millions of people will never get the chance to do–and at the end of the day here I am, sitting in the sun with my best friend, enjoying our third holiday in the past twelve months."

"Yes, we're like an old married couple. I'm sure a lot of people here think we're together. We should get notices put up next to our loungers saying 'These men are not lovers, so if you like what you see, please come forward.' Do you think that would work?"

"Actually in this place you probably get more interest if people think you are with a lover. It's one of the elements of our nature that we humans can be particularly proud of. The desire to get our hands on someone else's property. Have you ever done that thing when you're in a bar and someone on their own looks at you, and you're not particularly interested–then their friend turns up later and suddenly you see them in a whole new light?"

Alan laughed, touching his friend's plastic cup with his own in a miniature toast.

"Yes, but that could just be because you've drunk a shed load in the intervening time and you're seeing them through the old beer goggles."

"Always the best way of looking at the world, my dear!" They finished their drinks and headed back to the loungers. In a few moments George was sound asleep. Alan stood up and looked back towards the mountains. The clouds hadn't moved away from Roque Nublo, which meant that they were more or less guaranteed a day of uninterrupted sunshine. It was nearly time for lunch and a few people from the beach were starting to slope off into the dunes. He saw couples walking off together and knew that once they were out of view of the beach, they would probably split up and go in search of sexual contact with strangers. Could that work for him? If he had a lover, a man whom he needed in the way he used to need his wife, could he stand there on the beach and watch him walk away across the sand, becoming a speck in the distance and then finally disappearing behind a bush or a mound of sand? Part of him felt that no, if that person was his then by his side was where he should be. But another part said, why not? Wouldn't it be a great act of generosity, giving your lover something he wanted and trusting that he'd come back to you? Maybe that would be better than sneaking around behind one another's backs, simply to satisfy those basic compulsions that were inherent in all people. But what if you sat there on the beach waiting and waiting, until the Hamacas boys had taken away all the loungers and parasols... until the kiosks were all shuttered up, the sun had sunk beneath the horizon, and the only sound was the slap and hiss of the waves? The thought troubled Alan. He lay back down and opened his book.

*

GORDAS and Alexander talked until all that was left of the fire was a small pile of glowing embers. Despite his desolate feelings about the bloodshed at Chaeronea and the loss of Deridas, Gordas had gradually–aided no doubt by the wine–warmed to the young warrior prince. There was something beguiling about the way he listened to what the older man said with his head tilted slightly to one side, smiling and encouraging him to speak more about the Sacred Band, and what it had been like to be part of such an illustrious fighting force. When Gordas has finished Alexander looked deep into the remains of the fire.

"But is it not strange," he said, "how our fortunes wax and wane? One moment you are the most powerful force in the land, and the next you are nothing. It is the unending cycle of ascent and descent to which we are all subject, but I tell you this–I am in the ascendant, and I intend to use that good fortune to carry me to distant lands." He pointed at the sleeping soldiers behind them. "My comrades here have no idea how far I intend to go. They think that I, like them, dream only of conquering these lands and then returning to my wives, my lovers and my riches, to grow fat and live out my days concerned only with petty trivialities–but that is not how it will be. My dream is pure conquest, nothing else. I intend to take these lands, and the lands beyond those, and the lands beyond those, and to continue as long as the gods will allow it. Does that alarm you Theban?" Gordas shook his head.

"If anyone else told me these things, I would think they were deluding themselves. But coming from you, I can see the truth of it.

There is a sense of destiny around you that makes it seem natural–even inevitable–that such a quest should happen." Alexander put his arm across Gordas' shoulders and held him tightly.

"You are indeed a wise man. Let's discuss it further in my tent. These warriors can sleep off the wine where they lie." And so it was that Gordas came to have sex with Alexander. It seemed strange to him that two such warlike men, who just days before had faced each other on the battlefield, could share such tenderness. And Alexander, despite the strength of his character and the awe that he inspired among his own fighting men, turned out to be a surprisingly yielding lover. It was indeed a pleasure, but when they were finished the sadness Gordas felt about his comrades returned, along with a feeling of disgust at how he had betrayed them. He sat up.

"Why did you bring me here?" he whispered. "Your guards are asleep and I am the enemy. I could kill you now and nobody would know until the morning." Alexander did not move but only smiled in the darkness.

"You could kill me now but what then, Theban? Even if you escaped, you would have nowhere to go. And you would lose your chance to discover what became of Deridas in the fighting at Chaeronea. Only through me can you find the answer to that question, only through me do you stand any chance of being reunited with him." Gordas was stunned–he had made no mention of his lover during their discussion by the fire.

"But how can you know his name?"

"When you were found on the battlefield, you were taken for dead. Your body lay soaked in blood and surrounded by the corpses of others. But later, when my men tried to move you, there were signs of life. For many hours you were delirious. In your feverish state there were outbursts. You mentioned the name of this youth frequently."

"And do you know what became of him?"

"Truthfully I cannot say. There was much confusion and it will take some time to discover if he was among the slain, or if he was taken prisoner, or if he fled. I mean no dishonour by making that suggestion–but such a battle can wound a man's mind as grievously as it can his body." Gordas sat looking straight ahead, but could see nothing in the darkness. He imagined the fabric of the tent an arm's length away from his face, the snoring soldiers lying outside in their stupors, and the emptiness of the desert beyond. He spoke almost under his breath.

"And you will help me try to find him?" Alexander laughed.

"Of course! I won't lie to you Gordas, you can be very useful to me. My men may be good fighters but they lack experience–and you can teach them a great deal. And it suits me to have someone who has no connection with my people or with my father's people, with whom I can discuss my plans. In return for this I will gladly do all I can. And if we are successful I can count on the loyalty of not just one, but two former members of the legendary Band of Thebes." Gordas lay back down, his head spinning. What kind of pact had he made here, and with whom? This boy leader, who fought with such fury and talked of conquering the world and yet whose touch was as gentle as a blushing maiden's. How could Gordas, dispossessed as he was and fitter for the grave than for the field of battle, be of any use to such a man? As if answering the question, Alexander rolled towards Gordas and laid his arm across his chest, pulling the older man closer as he drifted back into sleep.

*

THE sun had moved further across the sky, in the direction of the lighthouse at Maspalomas, and the parasol that had been keeping Alan cool as he read was now casting its shade uselessly onto a patch of sand next to his lounger. He had become unpleasantly hot and could feel the droplets of sweat tickling as they ran down from his chest and belly, moistening the towel on which he lay. Experience had taught him that it was a difficult business to remove the spike that supported the parasol, and try to push it firmly back into the sand somewhere else. The Hamacas boys were always keen to help and he, of course, enjoyed watching them do their stuff, so he looked around. A sad truth of the place was however that they were rarely nearby when you needed them. He looked over at the kiosk to see them chatting to the fat lesbian, smoking and fooling around. What a perfect job that must be, thought Alan, dragging his lounger around so that the shade cast by the parasol was covering as much of it as possible.

Now he really was quite hot and with George still out for the count, another dip seemed like a good idea. He walked down towards the sea, quickening his pace because the baking sand was burning the soles of his feet. As he moved through the loungers, the odd person looked up from their book, or tilted their head to get a better look. One or two smirked at the strange, hopping gait he had adopted in an attempt to keep each foot down for as short a time as possible. He saw Frank and Steve, the couple from last night. Steve was lying on his belly so didn't see him, but Frank smiled and gave him a little wave. Alan was too far away to really examine the young man's shape, but from this distance it looked as if it might be as appealing as he had imagined. He thought, how great it must be to come to a place like this as a couple, to be able to reach out your hand and stroke your lover without fear of offending anyone or causing any problems. He carried on down the beach–suddenly realising that he had forgotten to put on his swimming trunks, as he usually did whenever he went for a swim. Down near the water's edge he came across a sandcastle that had been partially demolished by the waves. It was quite an elaborate affair, with crenellated walls and four towers that had been made with an upturned bucket. It had obviously taken quite some time and effort to build. Alan stopped and watched as another wave came in and washed away what was left of the walls. The water had gouged out the sand at the bottom of the last remaining tower, and the next time a sheet of water zipped up the beach it finished the job, chopping the column down at its base. The sand fell sideways in a heap. All that was left now was a small stick that someone had stuck into the sand to serve as a flagpole, poking up forlornly as the sand around it was washed away. Alan continued on his way and was soon up to his waist in water. When he looked back up the beach, the castle had gone. The damp sand was almost smooth once again and the stick had been uprooted and washed away.

*

TERRY arrived at the gay beach to find George flat on his back snoring loudly–much to the amusement of those lying on loungers nearby. He might have walked straight past, had it not been for the noise. He took off his rucksack and sat down on the other lounger, which he presumed belonged to Alan Reid. Alex and Dieter always packed up and went home at lunchtime. Now that they lived on the island, they'd adopted the rhythms of the Spanish–who did their sunbathing early when the rays weren't quite so strong and then went for lunch and a siesta during the afternoon. It was a more civilised approach than that of the tourists, who tended to gorge themselves because their time here was limited. Terry's arrival attracted a lot of attention. Before walking down to the beach he'd put on a pair of skimpy white football shorts, and the way the lightweight material slid over his buttocks, thighs and groin as he walked past the loungers had a few of the old timers stirring on their loungers. Many a young man in his position would have lapped up the attention, but Terry found it unnerving. He was really rather shy, and even though this stretch of the beach was nudist, his shorts would not be coming off. It was all a bit too public down here, not at all like the dunes in which you could easily find a quiet, secluded spot where people wouldn't gawp. He wasn't ashamed of his body–quite the reverse in fact–but he liked to preserve a bit of mystique. As he sat there Terry felt acutely the hungry eyes upon him, a sensation that did little to ease his nervousness about his imminent meeting with Alan Reid. He thought about waking George up, but then decided that would be unfair. He was only looking for a diversion after all, and the fellow obviously needed his sleep. Then he noticed a pair of binoculars hanging from the screw that was used to adjust the height of the umbrella. He lifted them off and took them out of their case, surprised by how heavy they were. He put them to his eyes, adjusted the width between the viewfinders, spun the focussing wheel and scanned the beach. He stopped when he saw a shock of white hair and a familiar shape walking out of the water. He sat a little more upright and gripped the glasses tightly.

Out of the waves and the windblown surf was emerging a tall, tanned figure. His head was down; his legs pushing forward against the force of the spent waves sliding back out to sea. As the water subsided, he saw calves that were still strong, curving slightly outwards below the knees. The thighs too had plenty of width and power, the stride was long and the stance erect. Further up, there was a roundness to the belly–what a casual observer would probably call a beer gut–but it was neither fat nor flabby; in fact there was a certain tautness to the curvature. After lingering there for a few fractions of a second, he continued his visual voyage north. The chest was broad and sprinkled with white hairs, which were highlighted by the dark brown–almost mahogany–skin. The neck was a little wrinkled, and there was a bit of sagging skin under the chin, but again that was all part of the attraction... signs of weathering. And then there was the face with its bold features, the white moustache, the high forehead and the hair, now a bright white, bleached to some degree by a couple of weeks in the strong sun. Terry had always been attracted to men who wore glasses, as Alan did, but he had taken them off to go for his swim and this too contributed to the dashing, rugged look. There were little droplets of water all over him catching the sun and twinkling, making this vision that had emerged from the waves seem other-worldly and magical. Terry gaped through the binoculars, thinking that, if anything, the ten years or so that had gone by since he had last seen Alan had made him even more attractive. He considered doing a runner before the figure made it up the beach. But despite his slow stride, Alan was now half way there. Terry slipped the binoculars back into their brown leather case and hung them up again. Get a grip, he thought, be yourself–turn on the charm. Do not, I repeat, do not revert to being an awkward teenager in the face of this man. Alan threaded his way through the rows of loungers, uncertain of where he was going. He looked confused for a second when he saw that someone was sitting on the edge of what he thought was his own lounger, so Terry spoke.

"Oh I'm sorry. I met your friend last night and I thought I'd wait while he was sleeping. This is your lounger." He got up.

"It's okay," said Alan. "I just need to get my glasses. I can see things in the distance perfectly, but close up I'm blind as a bat." He reached down to the lounger where, tucked under a fold in the towel, was a baseball cap with his sunglasses folded up inside it. He put them on and smiled–holding out his hand for a shake.

"Well, well. Terry Fowler isn't it? Strange to come across you here. How are you?"

"I'm fine, thanks. Struggling hard to resist the temptation to call you Mister Reid, like I used to when I was a boy."

"Yes, we're all adults now, lad. And how you've grown up." He gave Terry the once-over, raising an eyebrow appreciatively as he took in the lithe, gym-toned physique. There was absolutely no surplus fat anywhere to be seen and the flawless skin was just starting to turn from pink to a light honey colour as his tan developed. "Very athletic I must say!"

"Cheers." Terry felt himself blushing. He was bad at taking compliments–especially from a person who had featured so much in his adolescent fantasies, and even a few more recent ones. He soldiered on. "How are you, and how's the family? How's Jane?"

"Well, I lost my wife Marge two years ago. It was a terrible shock, but the girls were a big help to me. They're doing well. Jane's been married for six years now and has two daughters of her own. I'm afraid you missed out on a good one there, son." There was obvious pride in his voice.

"Yes I know," said Terry. "But it sounds to me like things have turned out well for her–and I think she's better off without my... complexities." Alan reached past the younger man and picked up a small towel which he had folded around his clothes to make a pillow. He started rubbing off the droplets of water on his body and legs. He then pulled out a bottle of sun cream and began putting some on his legs. He looked up to see Terry staring intently, and chuckled.

"Complexities, eh? How dull life would be without them." Terry felt a flutter in his stomach, an involuntary reaction to Alan's flirtatious tone. He was mildly annoyed that this man still had so much power over him.

"To be honest, sometimes I could do with fewer." He laughed. "But no, you're right, they're one of the things that make life interesting." Alan held up the bottle and smiled wickedly.

"Want some cream on your back, or would that be one complexity too many?" Terry ignored the quip.

"I suppose I should–otherwise I'll get burned to a crisp." He turned around and Alan started smoothing the cream on his neck and shoulders. Sliding his hands over the muscles, Alan started getting a bit turned on. By now the scene was being observed by quite a few sets of eyes. Plenty of people in their vicinity had books and newspapers in their hands, but not much reading was being done. Alan spoke gently.

"You should be more careful, you're a bit red around the shoulders. You don't want this lovely young skin turning all wrinkly like mine." George stirred.

"Did somebody say something about lovely young skin?" He sat up, rubbing his eyes. "Oh Lord, how long have I been asleep in the sun?" Alan raised his voice as if speaking to an elderly relative who was slightly deaf.

"Afternoon dear. We have a visitor." George put on his glasses.

"Hullo Terry, how nice to see you. What time is it?" Alan dug into the side pocket of his rucksack and pulled out a watch.

"Half past one."

"I've been asleep for an hour at the hottest time of the day without any cream on," muttered George, searching frantically for his hat.

"I don't think you'll have burned much," said Terry. "You've already got a pretty good tan, and your skin looks as if it can take it."

"Yes but you can still get sunstroke. I had that last year and I was ill for three or four days." Alan lowered his glasses and winked.

"Must have been all that walking around in the dunes admiring the flora and fauna, eh George?"

"Well you of all people should know how quickly the time can pass when one is engaged in such pursuits, Mr Reid." As they laughed, there was a loud chorus of beeping from one of the rucksacks. Alan looked down.

"Christ, George! What the hell is that?"

"My new mobile phone. I haven't worked out how to turn it down yet. Somebody's sent me a text." George fished the device out of the side pocket and squinted at it. He then shaded it with his hand so he could see the touch-screen more clearly in the sunlight. After a few seconds of faffing around with the device he spotted the smile on Terry's face.

"Laugh if you want to boy, but this age of digital information isn't just the preserve of you youngsters, is it Alan?"

"Good heavens no. We're even on the internet now. There's a site there for people who like oldies. We put a picture of George's privates on it, and got so many emails the bloody computer crashed." George put on his reading glasses and fiddled with the phone.

"It's your daughter checking up on you," he said. "Shall I tell her you're about to seduce her ex-boyfriend?" Alan turned crimson.

"Don't you dare!" Turning to Terry he spoke more quietly. "Ignore him–the bugger's gone senile." Just at that moment a slim man in his fifties with orange skin and a bottom like a baboon's walked past, wearing the skimpiest of white thongs. Alan stifled his laughter until the guy was out of earshot.

"Did you see that? He needs his head examined–walking around on a nudist beach with that piece of string up the crack of his arse. It can't be hygienic." George leaned forward and had a look at the man in the thong–who was heading towards Kiosk Number 7.

"He certainly seems quite proud of himself. And anyway, I'm sure they're perfectly okay if you keep yourself clean." Alan wasn't convinced.

"There's bound to be seepage if you're prancing around a hot sweaty beach like this all day." A man on one of the loungers in front of them, who was sitting under his parasol eating some sandwiches, turned around.

"Do you mind? There are other English people on the beach–and we're trying to have our lunch." Alan and George exchanged smiles like a couple of naughty schoolboys who'd been caught stealing apples. Alan turned to Terry.

"I'm afraid that when I'm on holiday I get into the rather bad habit of assuming that everyone is foreign–and saying outrageous things too loudly." George cleared his throat.

"What do you mean? You do it all the time at home too." The banter continued to flow–but George sensed that something big was in the air, and that it did not include him. He could see from their body language that Alan and Terry were forging a connection, and could also see that his suspicion last night at Monroe's that the lad was carrying a torch for his friend had not been unfounded. George had enjoyed his night with the boy, and at the time had pretty much accepted that it would be a one-off, but now that the cogs and wheels started to turn in his subconscious he felt slightly jealous. But–as with Mark the night before–he was also happy that Alan might at last be on the verge of something interesting. He decided once more to give him the space to get on with it, for better or for worse. What else could he do, after all? He just prayed that Alan would pick the ball up and run with it this time.

"Well chaps," he said. "I think I might head back." Alan looked concerned.

"Really–this early?"

"Yes. I've got some things to do in town, a few presents to buy–and I think I've had enough sun for today. I'll take it easy, maybe have a look around in the dunes on my way back."

"You don't have to go," said Alan, in tune with the way George's mind was working. George looked at the pair of them in turn–Terry smiling and Alan a trifle nervous, a trifle unsure.

"I know that–but I want to. As I say, I've had enough sun and I really must get my postcards written, or I'll be doing it in the departure lounge at the airport, as usual." Alan's face softened.

"Okay then—see you at the hotel."

"Yes, dinner at eight o'clock sharp. Bye Terry—maybe see you later in the usual dives. It's carnival night so be sure to wear your best frock." Terry smiled.

"Will do. Have a good afternoon." Lifting his fingers to the brim of his hat in a quick salute, George headed away from the beach, walking towards the dry riverbed that snaked its way back through the sand dunes towards Playa Del Ingles. When he was out of sight Terry moved around to George's lounger and sat down on it.

"Do you mind if I use this?" he asked.

"Not at all—it's paid for so you may as well, or the Hamacas boys will come and take it away. They're always keen to tidy up so they can bugger off as early as possible."

"Your friend's quite a character, isn't he?"

"Oh yes—George and I go back a long way. I've known him longer than I've known anyone else. I met him before I met my wife, even."

"I know, he told me about it last night. You met when you were doing your national service."

"Yes, well—things were different then. I never thought I'd do anything other than meet a woman, settle down and get married. It was just what everyone did. In that respect I think George was very much ahead of his time—he always said from the beginning that he didn't fancy women, and wanted only to share his life with a man. He hasn't compromised on that at all—but it's been a hard slog for him at times. I think it's much easier for your generation."

"You'd think so but I'm not sure. I mean, my family still don't know about me. I suppose I just haven't had the guts to tell them yet, in case they reject me." Alan looked out towards the blue sea and the hordes of people walking up and down the beach. He saw families, young children with their mums and dads, some of the dads sneaking quick glances towards the gay beach. He had seen the same thing in the Yumbo Centre at night. Men and women walking past the gay places, the women with stern faces as their husbands looked inside the bars, masking their curiosity with perhaps the odd dismissive comment. But the world continued to go round.

"People have this ability to put things into different compartments and get on with life if they really want to. After I met Marge I obviously looked at men and fancied them, but I was more or less able to keep my feelings in check. The trouble always starts when people don't have the self-discipline to do that, they just obey their urges to run off at the first sign of an infatuation—and then they turn around and say: 'Oh shit, my life is such a mess. What happened? Surely it wasn't my fault.' I don't judge that sort of behaviour, because it's none of my business, but I think you have to take responsibility for your actions." Terry reached out his hand and gently touched Alan's leg, began to stroke it.

"But to err is only human, wouldn't you say?" Alan put his own hand on top of the younger man's but he didn't move it away—he just pressed down on it to stop the caress, because of the effect it was having on him.

"Now you," he said quietly, "are a very wicked young man, whose actions have caused all these people around us to start looking once again at what we're doing."

"Well," said Terry, turning onto his side so that he was now facing Alan properly, and bringing his other hand over to touch the older man's body, "why don't we continue this discussion somewhere a bit more private?"

"But you're never going to improve your suntan unless you stay on the beach and let it develop."

"Getting a suntan is not my most pressing concern at the moment. I have some unfinished business to attend to—and I've waited a long time for the opportunity."

"Really? And what makes you think the opportunity has come now?" The little plane buzzed by overhead once again, heading from Maspalomas back around to Playa del Ingles. The Horst's Bierkeller banner had been replaced by one that advertised a disco on the

Avenida Tirajana called Boney M. Terry watched it move down the beach.

"I don't know. Maybe it's not going to happen–but I'm not the type to give up easily." Alan wrinkled his brow, mimicking Terry's earnest expression, but there was a smile on his face.

"Oh yes, and you look so sexy when you're serious. I'll bet you get what you want most of the time, one way or the other."

"I don't–but I'll keep trying until I've exhausted all the options."

"And as they say, God loves a trier. Come on then, let's take a slow walk down to Maspalomas and get the bus. If you're a good boy, I may even buy you an ice cream."

*

WALKING back from the beach towards the dunes, George decided to stop and have a drink of water. He sat down on a tree stump and opened his rucksack. It had been a funny sort of day. He was pleased to wake up with Terry, but less pleased that the younger man was in such a rush to get back to his friends' villa. He left without even having a shower. As soon as George lifted his head off the pillow the extent of his hangover became clear. He had missed breakfast–but he doubted anyway whether he could have managed to keep anything down. His stomach hurt, his back hurt, his eyes hurt, and waves of pain kept shooting up from his neck to the top of his skull. It was a particularly malicious combination. Every so often he would feel that it was subsiding, but then a few minutes later the agony would return. He felt sure that it had been those Flaming Inferno things they had drunk at the Block, and all the free schnapps they had been given later on. Alan often refused them, which was a pretty sensible move. The corrosive draught lager sold in many of the bars had not eased the situation, and of course the half-litre bottle of water that he had intended to drink before going to sleep lay untouched on his bedside table.

After Terry had left he rooted around in his toilet bag for the remedies–special powders that were dissolved in water and were supposed to be taken by people with diarrhoea–and strong painkillers.

He sat on the edge of the bed with the curtains closed, waiting for the medication to work, groaning and laughing at the pain and wondering whether it was worth following Alan to the beach–or whether he'd be better off staying at the hotel and sunbathing by the pool. Eventually he felt well enough to leave his room, but there was no way he was going to walk all the way down to the Riu Palace and through the dunes. He flagged down a taxi outside the hotel and was driven straight to Maspalomas. At least the walk along the beach on the flat, hard-packed sand near the water's edge was comparatively easy, and the sea air had freshened him up considerably by the time he arrived at the gay beach and found his friend. It had been the archetypal day after the night before, always catching up, catching up; just half a beat behind the rhythm of life–but what a difference it made to a man like George, who preferred to live an ordered existence. Last night's intrigues with Alan, Mark and Terry had also left him feeling unsettled. He looked back at the waves, at the heads of people in the sea, the small black dots being tossed around by the huge surges of water, and wondered at the unseen forces controlling the actions of humans. What was going on here? Why had Alan gone off with the guy that he fancied–Mark–last night? Why had George then gone off with young Terry, when he suspected that the lad was really after Alan? Could anything good come of it? Or was he taking things a bit too seriously–was it all just a bit of holiday fun? As that thought coalesced on the turbulent surface waters of George's mind, before he'd even had time to consider it, he felt a gentle tap on the shoulder. He looked up to see Mark smiling down at him.

"Hello there," said the younger man cheerfully. "I've been looking for you on the beach. Mind if I join you?" Gran Canaria had changed gear on him again.

*

IT took Alan and Terry about twenty minutes to walk to Maspalomas. Terry considered himself a fast walker but the speed at which Alan strode along the sand, weaving in and out of the crowds, impressed him–and once or twice he'd even had to break into a jog in order to catch up. First they passed the dilapidated building that served as the headquarters for the Red Cross lifeguards, who patrolled this section of coast. It reminded Terry of those derelict crofters' cottages in the high fells of the Lake District–apart from the fact that it was in the middle of a beach and had a big radio mast sticking out of the top. The lifeguards strutted around in their bright red shorts and their shades, immaculately tanned, chatting to women, smoking cigarettes and occasionally scanning the sea with their binoculars. Every few hundred metres there was another beach kiosk–each a carbon copy of Number 7, but without the rainbow flag, the thumping music, and the homosexuals posing in their designer trunks and shades. Alan and Terry passed one–Number 3 or 4 perhaps–that was a long way from the nearest section of loungers, and therefore wasn't getting much trade. Perched on the top of an exposed stretch of bedrock, with nothing but the dunes behind it and a few hundred yards of pebbly grey sand on either side, it seemed to Terry more like a forgotten border outpost than something you'd come across on a holiday beach. He couldn't imagine anyone wanting to stop here for a drink or a snack when there was so much life and activity nearby. Two old men were sitting playing chess at one of the white wooden tables in front of the bar–and as Terry and Alan walked past, some thirty metres further down the beach, they could hear slow classical music, perhaps a requiem, drifting on the breeze. The woman who ran the place stood with her arms folded, lost in her thoughts as she looked out to sea–but when she saw Alan she smiled and waved, calling out to him. Alan returned the wave. Terry was amazed.

"You know her?" Alan shrugged.

"I like to come down here sometimes, have a coffee and read my book–get away from all those queens at Number 7. And she needs the business." Further along, there was a huge lake–part of the wildlife conservation area of the dunes. In autumn and spring, migrating birds stopped here for a rest as they made their journeys across the continents. A few years ago during a particularly ferocious storm, the narrow stretch of beach which separated the lake from the sea had been washed away–and on his way to the nudist area the next day, Terry had been forced to put his clothes and shoes into his rucksack and wade across the water, carrying the bag above his head like a jungle explorer.

At Maspalomas the beach had gradually been eroded away, leaving the promenade, with its parade of shops restaurants and hotels, dangerously close to the high tide mark. Alan sat down on the low wall separating the promenade from the beach, took off his deck shoes and tapped the soles to get the sand out. Terry caught up with him.

"I'm starving," he said. "Do you mind if we stop for some lunch?" Alan was putting his socks back on, the quintessential Englishman.

"Not at all. I was just thinking the same thing. I can never manage much breakfast because I'm usually so hung over–which means that later on I fill myself with cakes and ice cream."

"Nothing wrong with that." Alan looked at the lad's slim figure.

"Easy for you to say, there's not a pick on you. Wait until you're my age and you start piling it on." They walked up the promenade into Maspalomas, into an area between the beach and the town itself which was like a miniature, sanitized version of a Moroccan Kasbah. Boutiques, pubs and snack bars were all squeezed together in a seemingly random way, some open to the elements, some covered, all reached by a rabbit warren of passageways. Terry had once been told about a gay bar in there that was supposed to be quite good, but in the few years since he'd started coming to the island, he had never been able to find it. They stuck to the main promenade, where there were a couple of bigger restaurants near the lido that seemed always to be busy. They were in luck. At the first one, a waiter came straight away and showed them to a table in a good position under the awning. He put down a basket of bread and an ashtray, and handed them a couple of menus.

"Now this meal is on me," said Terry. "After all, it was my idea. Let's have some wine." Alan looked surprised.

"Thanks–very kind." Terry asked the waiter for a carafe of rosé wine and some sparkling water, and then opened his menu.

"I love these places where they have photographs of each of the dishes like this." He pointed at one of the laminated pages in the slim, leatherette-bound volume. "It always cracks me up when the food arrives and it looks exactly like it did in the picture." The waiter arrived with the wine and poured some for them. He took their order and vanished. Alan removed his sunglasses and put his normal specs back on, so he could see properly now that they were out of the glare of the afternoon sunshine. Terry put out his hand.

"Do you mind if I have a look at those?" Alan handed him the glasses and Terry examined them carefully. The frames themselves, which were in a sort of wrap-around, teardrop shape, were made out of a tortoise-shell material, but the arms were metal with tortoise-shell panels inlaid into them.

"Very chic," said Terry, "very retro. They make you look like some kind of jet-set aristocrat." Alan laughed.

"No-one's ever said that before. They're ancient, like me. Used to be my normal glasses, but when I got a newer pair I had these tinted lenses put in. The optician was doing a special offer. George is always telling me to get some modern, trendy ones."

"Well he obviously has no idea about fashion–because stuff like that is right back in." Alan took a sip of wine, excited by the young man's exuberance.

"That look you just gave me," he said. "My wife used to look at me like that, many years ago."

"But I remember Mrs Reid. I don't look anything like her."

"I know that. But it was the way you looked at me. It could have been her." Terry smiled.

"Maybe it's just something you bring out in people."

"You must all be daft," said Alan, shaking his head and wishing he'd kept his mouth shut. Bloody fool, the wine was already going to his head.

"No–we just have good taste. Now if you'll excuse me, I must go to the loo before the food arrives." Alan watched the way the lad walked across the terrace and into the restaurant, pausing on the threshold to try to locate the toilet. He saw people, especially women, looking Terry up and down, admiring him–and why not? He was extremely handsome, exuding a sort of contained, muted masculinity. There was a degree of boyish charm there but he was most definitely a man. Alan wondered what these folk made of the situation–perhaps they thought that he and Terry were father and son. But some were bound to understand the nature of Gran Canaria's gay scene, and suspect that they were lovers. They would no doubt be wondering what on earth a gorgeous guy like Terry was doing with an old crock like Alan–and would probably conclude that money was changing hands somewhere down the line. But who cared what anybody else thought? The sexiest young guy there was buying him lunch, and nothing else mattered. People walked past on the hot pavement outside the canopy, beleaguered by the power of the sun. Alan and Terry had put their clothes back on before they left the beach, but Alan was rather disturbed to see that here, back in civilization, obese, middle-aged people were wandering around dressed only in skimpy swimming costumes. Alan smiled at the absurdity of it. Under the awning it was pleasantly shady and he felt cozy, bathing in the warmth and the sounds of the restaurant–a dozen different conversations, laughter and the clinking of glasses and cutlery. A cork popped. The waiters flitted among the tables, expertly opening bottles of wine, carrying stacks of empty plates and huge paella dishes. He sipped his wine and then poured a little more into the glass.

Inside, Terry was surprised by how big the restaurant was. The toilets were right at the back, next to the kitchen–which was separated from the dining room by a chest-high partition on which the cooks left dishes for the waiters to pick up, each with a small piece of paper slipped underneath to confirm where it was going. It was an infernal scene–a billion miles from the relaxed atmosphere of the terrace. A dozen or so men and women toiled in the heat generated by several massive ovens and ranks of hot stoves. Up on the wall was one of those machines for killing flies–an electrified metal grille with a circular florescent tube behind it that cast a queer violet glow on proceedings. There was a lot of shouting. A couple of waiters were skulking in the corner, hoping that their orders would emerge soon. Suddenly the head waiter, a robust man with jet black hair and a moustache that jumped around above his mouth like a small furry animal, charged across and started ticking them off–probably telling them to go and clear some tables instead of hanging around. Terry walked along a small passageway into the toilet. It seemed very dark after the brightness outside, and strange blue patterns pulsated at the edge of his vision as his eyes adjusted. He walked up to the urinal and looked at the tiles in front of his face. He was chuffed about being here with Alan. All the nervousness had slipped away and only pure, heady excitement remained–or maybe it was just the wine. Something told him that he would have to take it steady. If Alan found out how deep his feelings were and for how long he'd had them, he was bound to run a mile. And who could blame him? As Terry washed his hands he scrutinized himself in the mirror. There was a certain amount of giddiness there. He looked sternly into his own eyes.

"Just-keep-a-lid-on-it," he said slowly, under his breath.

Back at the table their starters had arrived. Alan smiled as Terry sat down.

"So, youngster, what's the story here? What are you doing hanging around with old farts like me, when you could have just about anyone you wanted?" Terry broke some bread over his soup.

"I'm not sure that there's an answer. Until I met the first older man I fell in love with, I thought I was just like everyone else. Meeting girls after school, showing off in front of them, trying to chat them up. And even after I realised that I liked older men, I didn't admit it to myself. It took me ages to do that."

"And had you realised by the time you were going out with my daughter?" Terry felt that he was on dangerous ground. He paused for a few seconds, thinking the answer out carefully, trying to compensate for the wine and the excitement.

"I'm not sure that I had," he said finally. "I didn't actually do anything about it until I went to university. When I got round to it, I realised that it was something that had been there for a long time." Alan shook his head.

"And you've never worked out why you feel the way you do?"

Terry giggled.

"I once went to see a psychiatrist about it, and ended up in bed with him. What about you?" Alan's eyes sparkled.

"Did I end up in bed with my psychiatrist? Never had one."

"No—when did you work out that you liked men?" Alan cast his mind back through that old familiar territory.

"At school we all used to play around with each other. It all seemed quite innocent—nobody thought it meant they were gay, it was a bit of relief and nothing more. Then later on I met George and that took things a little further. But when I met Marge I really fell for her. She was a smashing girl—smashing enough to take my mind off all the other stuff. I married her and everything else just slipped into the background."

"But did you carry on seeing men?" Terry blushed and looked down at the tablecloth. "Sorry, I shouldn't have asked that. It's the wine making me forward—don't answer if you don't want to." Alan laughed.

"Not at all. You've been very frank with me so I think I can manage it too. The answer is no. George and I had a bit of fun occasionally—usually when his love life was going through a slump. But my wife always knew him. They were great friends and she knew he was gay. I think she suspected that there'd been something between us, but Marge and I made a life together, and I really loved her. I didn't go with another man until after she died. George gave me the address of a hotel in Brighton he used to go to, and I thought—well, life's got to go on."

"That must have been pretty weird."

"Oh yes—suddenly parachuting into the gay scene at my time of life. I mean, it's very difficult to go back out there and look for company when you've spent most of your life with someone, and I guess that applies to both heterosexual and homosexual people who lose their partners. It was a way of thinking, a set of social skills that I had more or less forgotten about—if I ever had them in the first place. But on the other hand I was quite excited by it, by the novelty of it. Exploring a whole side of myself that I had only ever dabbled with–that's quite a liberating experience." Terry raised his glass.

"Here's to liberating experiences," he said. He'd often fantasized about sharing an intimate moment with this man, and now that it was happening it was nothing like what he had imagined. In his fantasies, it had all been visualized in two dimensions. There had been just the physical desire and the fulfilment of it, in some arbitrary scenario generated by his imagination. But actually to speak to Alan properly, to hear a bit about him, and to be able to look forward to the possibility of something physical later–that was truly thrilling.

"But hang on," said Alan. "You've not yet explained to me what the attraction is to older men. I mean, I was at my best decades ago, long before you were even born. I'm well past my sell-by date and yet you seem sincerely interested."

"That reminds me of a guy I met once in London," said Terry. "He took me back to his flat in Kensington–one of those huge, imposing red brick mansion blocks. His place felt more like a museum than somewhere you'd actually live, with polished parquet floors and statues and antique furniture–and in the lounge above the fireplace there was an oil painting, a portrait of a young man. So I asked him if it was a picture of his boyfriend or someone he'd known in the past, and he said no, that's me when I was twenty-five–wasn't I handsome? And I said, yes–but if you still looked like that I wouldn't be here. I wouldn't have even noticed you in the pub. Somewhere in his mind that was how he chose to see himself, as he was in his twenties. He probably looked in the mirror every day, thought about that youthful face, and cursed the passing years for what they'd done to him. But to me they had made him so much more interesting, so much more sexy–as they've done for you too." It was time for Alan to raise his glass.

"Here's to that." They finished the wine, had another carafe, ate and chatted and laughed–the ice by now well and truly broken. Afterwards they ordered coffee and Alan leaned back in his chair, smiling contentedly.

"George tells me you're on your own—that you don't have a lover. Seems a bit of a waste to me." Terry lit a cigarette and shrugged as he put his lighter back down on the table.

"I guess it's similar for me as it was for you. None of my mates back home knows I'm gay and I haven't told my family. It seems easier to stay single."

"Right." Alan regarded the lad over the top of his glasses. "But surely nowadays things are very different. I mean, homosexuality is accepted more readily now, everywhere you look there are TV shows about gays, articles in papers. Young straight guys going on about how they're in touch with their feminine sides. You could easily live a gay life if you wanted to—there's no need to cover it up any more."

For the first time in the conversation, Terry's voice became brittle.

"You'd think so," he said. "But it's not really like that where we're from, is it? It's not like London, where nobody knows who you are and nobody cares what you're doing. If my mum and dad found out about this, about the older man thing, it would break their hearts." Alan leaned forward, composing his words carefully.

"Look, Terry—this is none of my business so please feel free to tell me to bugger off if you want to, but you may be underestimating your parents. I mean, I'd want my daughters to give me the chance to know how they're living their lives, to share their experiences—however much their situation diverged from what I'd imagined. Do you understand what I'm getting at?" Terry looked under the awning at the people milling around on the promenade, checking out the shops and bars of Maspalomas as they made their way back home from the beach. He stubbed out his cigarette.

"Yes I do," he said. "It's hard, though, isn't it? I mean, what if things were flipped on their head, what if you met a nice guy that you clicked with—would you make a life with him, tell your daughters about that?" Alan laughed.

"That's not an eventuality I've ever considered." But Terry was not being put off.

"It could happen, though."

"I'm too old–what's the point of rocking the boat now?"

"What's the point of rocking the boat at any time?" The older man shrugged, lacking any decent riposte.

"Touché, I suppose," he said. The waiter brought their coffees, flashing them both a smile as he laid the tiny espresso cups and saucers down on the table. Terry had noticed that he was much friendlier to them than he was to the other diners–making an extra effort to clean the crumbs off the table between courses, and to top up their wine. He nodded towards the waiter's back as he walked away.

"Do you think he's onto us?"

"I was wondering that too. He's very smiley isn't he? But then again he's probably got a wife and eight kids at home. You know what these Spanish are like, they all swing both ways." Terry winked.

"Quite a few of those about, by all accounts." Alan laughed, relieved that after the seriousness of their words a few moments ago they'd regained their levity.

"I have no idea what you're talking about at all, young man." Terry downed his coffee in one and looked at his watch. He sighed.

"I feel absolutely blasted. I don't normally drink at lunchtime, and we've had quite a lot of wine. I think I'll head home and sleep it off. Are you going back to the beach?" Alan looked up at the sky.

"Looks like we've had the best of the day, eh? May as well go back to the hotel for a siesta. George and I still have more than a week left–plenty of time to get a good tan." They called the waiter over and asked him to bring the bill. When they stood up to leave, he shook hands with both of them. Terry looked as if he was about to keel over, so Alan took his arm and navigated him through the tables and out towards the promenade. Alan leaned over to whisper in the younger man's ear.

"It's obviously you he likes–he hardly looked at me when he

shook my hand."

"Rubbish," said Terry, squinting against the sunlight and groping around in his rucksack for the hard plastic box containing his shades. "Maybe he was just too embarrassed to make eye contact." They joined the crowds heading back towards the lighthouse–where there was a taxi rank and a couple of bus stops. Alan looked up at a digital sign that said it was half past three, and the temperature was 28 degrees centigrade. He turned to Terry.

"How do you want to travel back to town?"

"May as well get the bus, eh? It's still early so it shouldn't be too busy."

There was a huge crowd of people waiting at the bus stop but somehow they managed to squeezed their way on board–and even found an empty seat near the back. As the bus negotiated the curving roads and roundabouts on its way to Playa Del Ingles, its motion forced their legs and bodies together. Emboldened by the wine, Alan pushed himself harder towards Terry, and was delighted to feel that pressure returned. By the time they got to their stop, he was so turned on that it was almost an embarrassment to stand up and get off. He felt like a naughty schoolboy holding his rucksack in front of himself and pushing through the crowd–but fortunately things had calmed down by the time they got out onto the street. The bus dropped them off right outside Alan's hotel. They stood on the pavement smiling at each other as it drove off. Alan took a breath.

"Coming in?"

"Thought you'd never ask."

*

WALKING around in the dunes looking for a suitable spot to spend the rest of the afternoon, George and Mark kept bumping into people they knew from the bars in the Yumbo Centre, and stopping to chat with them. That was one of the things George loved about Gran Canaria–the self-contained social scene which he and Alan had become a part of. They would walk into Hummel Hummel on their first night and within seconds they would be saying hello to people they knew. Some were just familiar faces; others had played more significant roles in previous holidays on the island. These were often the most interesting cases. George would find himself sitting looking across the bar at someone with whom he'd had a fling—someone who perhaps he had even pined for after returning home—and wondering what it was that he had seen in them. The attraction had dissipated like a mirage. Perhaps they were a few years older, or had maybe put on some weight or met a new man, or changed jobs—but inevitably the circumstances had altered. Sometimes they looked fitter and sharper—as if life had been good to them in the intervening time, but sometimes they looked as if illness or bad fortune had knocked something out of them. It was also possible that the first time around George had met the person half way through their holiday, so they were already tanned and rested—relaxed and looking their best. The following year he would see them when they arrived, pale and worn out by the day's journey from the UK. But the wonderful thing about being a gay traveler was that wherever he had gone, there was always somewhere George could go where he would be sure of meeting like-minded people. Whether it was a sauna or a bar that he had read about in a gay guidebook, or a specific area of a park, or even a public toilet, there was more or less a guarantee of human contact. Similar opportunities did not exist for heterosexuals—a fact that had been brought home to him one morning in Playa Del Ingles when he was outside the hotel, and he came across an old widower who was sitting alone on his suitcase, waiting for the coach to take him back to the airport.

"How's your holiday been?" George asked cheerfully.

"Bloody terrible," said the man. "Hardly spoken to anybody for two weeks, and when I booked one of these excursions around the island, they forgot to come to the hotel to pick me up—as if I didn't even exist. To tell you the truth I'm slightly worried that they're not going to pick me up now. It's the last time I'll be coming here." George's heart had gone out to the man. He imagined that travelling alone would be particularly depressing for someone who had always had a companion—but at the same time George couldn't help thinking how different the guy's holiday would have been if he was gay. He was quite handsome really in a chunky, simple sort of way, with pleasant smile and a good head of grey hair–and George felt sure he'd have been fighting them off at Hummel Hummel or on the gay beach. But of course these possibilities were simply not open to him. But then, maybe there were plenty of opportunities for straight people too, and it was just a question of how you approached life.

Strolling through the dunes, George and Mark had eventually found a secluded clearing slightly off the beaten track, where they were unlikely to be disturbed. They spread out their towels side by side, and laid stones around the borders to stop them being disturbed by the breeze. They then stripped off and ate the fruit that Alan had left when he went away with Terry. They chatted for a while about the island and their different experiences there, and George was delighted to discover what easy company Mark was. He was older than Terry, probably in his early forties, and like the younger man was quite tall. But where Terry basically had a slim build, Mark was more powerful with strong arms and a broad, hairy chest. His legs too were very muscular and hairy, and he had dark brown skin, black hair and a black moustache. It was easy to see why George thought he was Spanish when he first saw him. Mark also had a fantastically cheeky, impish face which seemed all the time to be on the verge of breaking into laughter. Mark had fallen asleep after a while and George had been lying quietly for some time now, dozing in the late afternoon sun, watching the swallows dip and swoop just a few feet above their bodies as they flew over the dunes catching small insects. A sense of deep contentment flowed over him, and within minutes he too had drifted off to sleep.

*

GEORGE loved all birds, but swallows held a particular fascination for him. He would be out walking in April and he'd look up and see them zooming around, and know for sure that the summer had arrived, and that knowledge would lift his heart. When he was very young, probably about six or seven, he watched a pair build their wattle and daub nest in the apex of the roof of the house next door, where old Carter lived with his wife. The nest had the slightly aberrant look of nature gone haywire, like a termite hill or a growth on the trunk of a diseased tree. George was amazed at how the birds managed to get it to stick to the structure so solidly, without the aid of glue or the tools that a human would use. The swallows had it built within a few days and he would sit in his bedroom watching them flying in and out, squeezing through a hole that hardly seemed big enough, even for a bird's tiny body. Then one morning he heard voices outside, and saw through the window old Carter and his father talking over the fence. Above them, where the nest had been, there was an empty space. His father came into the house with a worried look.

"That bloody fool Carter's knocked the swallow's nest down, because his wife didn't like it." He grabbed the boy's shoulders and looked into his eyes. "Promise me George that you'll never interfere with swallows. It's a blessing if they choose to settle on your property, but it's very bad luck if you do anything to harm them." George didn't need to be told the gravity of the situation. His mind was filled with the image of the nest lying smashed in the yard, the little eggs inside all broken, the adult birds nowhere to be seen. He felt the strange ache in the back of his throat that came when he was going to cry. He ran straight to his room and looked out at the space where the nest had been. Old Carter was sweeping something up below it. George followed the fortunes of the neighbours over the following two years with a growing sense of dread. First old Carter had a heart attack while out walking the dog on the farm track one morning. By the time someone found him he was already dead. Then one morning, barely a year later, Mrs Carter went out early and slipped on the damp paving stones, breaking her hip. She went into hospital, but caught pneumonia and passed away some weeks later. The incidents–which were in all probability coincidental–left young George in no doubt about the strange power of the swallows. For quite a while he feared that some of the bad luck might have rubbed off onto his own family merely because they had been associated with the Carters. When bad things happened he would lie awake in bed and pray for the birds' forgiveness. But soon a new family moved in next door and the memory of old Carter and his wife gradually faded.

Strangely, some years later, George was given the chance to make his peace with the swallows. He was out walking on the farm track one summer's evening when he came across one of the birds, lying exhausted on the ground. The creature had become starved of oxygen because its gaping beak was so full of flies, and it had dropped out of the sky. It was too tired to move and was lying on its belly, wings outstretched, utterly helpless. George shuddered to think what would have happened to it if a dog or a tractor had come along before he did. He gently picked the bird up. He could tell it was a female because it had shorter tail feathers than the males had. Although there was fear in her tiny eyes, she didn't have the energy to struggle. He admired the contrast between the dark, metallic blue feathers on the upper parts of her body, and the creamy white ones underneath. With his thumb and forefinger he gently teased out the sticky mass of insects that had become wedged into the bird's mouth, and let them fall to the ground. Straight away she began to suck in air to fill her lungs. He heard a little gasp, felt the small body changing shape in the palm of his hand. The bird was suddenly alive again, shaking itself and looking around. For a fraction of a second its eye held his; there was a brief moment of contact, of communication, and without thinking he gently threw the bird up into the air. Immediately her wings caught the delicate currents of the breeze and she climbed twenty feet or so, before swooping and changing direction as she re-gained her bearings. Moments later she was away across the fields–heading most probably back to the waiting brood in some outbuilding over at the farm.

From that moment on George felt that he had a secret kinship with the swallows. When he was out walking in the summer, they would flash by above his head, twittering and chit-chitting as they did. He knew this was a common experience for walkers in certain parts of the country, but it stirred something deeper within him. Then one day in November he was walking around stark naked in the dunes of Maspalomas, enjoying the hot sun on his body and vaguely cruising a young man who was sunbathing nearby, when a pair of swallows zipped by overhead. On his way back to the hotel he had gone to the information centre near the Riu Palace hotel, and a pleasant lady there had confirmed that the swallows did indeed come to the island. It seemed perfectly fitting to George that his own winter migration patterns would eventually synchronize with those of the swallows–both in the late autumn, when they were on their way to southern Africa, and again in the early spring when they were travelling back to Britain. It was another reason why he always felt when he arrived in Gran Canaria that he was coming home.

*

GEORGE felt a hand stroking his chest gently. He opened his eyes to see Mark propped up on one elbow, looking down at him and smiling, shaking his head from side to side.

"What?" said George.

"Boy, was I jealous when I saw you leaving the Yumbo Centre with that young guy last night." George chuckled, rubbing his eyes.

"Well–you had gone off with my best friend. How was I to know that it was going to be a disaster? Might have been the start of a beautiful thing."

"Oh sure, I couldn't blame you–he was gorgeous. I thought to myself: 'how can I ever compete with someone like that.' It was a depressing moment. But now here you are, things worked out all right in the end."

"Don't count your chickens," said George. "I still haven't decided whether or not I'm going to forgive you for abandoning me. Maybe if you keep stroking me for another hour or so." Mark gave him a light slap.

"You were the one who went off in a sulk while we were on the Sky Rider. If you'd waited for us, we probably wouldn't have gone back to my apartment. Why did you leave, by the way?" George brushed some sand off his legs.

"I'm not sure, really. I was a bit miffed. It seemed to me as if Alan had only gone for you because I'd expressed an interest. He normally only likes guys in their twenties and thirties. But then I thought I'd give him a chance, because he doesn't have much luck in these matters."

"I know the feeling."

"What? Don't tell me you have a hard time when you're out on the pull. They must be queuing up." Mark shook his head.

"No way! They used to when I was in my twenties, and I suppose even into my thirties. But once you get into your forties you're in a sort of no-man's land. You're too old for the ones who like youngsters, and you're not old enough for the ones who go for the more mature man. It's a bit of a weird time, really. So you can understand why I was so annoyed when I saw you going off with that lad. I was kicking myself for missing a good opportunity."

"I can see your logic but I don't agree. Alan's always moaning on about being over the hill, but it's all up here." He tapped his head. "I think that whatever your age, if you've got something about you, there'll be someone after you. And you've got plenty going for you." Mark smiled.

"Glad you think so. But there's another reason why people tend to run a mile when they get to know me a bit better."

"Really?"

"Well, yes." Mark stopped stroking and looked off into the bushes. "I may as well tell you this now. I have a boyfriend. But it's not a straightforward situation. He has senile dementia. He's in a nursing home now. That's why I'm here on holiday on my own."

'Oh. I'm sorry to hear that."

"I couldn't look after him any more. I would get home from work every night and the same thing would happen. He'd have taken a load of his clothes out of the wardrobe and packed them into a couple of suitcases, as if we were going on a journey, and tell me as I came into the house that it was time to go home. Of course we were already at home–the place he was thinking about was somewhere he'd lived years ago, when he was much younger. When it first started to happen I tried to reason with him, but it was no good. Eventually I started taking the cases and putting them in the car and driving out of town with him. After a few miles I'd turn around and bring us back and say: 'Okay darling, we're home again,' because that was the only way I could get him to settle. But it would be the same again the next night, and that went on every day for three years." George suddenly felt humbled—his own affairs and concerns seemed rather trivial in the face of such a bleak situation. It was his turn to give Mark a gentle caress.

"That must have been very difficult for you."

"It was but you know, in some ways it's a privilege to be given the chance to express your love for someone in that way. I mean, we go through our lives being so independent, so selfish, thinking most of the time about how to take care of our own affairs—it's a blessing to be really needed by somebody for once." George moved his hand to Mark's leg.

"Your story doesn't put me off at all. On the contrary, it's nice to meet someone genuine for a change."

"I still go to see Paul a few times a week, but he doesn't recognize me at all and it breaks my heart. We just have to get on with it, though, I suppose." There was a rustling in the bushes behind them. They both sprang up and stood staring, to see what it was. A large lizard poked its nose out of the shrubs—attracted no doubt by the smell of the remains of their fruit. Mark let out a huge laugh and bent down to his rucksack. He brought out a packet of biscuits, broke one into pieces and started feeding the animal, which had now crawled into the open. George watched him as he crouched down and spoke softly to the lizard, while letting it take the bits of biscuit from the palm of his hand. He thought about all the things that had happened to this man, who was so kind and so good-humoured, and imagined the pain of watching a lover's mind fall apart. He walked forward and laid his hands on Mark's shoulders. Around them the shadows had lengthened.

"Isn't it beautiful here at this time of the evening?" said George softly. "When all the other buggers have gone back to Playa del Ingles?" Mark clapped his hands together gently to brush off the crumbs.

"Yes," he said as he stood up. "It's a magical time. And there's still quite a lot of heat in that sun." He turned around and they hugged, George really pulling Mark into him, enjoying the smells of sweat and suntan oil, rubbing his hands all over his back, feeling the muscles. Presently they began to kiss, and after a minute or so Mark broke off and spoke in a whisper.

"Let's lie down." And then they were in one another's arms again, intoxicated by the sensation of being so close out in the open, with nothing between their skin and the sky, caressed by the breeze, observed only by the swallows that flitted through the clearing. They stayed there for another hour or so as the sun dropped below the level of the trees, and the odd straggler from the beach treaded quietly past the bushes that surrounded the little clearing, oblivious to the tenderness being expressed just yards from where they walked.

*

TERRY fell asleep moments after he and Alan finished making love. Alan shut his eyes and tried to do the same, but he'd left the balcony door open a tiny bit, and the noise of a scooter buzzing past jarred his senses just when he was about to drift off. He lay there for a while starting to feel the circulation in his arm being cut off by Terry's weight on top of it. It had been terrific sex–better than anything he could have hoped for after the previous night's fiasco with Mark–but the giddy intoxication of the afternoon and its physical crescendo had all but melted away, and he was once again seeing things as they were. Thoughts began to flow through his brain demanding his attention, and before long sleep was impossible. As he tried to gently disengage himself, Terry made the task easier by rolling onto one side so that he was facing the wall. He was out for the count–which was unsurprising considering the pace of life here. People talked about restful holidays in the sun but really they had no idea. It could take weeks to recover from a stint in Gran Canaria and as George often said, to be a true hedonist you had to have the stamina of a military commando. Alan reached down to the foot of the bed and retrieved one of the crumpled sheets, pulling it over the boy's body. He got up and padded into the bathroom, had a pee, then picked up a half-empty bottle of mineral water next to the basin and drank it all in big gulps. He walked back into the bedroom, stopping in the doorway to look at the boy on the bed. Only the back of Terry's head, one shoulder, and his neck were visible. The rest was hidden by the white sheet which followed the contours of the body underneath, reminding Alan of the flowing robes he had seen on carved marble sarcophagi in Italian cathedrals. The curtains weren't fully closed and an intense, golden sunlight was flooding through the gap, hitting the wardrobe doors at the far end of the room, and then diffusing into a soft orange radiance. He picked up his cigarettes and sat down behind the little circular wooden table in the corner of the room. Staring into space, he heard muffled noises in the building around him–doors opening and closing, the scrape of furniture being moved, a swooshing sound that he guessed was somebody having a shower or flushing a toilet, then footsteps in the corridor and the sound of laughter. This was always a strange time, when the day had ended but the evening was yet to begin. People were returning to their rooms, having a nap or making love, watching television, sprucing themselves up for the evening ahead. When his wife was alive Alan had loved sharing this quiet time with her. Maybe he would doze on top of the bed while she sat reading, or they would sit on the balcony and have an aperitif together. But now he felt suddenly alone, as if there was no one he could really turn to. To wake the boy on the bed would be wrong. What would he say? Talk to me because I feel confused and somehow dislocated from the rest of human society? He believed (and here he was doing Terry a great disservice) that a boy like that would be unable to understand. What about George? Alan had no idea whether or not his friend was in his room. If he was, he would probably be cursing the fact that Terry wasn't in his arms–so to go and knock on his door would be at best insensitive and at worst, downright mean. He lit a cigarette and thought, come on Reid, get a grip. You've got yourself to this point, and you're going to have to handle it on your own. But handle what? A sense of doubt, a feeling that he was unprepared for the events that were unfolding. He stubbed the cigarette out and walked back into the bathroom, where he stood in front of the large mirror, staring at his reflection. It was body he was still secretly quite proud of, a lovely dark tan, but the face–my goodness there was such a story of anxiety and bewilderment spelled out in the creases and the wrinkles! He looked himself in the eye. What are you going to do now, eh? He had the feeling that there was some potential here, that with this lad he was on the verge of finding something he needed, but he had family, friends, and neighbours to think about–a life so established that it seemed like an impossible task to embark upon something new. There was also the age gap–he could just imagine how people would sneer when they heard about that. Goodness only knew what the rest of Alan's family, indeed both of their families, would think of it. And would an affair at this time of life not somehow be cheapening his marriage, insulting the memory of his dead wife? George was clearly carrying a torch for Terry—so maybe it would be better just to forget the whole thing and let them go off together. They'd all be friends and everything would remain as it had been—unresolved and unsatisfactory, in other words.

He heard a cracking sound, the noise made by the tiny bones in people's feet when they walk around with no shoes on, and turned to see Terry standing in the doorway. In the neon light of the bathroom the boy's skin seemed quite pale, with redness from sunburn on his shoulders, forearms, and face. He really had a perfect young body. Marge would have said that he was too thin and needed feeding up—George would have grinned wickedly and said that yes, he certainly did need something hot inside him. Terry's eyes were puffy, and his hair was all spiked up on one side where he had been lying on it. His voice was hoarse with the cigarettes and the wine and the doze.

"Are you okay?"

"I don't know. I feel a bit lost. Why are you here? Why are you interested in me? What have I got that you can't find in someone younger—someone who would suit you more?" Terry saw that Alan was upset, and came forward to put his arms around him.

"Don't be like that. I'm enjoying being with you. I like you." The young man made it all sound so simple but Alan's doubts went too deep.

"Come on! I've lived my life—I've done everything a man can expect to do, and things are winding down for me, but then you turn up, some young guy from the past, walking in and giving me one of the nicest afternoons I've had in a while. I think I could be forgiven for thinking that it was all some kind of put-on." For a moment Terry was tempted to tell Alan how deep his feelings were, and for how long he'd had them—to reassure him that he wasn't playing around, that his interest was real. But then he realised the folly of such a move. From Alan's point of view the situation was already weird enough, so Terry would have to keep it all under wraps, certainly for the time being.

"Look," he said, "I know this has all been a bit strange, meeting here by chance, but I'm delighted to see you again–it's made my holiday. And I hope this isn't just a one-off, that we can see each other later, maybe spend the night together. But just see how you feel, take it at your own pace." Alan laughed–but it wasn't an expression of amusement, more a sort of acknowledgement of the absurdity of life.

"Oh God–I don't know, I give up." He opened his arms and they embraced once again, standing naked in the middle of the bathroom. After a few moments, Alan pulled away and looked in the mirror, waving his hand in the direction of his own reflection. "Seriously, though, look at me–a wizened old fart, practically putrefying on the spot." Terry raised his eyes, exasperated.

"That's such rubbish, and you know it! You're in excellent shape."

"Go on, complete the sentence."

"What do you mean? There's no more."

"I'm in excellent shape for my age. Isn't that what you intended to say?"

"You said that, not me. And anyway, why have you got this hangup with age? You should take a leaf out of George's book. He obviously doesn't let it get him down, or at least if it does, he doesn't show it."

"I know–back home they all call him Peter Pan. But be honest, lad, there's not much of a future in your relationship if one of you is a pensioner–none of us can do anything about the old anno domini."

"But who knows how long any of us has got? I could walk outside and get hit by a bus, or die of a brain haemorrhage at breakfast tomorrow morning. You just have to do the best you can, enjoy what comes along."

Such wisdom in one so young, thought Alan. And he was right, really–the whole of life was lived in the face of uncertainty, and it was pure folly to think you had any idea how it was going, or what was likely to happen next. Marge's death had left a huge hole in Alan's life, and the sense of despair and loneliness often returned. But the acute, stupefying feeling of loss, the initial impact of her departure, had departed surprisingly quickly. It was now time to rebuild himself, to get up and carry on with his life. It seemed that the story was still unfolding, demanding that he take part, regardless of his confusion.

Through the open window they heard the sound of drivers blasting their horns, crowds of people cheering and clapping, music and a pounding disco beat. Of course tonight the carnival arrived in town, and the parade of floats would be on its way down the Avenida Tirajana, past the hotel and into the Yumbo Centre. Terry slipped on a white T-shirt and a pair of underpants, and headed out onto the balcony to see what was going on. Alan lingered in the bathroom for half a second and glanced in the mirror. This time he smiled and gave himself a little wink. He grabbed a bathrobe and followed the boy outside–and was surprised by how warm it still was. Just as he was about to sit down, he remembered something.

"Fancy an aperitif? I can't do you a gin and tonic because I don't have any tonic, but I have Campari and fresh orange juice."

"Sounds lovely." Alan disappeared through the patio doors again–re-emerging a few minutes later and handing Terry a cool glass containing a drink the colour of blood orange juice. An unlit joint hung from his lips. Alan smiled at Terry, the mischief back in his eyes.

"A little sharpener," he said out of the corner of his mouth, sitting down and lighting it up, blowing a huge cloud of smoke across the balcony. "Let's see what the Canarian night has in store for us."

"That's more like it."

As it happened, the parade hadn't arrived yet–and all they could see were the crowds milling around on the pavement. Terry's attention shifted to the people sitting at the poolside bar, and the balconies on the other side of the swimming pool area. Suddenly his arm shot out.

"Look over there—outrageous!" Alan realised immediately what had caught Terry's eye. Balcony Man was up to his usual tricks, and seemed to be putting on an extra display because he had a handsome new admirer. He was standing in the corner of his balcony, out of sight from the bedroom windows, playing with himself in full view of anyone on their side of the hotel who cared to look. Terry giggled.

"I can't believe it, you'd get arrested for that back home! Where are your binoculars?" Alan nipped inside and grabbed the leather case, which was hanging over the back of a chair. Terry put them up to his eyes.

"I wish I had a camera—but hang on. Oh dear! Someone else is there." Alan looked across and sure enough, Balcony Man's gibbon-faced wife had come outside and caught him in the act. Well—it had been a long time coming. She had rolled up a magazine and was hitting him repeatedly over the head with it, her short fat arm pumping up and down like a fleshy pink piston. They could hear the impacts even across here. Terry continued to watch the scene through the binoculars, fascinated.

"Shit—she's really getting stuck in! I think you'd better ring for an ambulance." Within a few seconds the woman had pushed her husband back inside their room. Alan touched his forehead, disturbed.

"I dread to think what's going on in there. Maybe we should go round and rescue him." Terry put the binoculars back in their case.

"I'd travel to the other side of the planet to get my hands on a cock like that—but there's no way I'm taking her on, she'd have us all for breakfast. I'm afraid he's on his own." Alan handed the joint over.

"Here—that'll take your mind off the fate of poor old Balcony Man."

"Cheers," said Terry. "Do you ever see him around the hotel?" Alan shot a sideways glance at Terry.

"You'll be asking for his phone number next."

"Relax, I'm not after him. He's married anyway."

"And when has that ever made a difference, young man?" Terry laughed.

"Touché."

"In answer to your question," said Alan, "he and his wife eat dinner a few tables away from us in the dining room. He acts as if butter wouldn't melt in his mouth."

"That may be so–but next time you see him I reckon he'll be all wrapped up in bandages, with big black panda eyes." Alan leaned back, breathing out in a long sigh. He looked shellshocked.

"I've been smoking that dope all week and I've still not got used to the strength of it. I'm quite squiffy already and I've only had a couple of puffs." Terry was now scanning the dense crowds that had gathered with the binoculars.

"God," he muttered, "how are all these people going to get into the Yumbo?"

"Yes, they come from far and wide to watch the burning of the sardine."

"The sardine?"

"Haven't you ever been here before at carnival time? The whole point is that they have this huge papier maché sardine, which is the focus of all the celebrations. They start off by worshiping it, but then it gets ill and a bunch of people dressed as doctors and nurses try to save it. But it dies anyway, and they burn it on a massive bonfire in the Yumbo Centre. I'm not sure what it's all about. Maybe it's an offering to the gods, to try to ensure that the fishermen get good catches or something." Terry, who was now starting to feel the effects of the dope, had no idea what Alan was talking about. It sounded like gibberish, but he suspected that his difficulties in making sense of it were more to do with the state of his own head. He remembered that he had arranged to meet Rob and Helen at the Norwegian bar across the road, to watch the parade and have a few beers before they went back to the villa.

"Listen, Alan–I think I'm going to head off. I promised I'd meet the people I'm staying with and go back home with them for dinner. Is that okay?"

"Of course. George and I are supposed to go down to the dining room at eight o'clock anyway." He looked at his watch. "I'm sure you could eat with us if you wanted to, but you can't go in wearing shorts, and I don't suppose any of my trousers would fit you. How big is your waist?"

"Thirty-two." Alan shook his head.

"Thirty-two. I can't even remember when my waist was that size."

"Yeah, but look at it this way, if you were a thirty-two I'd probably not be interested in you. I don't think older men suit being too thin. It looks unhealthy, makes their heads look too big."

"We'll see if you still think that when you're my age, and it becomes a constant battle just to stop everything sagging."

"I'm not getting dragged into that again. You know how handsome I think you are, you're just fishing for compliments." Alan paused.

"No, I get plenty of those every time I go into one of these bloody bars in the Yumbo Centre. You're all perverts. You need your heads examining, or maybe your eyes tested–or both." Terry smiled.

"Okay you win. Can we meet up later?"

"Of course–we'll probably be in Hummel Hummel a little earlier tonight so that we can get a table and watch the comings and goings."

"I might have a look around before I come to the bar–check out the carnival."

"That's fine, take your time. We're bound to be there at least until midnight." Terry walked into the room, put his shorts on and grabbed his rucksack. A few moments later he came back out and kissed Alan goodbye.

"Okay then–see you later. Say hello to George for me." Alan wondered where George was and what sort of reception his friend would give him when they met for dinner. He felt a pang of conscience about the time he had spent with this boy.

"I will," he said, standing up and following Terry to the door. Alan watched the lad turn the corner at the end of the corridor, and then went back to the balcony to finish his drink. After a few minutes he noticed that it was getting a bit cooler. He went back inside and sat on the edge of the bed, where he hesitated for a moment and then picked up the telephone. It was quarter to seven and he guessed that his daughter and her family would have eaten their dinner by now. He was surprised to hear that the ringing tone sounded the same in Gran Canaria as it did in England. Jane picked up the phone after three rings. Through the receiver he could hear a mechanical whirring in the background, probably the dishwasher, and somewhere else a high-pitched young voice chattering away–obviously one of the granddaughters.

"Hello darling," said Alan, "it's only me."

"Dad! How are you? How's the holiday? George keeping you out of trouble?"

"Oh, you know us. The quiet life and all that." There was laughter at the other end.

"Yeah sure. How many gin and tonics have you had?"

"None so far. Thanks for the text–George got it this morning on the beach."

"No problem, he replied straight away saying you were having a good time."

"How are the kids?"

"They're cool, thanks, except that Daisy's had a tummy ache. Polly drew a picture of you today at school. She's going to give it to you next time she sees you. It's quite a good likeness, except that your head's blue and shaped like a boat." Alan smiled.

"It felt more like a sinking ship this morning, I can tell you." The sounds coming from this family home, and the thoughts of his granddaughters, lifted his mood.

"And what about you?" asked Jane. "Are you nauseatingly brown yet?" There was a short pause before his voice came down the line. Jane marvelled at the thought of it zooming through all those cables, or bouncing off a satellite, in order to reach her ear.

"Getting there, love. We've had a couple of rainy days, but it's been really hot for the rest of the time."

"Sounds absolutely awful." He ignored the sarcasm.

"And I've met a lad here who I think you used to know. Terry Fowler. Can you remember him?" Jane thought of the boy who drove an old Morris Minor and played rugby for the school team.

"Blimey, that's a bit of a blast from the past. How did you meet him?" Alan thought for a second, but the joint had befuddled his mind.

"Oh, we just bumped into him in a bar last night. An Irish place. He was there with his girlfriend." The poorly thought-out lie sounded somehow pathetic to him as he said it.

"Great–look dad, is everything okay? You sound a bit...distracted." Alan looked around the quiet room, at the crumpled bedsheets behind him, and the feeling of emptiness returned. On the table next to the television he could see the big duty-free bottle of gin he bought on the way out, the smaller bottle of Campari next to it. He thought about an old German guy he and George knew who had come here for three weeks, and after a couple of frustrating nights in the bars, had spent the rest of the time locked in his room drinking duty free booze. Who could blame him? The sense of isolation must have been unbearable. Alan was brought back to his senses by the sounds of cheering and music coming in through the open window.

"I'm fine–honestly. It's the carnival tonight, so George and I are going to that. Should be fun."

"Well you enjoy it–and if there's anything you want to talk about, you know where we are."

"Thanks Jane. I know that. I love you."

"Love you too dad. Take care."

Jane's husband Keith walked into the kitchen as she laid the cordless phone back into its recharging cradle. He had been in the garden, and went straight to the sink to wash the muck off his hands.

"What news from paradise island?" Jane stared at the phone, slightly troubled.

"I don't know, really. He says he's fine. He phoned to tell me he and George met a guy I went out with when I was at school. But it sounded like... a confession."

"Maybe they met in one of those dodgy bars." Keith smirked. "Maybe this lad's turned into a lady boy. Maybe they ended up in bed together." Jane looked up–and she wasn't laughing.

"It wouldn't surprise me if Terry was gay, to be honest. There was always something a bit awkward about him–more than the usual adolescent awkwardness. And dad's relationship with George–even mum used to talk about that."

"The plot thickens. But how you feel about it if they were together?" Jane picked the phone handset up again and started sliding the plastic battery cover open and closed with her thumb–something she often did when she was thinking in the kitchen.

"Don't know, really." She shrugged. "I'm not sure that I'd mind. I mean he's had a terrible time these past few years and in a way he deserves something to perk him up a bit. Life's always moving and you can't keep things the way they are. He loved mum–and whatever he does now isn't going to change that. She'd want him to be happy anyway."

"I suppose so. But if it was a woman his own age, or even a

younger woman, I could see it. But a young man? What can be in it for him, whoever he is?"

"I see what you mean. Well, it takes all sorts. And if he was a gold-digger I think dad would spot it–he's not that desperate for company after all. But even if he was, what difference would it make? We're doing okay–mum and dad have already given us so much. If he spends all his money or gives it to someone else, who cares? As long as he's happy." Keith raised an eyebrow.

"A very enlightened point of view."

"It's the only point of view. What could we do about it anyway, even if we didn't like it?" Keith laid down the tea towel he'd been using to dry his hands.

"This is probably all pie in the sky anyway," he said. "Alan and George most likely spend their afternoons playing bingo at the poolside bar, or doing those geriatric stretching exercises that they lay on at hotels like that. He'll be all worn out by now I expect–too much sun and sangria. Now come and see what Polly and I have done to the rockery." He led her out into the garden. It was already dark and there was a nip to the air. Their daughter was playing with the cat–which was purring and rubbing itself on her legs. Keith had finished putting the stones in place a few days ago–now he'd put the earth in and planted shrubs and flowering plants. It would look fabulous later in the year. Jane's concern about her father quickly receded into the background.

*

GEORGE and Mark parted company with a hug and a very European kiss on both cheeks. The younger man was having dinner with a couple he and his boyfriend Paul had befriended in Gran Canaria nearly ten years ago–before Paul began to show the early signs of dementia. Mark had invited George to join them and he would have loved to, but somehow it seemed inappropriate. In any case, George was keen to catch up with Alan and find out how his afternoon had gone. There was also a sense in which he quite fancied taking a step back from what had been going on throughout the afternoon. It had been a heady few hours and George had been so caught up in it that he relished the chance to go over things in his mind, to catch his breath as it were. He hadn't felt like this in ages. As he walked–or practically skipped–along the Avenida Tirajana, a huge grin spread across his face. Mark was a real find! George had been physically attracted to him from the start, but to discover that he was such a great guy had taken things onto a completely different level. And despite that fact that many times in his life he had met people and thought there was some kind of bond there, only to find that they disappeared without a trace, this time George believed there was a definite rapport. People often spoke of feelings being reciprocated, and that was all very well–but it did imply that there was some kind of transaction taking place. George felt in his heart that this was more a case of feelings being generated in both men simultaneously, because of their involvement with one another. No one needed to do any reciprocating, because it was coming from both of them at the same time.

Crowds were already gathering on the pavement to watch the carnival parade make its way into the Yumbo Centre. George–who was a very quick walker–weaved through the ditherers expertly, sometimes jumping off the pavement and walking up the road for a few yards when there were no cars coming, so that he could keep up his pace. As he approached the entrance of the hotel, the front of one of his flip-flops snagged on the edge of an uneven paving stone, flicking the shoe up against the sole of his foot with a loud slap, and causing him to stumble forward.

"Careful, silly old fool," he muttered to himself as he jogged down the wide staircase that led into the lobby. The place was packed with Germans, already perfumed and dressed in their evening clothes, milling around aimlessly, having eaten their dinner at six o'clock–the first available sitting in the dining room. George felt disapproving eyes following him as he marched across to the reception desk. He revelled in the role of the beach bohemian, coming back at this late hour oily and unshaven and covered in sand, smelling slightly unsavoury because of his wonderful liaison on the dunes. These people with their metronomic rituals could only dream about such a life. Having collected his key, he decided to go for a swim in order to wash off all the oil and sand. Few things were more annoying than getting out of the shower and walking back into your bedroom, only to feel under the soles of your feet the roughness of the tiny grains that had been scattered all over the place when you took off your beach clothes. George loved swimming anyway, and he also liked the idea of people looking down from their balconies, seeing him on his own in the pool in the early evening, despite the fact that guests were not supposed to go in after six. There was also always the chance too that some young hunk might spot him and invite him up to his room.

He popped into the poolside cubicle where people went to change their bathing costumes and took off his shirt, shorts and flip-flops. At the beginning of the holiday he'd bought some splendid orange and pink Speedo trunks–and although Alan had shaken his head and said they were meant for someone younger, George loved the colours and knew that when his suntan had developed sufficiently he would really suit them. Anyway, Alan was only jealous because they showed off George's packet so well. He pulled out his beach towel and then stuffed all his other things back into the rucksack. After the swim he would cause even more outrage in the lobby by walking in and waiting for the lift, barefooted and wearing only a T-shirt and the towel wrapped around his lower half. One evening George was on his way upstairs from the pool when a sexy young guy in the lift had laughed and asked him if he was wearing anything under the towel.

"Why don't you come to my room and find out?" George replied. The stranger did and they had the most marvellous half-hour on the bed. The next day George saw him down by the pool with his wife and two young children. George stepped out of the cubicle, walked to the edge of the pool and dipped his toe in. The brochure claimed that it was heated, but the water felt pretty cold. Mind you, he'd had a lot of sun–and the first few seconds in the water were always going to be a bit of a shock. He decided that the quicker he got in the better, so he went around to the deep end, stood right on the edge, and did a perfect shallow dive into the pool. Suddenly there was the huge babbling cacophony of the water in his ears, and the coldness of it sliding over his flesh. All he could see was a pale blue blur and the bright glow from the underwater lights set into the sides of the pool. He allowed the momentum to carry him forward under the water then, with one strong stroke of his arms and a flick of his legs, he brought himself to the surface. There was a sudden burst of cheering and clapping–but it wasn't for his dive. The crowds lining the street outside had spotted the first floats turning the corner and heading up towards the Yumbo Centre. George put his feet on the bottom and quickly stuffed his hands down his trunks, dislodging with his fingers any sand that had got into the nooks and crannies. Anyone standing on their balconies would be looking at the parade, and in any case he doubted whether they would be able to see what he was doing under the water. The job complete, he pushed himself off with his feet and began swimming lengths of the kidney-shaped pool–first crawl, then backstroke, then breast stroke. As he neared the far end, he heard a gruff voice somewhere above his head.

"I saw you cleaning out your crack, dirty old bugger!" George looked up to see Alan Reid with a drink in his hand, looking down from his balcony. Trust Alan to have spotted his indiscretion in the middle of the pool! George swam to the side and leaned his arms on the edge.

"Darling, the water's freezing. I hope you've got something to warm your auntie up." Alan laughed and waved a small object in the air that looked like a joint.

"I've got all auntie's favourite medicines up here." He was delighted to see his friend. After the phone call to his daughter, Alan had sat for a while feeling sorry for himself–but the sight of George posing in his new trunks had fairly lifted his spirits. And he had to admit that George was a wonderful swimmer, so at one with the water and so graceful in it. And yes, the trunks did suit him now that his skin had darkened. Actually, Alan had been thinking what good shape George was in for a man his age. He had a little bit of a paunch but a life spent working out of doors had done wonders for his body. He had well-proportioned legs, broad shoulders and fantastically powerful arms. And the tattoo he'd had done on his shoulder during his national service (Alan and George had made love that night, in a bed and breakfast in Blackpool) really suited him. Although Alan tended to be attracted to younger bodies, he glimpsed for a fraction of a second just how sexy a man his friend still was–and he could see why the kids in the bars who went for older guys were queuing around the block. George was now out of the water and rubbing himself dry with his beach towel.

"How did the afternoon go?" he shouted.

"Get yourself up here and I'll tell you. Do you want Campari or gin and orange? There's no tonic, I'm afraid."

"Campari please."

"Hurry up then. It's only three quarters of an hour until dinner."

"I'll be there in five minutes–that's if I don't get waylaid by someone gorgeous on my way up."

When George arrived the bedroom door was already open. He went straight in to find Alan pouring the drinks. George surveyed the rumpled pile of bedclothes and raised an eyebrow.

"Looks like somebody's had a successful afternoon then." Alan stirred the drink and handed it over with a holier-than-thou look on his face.

"Why must you always reduce things to their base level?" he said. "We had a very nice afternoon–a lovely lunch, a pleasant bus ride back, and then I thought I'd invite him up to see the room." Alan reached down and picked up his own tumbler. They went out onto the balcony and sat down at the small plastic table. Alan had bought a couple of those cheap candles in glass jars from the supermarket opposite the hotel, to give their nightly aperitif sessions a bit more atmosphere. There was also a bowl of pistachio nuts on the table. Out on the street the carnival floats were moving past. They could hear cheers and shouts and pumping dance music. George got the odd glimpse of scenery or a colourful costume through the tall trees that separated the swimming pool area from the street.

"Well, it's about time you pulled off a successful seduction–and he's a lovely boy."

"Do you think so?"

"Oh yes. Could have quite gone for him myself. I did–until I realised that he only had eyes for you."

"I know. It's a queer situation, though. I thoroughly enjoyed the afternoon but when he left I couldn't make head nor tail of it, especially the fact that he knew me years ago. I ended up phoning Jane and that made things worse." George looked surprised.

"You didn't tell her what had happened, though?"

"Oh good heavens no. But I told her we'd met him. Lord knows what she thinks."

"Well look–he's a perfectly nice bloke and his interest is genuine. At least we know that. Why not just enjoy it?" Precisely what Terry had said before he left. At that moment it seemed to Alan that everyone knew more about how to handle the mysteries of existence than he did. He stuck a finger into his drink and stirred the ice cubes around slowly.

"Dearest George. You always see things so clearly, I don't know where I'd be without you."

"Now look–don't start all that nonsense. We've known one another a long time and a lot of water has gone under the bridge. You've had a few difficult years–I just want to see you happy, that's all." Alan suddenly felt guilty about wallowing in his own problems all the time. Poor George had put up with it for five decades. In some ways, it was his force of character that had kept them both afloat.

"Thanks for that," said Alan quietly. "Anyway–enough of my rubbish. What about you, how was your afternoon?"

"Great thanks. On my way back to town I met Mark, the lad you went on the Sky Rider with. We went into the dunes and had a bit of a picnic, sunbathed for a while."

"Was he annoyed about what happened last night?"

"Not at all–just the opposite in fact. But he was relieved that he bumped into me, so he could set things straight." Alan raised his tumbler.

"Bravo, George. As long as you got what was coming to you in the end." George smiled.

"You know I always do." He raised his own tumbler and clinked it against his friend's. "And hopefully there'll be more later on. Mark's going out for dinner but he's meeting us afterwards in Hummel Hummel."

"Sounds like you've got everything worked out nicely–I wish I could say the same." Alan stood up and looked over the balcony. In the distance he could hear plates clinking–the kitchen staff were obviously doing the dishes from the first sitting, so they would be ready for the next set of diners. George had heard the sound too.

"Christ," he said, "what time is it? I've got to shave and have a shower." Alan looked at his watch.

"Ten to eight."

"Tons of time," said George, downing the remainder of his drink in one and standing up. He eyed the unlit joint lying in the ashtray. "That'll have to wait, though."

*

TERRY'S mobile had begun to vibrate in the pocket of his shorts when he was on his way out of the hotel. It was a text message from Rob and Helen, saying that they were already at the bar, and wondering what had happened to him. They'd chosen the Norwegian place because it was next to the roundabout that the floats would have to negotiate before they headed into the Yumbo Centre, and the position would give them the best possible view of the procession. Terry was glad of the opportunity to catch up with his friends–he was bursting to tell someone about the events of the past twenty-four hours. He had known Rob since his first day at university, when they met while queuing up to register at the hall of residence where they'd be living, and collect the keys to their rooms. Although Terry was very much in the closet at home, Rob and Helen were among the few people who knew about his love for older men. They'd never been judgmental about it, although Rob apparently believed it was a phase he was going through–and that he would eventually end up with a girlfriend. This had been proven when, just after the truth had come out during their second year at university, Rob had given Terry a birthday card with a topless woman on it, standing waist-deep in the sea. It could have been quite tacky but the photographer had done a decent job. On the inside Rob had written: "Happy Birthday, Mate. Get yourself a good woman like this, and everything'll be fine." Now he and Helen listened patiently as Terry poured forth about how he'd bumped into Alan Reid, this monolithic figure from his past, how he had spent the night with Alan's friend, and then how Alan and he had hit it off during the afternoon and ended up in bed together. When he finished, they sat for a while in silence. Terry was so filled with excitement that their sombre reaction caught him a little by surprise. Helen was the first to speak.

"I don't know, Terry. Normally I'd say that meeting anyone you've been in love with in the past is really unlucky. In my experience, not much good ever comes of it. But then, you never had an affair with this guy—so it's not like he's your ex or anything. And from what you've said, it seems like things have gone quite well. But I'd be careful, this meeting probably has a lot more significance for you than it does for him. You don't want to get hurt." There was a sudden burst of clapping as twenty feet away a float went past depicting the Flintstones. A woman dressed as Wilma was standing at an ironing board looking furious, while Fred and Barney sat on a sofa watching television, their feet up, bottles of beer in their hands. Terry's eyes followed the float around the roundabout.

"I know that but what can I do? I'm in love with him and I always have been. In many ways, he's the man who I've judged all the others against. I deluded myself that I'd put those feelings to the back of my mind, but I guess they stayed there all the time." Rob leaned forward with a serious look on his face, and blew smoke across the table.

"The dreaded archetype," he said gravely. "The first person you fell in love with, and from whom you will never be truly free until someone else fucks them out of your system." Helen chucked a beermat at her boyfriend.

"A fat lot of help you are! Sure you didn't get your degree in psychology, instead of philosophy?"

"It's true," insisted Rob. "As far as I can see, all Terry can do is ride it out for better or worse because this guy has too big a hold on him."

"Yeah," Terry agreed, "in an ideal world I'd just like to see how it develops–if I get the chance." Helen was thinking things through, utilizing that amazing gift women have for getting down to the brass tacks where emotional matters are concerned.

"Does he know you had a crush on him when you were in your teens?""I don't think so. Maybe he suspects but I haven't said anything. I mean, I don't want to chase him away." Helen clapped her hands.

"Good lad! Try at least to preserve a little bit of nonchalance, just for the sake of your own dignity."

"I think part of the problem is that he's always been in the closet," said Terry. "He's never had a boyfriend and he didn't come onto the gay scene until after his wife died. But I get the feeling that he's ready for something new now." Rob laughed.

"Easy, tiger. You're sure that's not a touch of wishful thinking?" Terry looked uncertain.

"I can't be sure–but I may as well stay optimistic." Helen reached across the table and took hold of Terry's hand.

"Absolutely. Some people go through their entire lives carrying a torch for somebody, and never getting so much as a kiss. You've already gone further than that."

"But that was just the hors d'oeuvre–now I want the rest of the banquet!" Rob raised his eyes in exasperation.

"Oh God. What's with this older man thing, anyway? What you need is a stint in a boot camp. That would knock it out of you." Helen snorted.

"I hope you're joking–that's the sort of rubbish my dad would come out with."

"Of course I'm joking," said Rob. "I accepted long ago that Terry here is a deviant." Rob looked across the table expecting some form of reprisal from Terry, but his friend's attention had been diverted from the banter by another float that was moving slowly past the bar. A replica of a Greek temple had been built on a flat-backed lorry, complete with classical columns supporting a crumbling roof. Terry presumed that the scenery wasn't made of stone, because that would have weighed the truck down too much, but it certainly looked pretty authentic. Dancing about in the ruins were four very good looking youths, dressed in skimpy white trunks–and Terry could also see several other people, both men and women, in more complex costumes, presumably the gods themselves. But lording it over the rest, seated on a large throne just behind the cab in which the driver sat, was a giant of a man, with white hair and a fabulous white beard, holding a huge carved staff that had been fashioned to look like a bolt of lightning. Kneeling by his side was a young man wearing golden trunks, holding in his right hand a small bronze cup. Terry immediately recognized the god Zeus and his cup-bearer, Ganymede. Near the back of the float a harpist strummed away, but her music was drowned out by dance tunes booming out of several stacks of speakers, which had been covered in rubble to make them look like piles of debris that had fallen from the roof of the edifice. It was all very authentic, and the people that had made the float had obviously set out to win first prize. But it was the man dressed as Zeus, nonchalant and regal, nodding his head in time to the music as he looked down on the crowds, who held Terry's eye. He looked to be at least in his mid-fifties. He was also extremely broad, and although he was sitting down appeared to be well over six feet tall. As Terry watched, Zeus looked over in the direction of their table, and raised his free hand in a little wave. Terry suspected the gesture was aimed at them, but he couldn't be sure. Rob evidently thought the same thing, because he leaned forward and raised an eyebrow.

"Looks like you're on there, mate," he said conspiratorially. "If you can put lover boy out of your mind for half an hour or so." Terry laughed.

"He's good looking I grant you–but I'd have to get past his acolytes first."

"Shouldn't be any problem for a northern lad like you. They look like a right bunch of pansies." Helen shook her head.

"Hardly the kind of comment I'd expect from someone who claims to be gay-friendly."

"Darling my best friend is gay, and I spend my nights in a gay bar stripping off for the delectation of lecherous old queens, so I think that entitles me to use the word 'pansy' without being accused of homophobia."

"A good point well made," said Terry, looking at his watch. "So what's the plan then?"

"Well," said Helen, "Rob has to work tonight because the other stripper's still off his eggs–so we're going to go home and have some dinner, then we'll come back to the Yumbo Centre later. Might have a nap first because it's probably going to be a long night." She gestured at some plastic bags around her feet under the table. "I've been to the supermarket and got a load of stuff in, and there's plenty for you if you want to eat with us, instead of drifting around Playa Del Ingles on your own, looking for more mischief. Sound good?" Terry smiled.

"Sounds great! Do I need to buy anything–maybe some wine?"

"I wouldn't bother." Helen nodded in her boyfriend's direction. "Rob never drinks too much before his performances, and I don't want to get started until later on."

"Okay then," said Terry. "Why don't I get us another round of drinks while we watch the rest of the floats?" Rob rubbed his hands together.

"Thought you were never going to ask. I'm dying of thirst here." As Terry flagged down the waiter an ancient bus trundled past, painted in garish designs. The windows and seats had all been removed, and the inside of the vehicle had been turned into a miniature nightclub. There was no attempt on the part of these people to give their float a theme–the whole thing was dedicated simply to the pleasure of dancing. It reminded Terry of the Chiva buses in which revellers traveled around the cities of South America at night, stopping off at each of the clubs on their route, fuelled by Aguardiente–a cheap liquor that set your teeth on edge, burned your throat and made you gag. An enormous sound system had been installed at the back of the bus, and they could see a young DJ with an afro hairdo surrounded by women, some sitting on top of the enormous speakers. The bus was crowded with people, none of whom were over the age of twenty-five, gyrating their bodies to pumping Balearic house music, and strobe lights inside the bus gave the whole thing a frantic, ecstatic feel. Terry raised his eyebrows.

"Blimey–they've certainly started early."

"And you know these islanders," said Rob. "They'll probably still be dancing at ten o'clock tomorrow morning." Helen sighed.

"What it is to be young."

"I don't know," Terry muttered. "There are plenty of old timers here who could probably give them a run for their money." Rob nodded.

"I'm sure there are–but the thing is, once you've retired you've got as long as you want to sleep it off every day. And you've got your ecstasy, your Viagra, and your goodness-knows-what other pills, potions and powders to help you turn the clock back each night."

"I once knew an older guy from Manchester who swore blind that horse tranquillizers were the answer," said Terry. He took a swig from the fresh bottle of beer the waiter had put down in front of him. "One night he was standing on the podium in a nightclub, gurning and waving his hands around, absolutely out of his face, and he just keeled over and died on the dance floor. Apparently the old ticker could take it no longer."

"Wow," said Rob, "what a way to go. Wonder what his last words were?" Terry raised his hands in the air like a raver.

"Turn it up, you fuckers!" He and Rob burst into laughter and gave each other a high five. Helen shook her head, unimpressed.

"You two are sick."

"Come on," said Rob, "you've got to laugh. Anyway, I have a lot of respect for that kind of attitude. Why shouldn't he enjoy his life to the end? Better than ending up stuck in a nursing home, relying on other people to do everything for you."

"I suppose you're right," admitted Helen. "I get depressed when I think about some of the people I went to school with–they're still in their thirties and they've already got one foot in the grave. When they get home from work they're too knackered to do anything except sit in front of the television."

"I guess it depends on what you want out of life," said Terry. "It may seem a waste to us but they're probably quite happy doing that." It was getting darker now but the floats were still coming in thick and fast. Rob got his camera out and wandered off into the crowd, trying to get a decent close-up of some of the more outlandish costumes. Helen allowed him to move beyond earshot before she spoke.

"Terry, I'm not trying to be funny or anything–but I'm a bit worried about where you're at." She kept her voice low. "Are you sure you're okay? I'm not just talking here about this guy Alan who's turned up–this is more to do with some of the things you've said since you got here about life back home, how it's slowly driving you out of your mind. Have you thought about making some changes, maybe telling your family the truth about yourself?" Terry watched as a space rocket full of people dressed as astronauts trundled past. The smooth, luscious opening bars of Jean Michel Jarre's Oxygene reached his ears. The world of make-believe surrounded him.

"You're right," he said eventually. "I need to come clean, don't I?"

"I think so–for your own sanity as much as anything else. You're in the second half of your twenties, maybe it's time to start building a life for yourself, or finding someone you enjoy being with for more than one night." She shrugged. "This guy Alan, you're obviously keen on him–what if he wanted to take it further, would you be ready for that?" He looked nonplussed.

"Chance would be a fine thing. I think his life's even more

complicated than mine."

"Okay–but you can see where I'm coming from, can't you?"

"Yes–and I must admit that I'd started to think the same thing myself. I've been living in denial and it's not doing me any good at all. But what about my family–you've met them, do you think they'll disown me?"

"I'd be very surprised–but even if they did, at least they'd know who you really were, instead of carrying on with this false idea that you're some kind of jack-the-lad who just hasn't met the right girl." Terry stared at the floats and the party crowds drifting by a few yards from their table, lost in his thoughts.

"The thing is," he said, "they may be able to accept the fact that I'm gay–but the older man thing is the hard bit. I'm sure they always imagined me settling down with a woman my own age, maybe having some kids–but the truth about my lifestyle, that I actually fancy old men with white hair and pot bellies and wrinkles, it's going to be a jolt."

"Yes but look–they love you and that means they want you to be happy. So you find happiness in the way that suits you, and if they can see it working with their own eyes then they'll find it easier to accept."

"Blimey," said Terry. "You make it all sound so simple."

"In a weird kind of way it is–just like a lot of the things in life that we allow ourselves to get horribly messed up about." Out of the blue Rob emerged from the crowd nearby and strode back to the table.

"What's this about getting horribly messed up?" he demanded. "Sounds like my kind of night." Terry smiled–his friend's bright-and-breezy manner was a breath of fresh air after the heavy conversation.

"How did the photography go?" he said.

"Got some great shots of that Darth Vader dude over there. These people–they must spend months making their costumes. Don't they have jobs to do?" Helen laughed.

"Well, I hope your photos turn out better than they did last year. For some reason most of them were blurred pictures of your own crotch."

"I think the shutter button got stuck. Oh well–c'est la vie. Shall we head back then, or do you want another drink?"

"Let's go," said Helen, "I'm starving." Terry finished the last of his beer.

"Ready when you are," he said.

PART 3 – CARNIVAL

NORMALLY ALAN AND George were able to stroll casually into to the Yumbo Centre after dinner, but on carnival night that was impossible. They could barely negotiate the cracked marble staircase down to the central plaza, because in places the crowd was so dense that they were unable to see where they were putting their feet. As they inched their way through they found themselves first in the middle of a large group of Carmen Mirandas, all with huge fruit headdresses; and then surrounded by a crowd wearing winged Valkyrie-style helmets and golden battle gear, but carrying plastic saxophones instead of swords. It was pointless trying to fight against the flow of bodies so they resigned themselves to being carried into the square, where the sardine burning ceremony would take place later that night. Alan knew from past years that there would also be a big firework display. He felt like he needed something to get him into the party mood–so he pulled out one of the large, badly-rolled joints that he had put together hastily when he went back to his room after dinner. As expected, all the bars in the square were packed, so they decided to go straight to Hummel Hummel. The most direct route, however, involved walking in front of the stage, where there were so many people that Alan feared they might never come out of the other side of the crowd. They agreed to go around the long way which would at any rate give them time to finish the joint. Alan took several big drags before passing it on to his friend. He normally enjoyed the chaos of the carnival but tonight he felt slightly edgy, and as the effects of the weed kicked in he began to wonder whether it had been wise to smoke so much–or even to light the damned thing in the first place. But it was too late now to have those kind of doubts because events were moving forward with their own unstoppable momentum. They walked along past stalls selling tins of sweets, candy canes and caramelised nuts, past overflowing popcorn machines, fluorescent rubber rats, laser guns that lit up and made zapping sounds, yo-yos, slinky springs and pots of brightly-coloured slime. Children tried to win prizes by shooting pellet guns at targets, while thirty feet behind them in one of the bars, adults gawped at a young stripper wearing a cowboy hat–who removed his thong and started firing two cap guns at the audience. The fact that such a spectacle could be going on just a few yards from where children were playing sideshow games was, thought George, a huge tribute to the Yumbo Centre carnival. All pleasures were catered for no matter how innocent or how depraved–and all under the same roof, or at least in the same building. It could never have happened in Britain.

They moved onwards through an atmosphere that had a thick, almost fluid quality. There were the smells of cigar smoke and hot toffee, pungent wafts of aftershave and sweat, steam from a simmering vat of hot dogs, the occasional whiff of the drains, and everywhere the subtle reek of alcohol seeping out of people's pores. A young guy walked past in a sheriff's outfit with a gold, star-shaped badge pinned to the breast of his black shirt.

"Seems to be a bit of a wild west theme this year," commented Alan. "I noticed on the way past that Juan and the other waiter at the Block both had ten gallon hats and leather chaps on."

"Ride 'em cowgirl!" shouted George, turning around to admire the bottom. He was still on a high because of his meeting with Mark, and the prospect of seeing him later. He took the joint out of his mouth and inspected it closely.

"Did you make this? I thought you never rolled them." Alan looked shifty. "Well I smoked the last of the pre-rolled ones this afternoon, so I made a batch of my own. Not very good, is it?" George smiled.

"Seems to be doing the job." His eyes took in row upon row of coloured light bulbs strung up along the front of the market stalls, and the people passing by in their weird and wonderful costumes. So much glitter, so many wigs, so much colour. It was like being immersed in a psychedelic cartoon. He and Alan were now walking directly behind the stage, and although the big stacks of speakers at either side of it were pointing away from them, the bass boomed in their ears. George spotted a group of firemen standing around, obviously there in case anything went wrong when the sardine was set on fire. They were wearing one-piece protective suits in readiness for such an eventuality–but several of them had the upper portions unzipped and hanging down over their waists, so that the tight-fitting dark blue T-shirts underneath were visible. George eyed the contours of their chests and flat stomachs. They looked nonchalant and unimpressed, surrounded by all this revelry but unable to take part themselves. Instead they drank coffee and flirted with a group of pretty girls loitering nearby. Alan and George walked on past the drag shows, past children having water pistol fights, past a stray dog having a shit in the middle of it all. Turning a corner they saw that Hummel Hummel already looked quite busy.

"Blimey, no room at the inn," said Alan. "Shall we go back to Na Und? It looked fairly quiet." But George was not going to be put off so easily. He walked straight into the bar, smiling and saying hello to the owner–a severe-looking, slightly hunched character who was there every night, sitting alone at a table near the bar, drinking a bottle of mineral water and watching the waiters to make sure that no one was on the fiddle. The guy always went home at eleven sharp, and spoke to very few people. Alan watched the owner flag down a waiter and gesture towards them. The lad came over, greeted them and ushered them to an empty table in the far corner which neither had spotted. Alan managed a smile.

"Pulling strings again, Hope? Excellent stuff."

"It always pays to hobnob with the management–although I hope he's not expecting any favours in return." Their table was under the awning at the front of the bar, out of the way of the people that were always squeezing past on their way to and from the video rooms, but they still had a good view of what was going on, and as they ordered their drinks Alan spotted young Steve sitting at a table not far away with his friend Frank. Steve caught his eye and waved and Alan responded with a little salute, grinning as he remembered how lovely the young man's body had felt while they were dancing in Na Und last night. He could see the sexual interest in Steve's eyes, and it excited him very much. George chuckled.

"Something's put the smile back on your face. Wonder that could be?"

"Am I so predictable?" Alan lifted a huge glass of sangria–more like a bowl, really–to his face and sucked some in through the bendy straw that poked out of the top, in between a miniature parasol and a tinsel bird. As he put the glass back down, a couple of bright red droplets fell on his pristine white trousers.

"Bollocks!" he shouted, brushing at the stains and moaning that he would have to take them back to the laundry tomorrow morning. George watched his friend fussing around with a napkin and shook his head.

"Doddery old bugger. But don't worry–they won't be able to see the stains when you go into the dark room." Alan looked past George, to see young Steve standing up and walking away from them around the other side of the bar, towards the younger man's video room. He was slightly annoyed by George's comments and felt like staying at the table just to prove him wrong–but experience had taught him that missing chances like this was sheer madness. The longer he lingered here, the more likely it was that he would never touch Steve's skin or kiss him, or do any of the things he had thought about during the past twenty-four hours. He had left it too late on several occasions, and had headed around to the toilets or the video room just to see the person he was interested in coming out, going back to his table, mystified by the fact that Alan had taken so much time to follow him in. Other times he had arrived in there just in time to see the object of desire, recognizable in the darkness only by his outline, being whisked into a corner by someone else. Steve's friend was facing in the opposite direction and that was all that mattered.

Alan pushed his chair back carefully and stood up, walking in the other direction, towards the older man's video room. With a bit of luck, Steve would have a quick look in the younger man's video room and then walk around the back of the bar for a quick peek in the other one, before returning to his seat. It was a kind of criss-cross manoeuvre, or a pincer movement. George looked up with a self-satisfied smile on his face. He had known that Alan would be unable to resist.

"Have fun," he called out. Alan moved around the bar, acknowledging people who said hello so as not to be rude, but rather deftly staying on the move. Now was not the time to get caught up in a conversation with one of these ponderous old buffers, about arthritis or how much the prices in Gran Canaria had gone up since the euro was introduced. He had that exciting judder in the guts, the jangly nervous energy that came on when sexual possibilities were in the air. He squeezed behind the backs of people sitting at the bar, paused to let a fat German puff his way past through the narrow gap, then flicked back the curtain and voila–he was at the urinal, reading the poster which told patrons to please be careful of their values. The journey had taken less than a minute, surely a record. There was, of course, a chance that Steve had been waylaid in the other video room, and if he had then all these manoeuvres were futile, but Alan's finely-honed instincts told him that the young man was thinking what he was thinking, and would be popping in here any moment now. Alan had a quick pee and then turned and whisked aside the curtain that kept the light out of the small TV room. There were a few people sitting on the stools to the right, watching a film he had seen many times. They were played using a machine behind the bar, next to which sat a big stack of porn videos. There was a second machine, with its own stack of tapes, which was used to play the films in the younger man's video room. When the tapes ran out, eventually a customer would come and tell the boys at the bar and they would slap a new cassette in without even looking at it. As Alan moved beyond the curtain, a couple of the guys on stools turned round to see who had just entered, and he made a gesture as if he was tipping an imaginary hat to them. No one responded; they just turned back to the television screen. Alan moved further into the room, but he could sense already that the bit around the corner, where he had hoped to lie in wait for Steve, was full of bodies. Damn, he thought, if only the lad had given it another half-hour, until the strip show had started, it would be empty in here. He moved backwards and eased himself up onto one of the high stools, wondering what he was doing here among these people–sneaking around like a teenager trying to get that first kiss behind the bike sheds. Only it wasn't the first kiss, and he should have known better at his age... at his age. But did people ever grow out of this sort of thing, or did most just accept what they had because they feared they would be unable to get anything else? He had the feeling that somehow he was selling himself short, chipping away at his own dignity like a deluded prospector trying to find a hidden seam of gold–but in danger of bringing the whole cavern down on his head. He considered leaving, going back to George and continuing the evening with everything intact. But then the curtain was pulled to one side and Steve was in the doorway, his white shirt glowing in the ultra violet, that big smile moving forward into the darkened room.

"I thought I might see you in here," said Steve under his breath. And Alan, made giddy by the adrenaline knocking around his system, the dope, the alcohol and the sheer fact that for once things had panned out the way he hoped they would, drew the young man close to him.

Outside in the bar, George sipped his brandy and watched the assortment of unusual specimens passing by. He was amazed by the inventiveness that had gone into many of the costumes. A small group of young men wearing hard hats and the sort of clothes normally seen on a building site stopped a few feet away, and laid out a circle of orange and white cones and a pair of home-made traffic lights. They then pretended to start drilling the asphalt. Nearby a group of surgeons wandered past, decked out in green robes with stethoscopes around their necks, and wielding an assortment of medical instruments. They were followed by a group of young men dressed as nuns, who made a great but irreverent show of kissing their Bibles, and fondling their rosary beads as they walked along. As George looked on he realized that they were clustered around somebody, keeping pace with him, clasping their hands and bowing towards him in mock worship. Suddenly with a start he saw who it was–young Terry! The boy smiled as he approached, but he had a hunted look and he moved quickly, desperately trying to get away from his tormentors. The nuns laughed hysterically and disappeared off up the nearest staircase, looking for another victim. George sat up and waved.

"Evening," he said, "how are you doing?"

"Fine thanks." Terry looked over his shoulder. "Pleased to get rid of them."

"Carnival night's not for the faint-hearted." Terry sat down and composed himself, adjusting his clothes, taking out his cigarettes and putting them on the table. Maybe it was just the light but to George he looked worn out–pale and hollow-cheeked, with shadows under his eyes and a slackness about the mouth. The sparkle that had been evident the previous night when they'd chatted outside the chip shop seemed to have disappeared. George leaned forward, scrutinizing the boy's face.

"Are you okay?" Terry, who was finally satisfied that the nuns had gone for good, tried a smile.

"Actually, I'm a bit tired. I had a few beers with my friends before dinner, when we were watching the parade coming in–and they really seemed to take it out of me. I went to bed for a while before we came out, but if anything that's made me feel worse."

"Yes," said George, "you've got to watch those siestas. Sometimes they can do more harm than good. What you need is a sharpener, like one of these high-power sangrias. That'll certainly get you back into the mood–as long as you don't mind losing all feeling below the waist for an hour or so."

"Sounds good–but what I really need is to lose all feeling above the waist. Above the neck, in fact."

"That's more like it! Nice to see that lovely smile again." Terry glanced around the bar, his face growing serious again. He leaned forward and looked George in the eye.

"Do you mind if I say something?"

"Not at all."

"I feel bad about the way I disappeared off with Alan at the beach, after you and I had had such a nice night together. I know it was a bit rude but, well, I've always liked him–and I was so relieved to have got the ball rolling again that I just let things take their course without really thinking about it." George smiled–Terry was a sweet lad.

"No problem. I knew something was going on, which was partly why I left. As long as you enjoyed it. That's what holidays are for, isn't it?"

"What about you? Did you get your postcards written?" George winked, ready to make his own admission.

"Well–after you left I bumped into another friend and we spent the afternoon together in the dunes." Terry looked at the empty chair, and the half-finished sangria in front of it.

"Where's Alan?" George hesitated for a second, thinking about what might be going on in the darkroom. It was sod's law that Terry would turn up at the very moment his friend was committing an indiscretion.

"I think he's round at the other side of the bar talking to some friends. You know what this place is like–it's impossible even to go to the toilet without having about ten conversations on the way. Would you like a drink?"

"Yes please. I'll try one of those sangrias if you don't mind–but I just need to pop to the loo first." For a split second George felt like warning Terry not to go into the dark room–but to do so smacked of telling tales on Alan, of breaking an old bond of loyalty. He had no desire to see the boy hurt, and in a sense he had the knowledge that could avert a crisis–but how could he use it? There was simply no time to work that out. Terry was already half way to the toilet, obviously heading for the one attached to the older man's video room where, no doubt, Alan and young Steve were. Terry was bound to take a quick look behind the curtain–everyone did despite any protestations they might make to the contrary. George sat back feeling concerned, the thoughts of what might happen weighing heavily. But it was too late to do anything and at the end of the day, it was their business. They were all adults after all, and would just have to work it out between themselves. Maybe Alan and Steve had the sense to go around the corner into the really dark area at the back of the room, so they wouldn't be spotted.

Terry tried to look as casual as possible as he headed towards the video room, but he was overtaken by feelings of doom. The way George had hesitated before he said where Alan was, the sight of that half-finished drink–the whole thing felt ominous. He wondered if he should just use the loo and go back to the table without looking behind the curtain, but that was impossible. He felt in a sense that he was on a pre-determined course, that it was inevitable that he would have a look. Part of him clung to the hope that Alan would be just sitting there on a stool, watching the film, and they could maybe have a hug and a kiss before going back to the table together. He moved the curtain aside and slipped into the room, waiting for a couple of seconds just inside to allow his eyes to adjust to the darkness. Almost immediately he spotted the two figures right under the TV set, oblivious to the three or four people sitting on the stools watching them. What had happened had obviously just come to an end, because Alan was pulling his trousers up, giggling in a way that suggested a mixture of relief and embarrassment. The younger man was zipping up his trousers, tucking in his shirt, feeling around to make sure his wallet was still there, and checking if his clothes were arranged correctly. Then the pair of them shared a final hug and Terry heard muffled laughter and a few words. Alan walked towards the curtain, not seeing Terry sitting there until he was almost outside. He realised immediately that the lad had seen what had been going on. He grinned guiltily and then looked away, spluttering something about being chatted up, and pushing past as quickly as he could. Outside in the toilet he moved into the little alcove where there was a wash hand basin, so he could tidy himself up. As he looked in the mirror he saw Terry emerge from the video room and disappear out into the bar without looking up. Now that Alan had had his knee-trembler, the whole thing seemed rather pointless–and it looked as if he might have blown his chances with Terry.

"Damn, damn, damn," he mouthed to himself, washing his hands and then realizing there was no towel to dry them with. He looked up at his own reflection and spoke quietly to the mirror. "How am

I going to sort this out?" A slim, straightforward little man from Liverpool with thick glasses, a hearing aid and a Bobby Charlton hairstyle walked out of the video room.

"You can stop talking to yourself for a start, you silly old fool." The pair of them roared with laughter. The man, whose name was Keith and who knew Alan and George well, walked to the urinal. "And don't go wiping your hands on my back when I'm not looking. I know what you and that pal of yours are like." Something about Keith's light Scouse touch–his basic warmth and humanity–prompted Alan to ask his advice.

"What am I going to do? A young guy that I really like has just seen me in the darkroom mucking around with someone else. I think he's really upset."

"I know. Terrible, isn't it? Thirty years ago when we were in the prime of life nobody was interested, and now they're queuing up. I can't cope with this place." It wasn't quite what Alan was looking for, but the irony suited his mood. He headed back to the table. George had seen Terry disappear into the crowds with a face like thunder, but he decided to play dumb.

"Any sign of young Terry on your travels? I think he was looking for you." Alan looked forlorn.

"He walked in while Steve and I were playing around. Saw the lot." George remained silent. Alan sucked some sangria through the straw. More drips on the trousers. He looked down and noticed that ugly grey smears had also appeared on the fabric–obviously some sort of residue from the video room, probably off the walls, which were somewhat less than immaculate.

"Look at me," he whined. "We've only just come out and I'm already a wreck!" He brushed in a futile way at the stains, continuing his monologue, speaking almost to himself. "Well it's not like I'm going out with him or anything, whatever he might think. I'm free to do what I want. And I don't know how much time I've got left–I've got to take these chances when I can."

"I'm not the one you need to be explaining yourself to," said

George. "In fact, I'm surprised to see you so rattled. This is the sort of thing we normally laugh about." Alan continued to fuss over his trousers.

"I can't say it was one of my proudest moments." George was looking closely at his friend.

"But you've been in that sort of situation before. I'm sure a gorgeous young guy like Terry will have been too. It's bound to happen in a place like this. It shouldn't matter too much—unless your feelings for him are stronger than you're letting on."

"I'm not sure what I want any more. I swore after Marjorie died that I'd never get close to anyone again. But then this guy comes along from the past and I get on with him and it makes me think, well, maybe there's more to life than these little flings in the darkroom and on the dunes." George nodded.

"But you couldn't resist one last foray. Nothing wrong with that at all, it's what people come to this bar for." George thought how strange it was to be having such a conversation with his hell-raising friend. The jealous part of him had secretly quite enjoyed watching Terry go into the darkroom, but Alan's comments had brought him back to his senses. He considered the situation.

"The boy loves you which means he'll give you another chance, I'm sure of it. But you have to decide what you want before you make the next step. Don't toy with him. If you have feelings towards him then go after him but if there's nothing really there, or you don't want to let things develop, then leave him alone. You know how these things work—we've discussed them often enough."

"What would you do?"

"I like him. He's genuine, intelligent and not a sponger. He's what most gay men in search of a partner would give their back teeth for. But I understand that the pair of you have a history which is... unusual. I'd probably carry on with it, see what happens. If it doesn't work out, you'll not have to worry about what the family will think—and if it does, well, these things can always be overcome. But as I say, it all depends on what you want." Alan looked out into the square, at the crowds, the confusion. The busiest night of the year, and he was going to have to go chasing cap in hand after young Terry. He finished the sangria and picked up the magic glasses case.

"I'd go easy on that if I were you," advised George. "This is a sensitive mission." Alan laughed.

"Well if it all goes wrong I can just go upstairs and blow myself away."

"Spoken like a true father of the revolution!" Alan winked as he stood to leave.

"Expect nothing less," he said. George gestured for his friend to lean down, so he could speak quietly into his ear.

"By the way—was young Steve worth all the aggro?" Alan raised his eyes to the heavens.

"Beautiful," he said, "see you later." And he was off into the crowd. George raised his glass to his friend's back. He wished him luck, but something about the turn of events was troubling him. Terry's reaction to what he had seen in the darkroom seemed quite extreme. No matter how nice his afternoon with Alan had been, it was hardly as if they were an item just yet. And whatever had gone before, during the period when Terry was going out with Alan's daughter, they had only just met as a pair of consenting homosexual adults. So was Terry's behaviour a sign of something darker, more sinister? He had said something just before he went into the video room about getting the ball rolling again. An adolescent crush could have stayed dormant for all these years and now with its consummation, re-surfaced as a full-blown obsession. George had come across such instability before—there were a lot of fragile psyches on the gay scene—and he had no desire to see his best friend sailing into those murky waters. But it was also possible that George was reading too much into what he had seen. He was probably letting his thoughts run away with themselves. And how would he have reacted had he seen young Mark in the darkroom, getting off with some white-haired stranger? Disappointed certainly, maybe even a little angry. He would have covered it up better, of course—but that would have required a level of self-discipline that Terry had perhaps not yet developed. It was hard to put one's finger on the exact point when a person fell in love with somebody else. First sight was, George had always felt, pushing it a bit, but first kiss was possible and first fuck even more so. At the end of the day it could always emerge unexpectedly–a sneaking realization that crept up on you, hours after the object of the affection had gone away. As the thought coalesced, someone at the bar burst out laughing and brought George back into the moment. He sat back, enjoying the soft burble of people talking in different languages, watching one of the waiters making fun of a punter sitting at the bar. Sooner or later the life that was going on around him would interact with him–someone would come and say hello or try to chat him up. Years of going to gay bars alone had taught George one of the most valuable lessons of all–how to set his face. It was impossible to sit on your own smiling from ear to ear, because people would think you had gone bonkers. Neither could you allow yourself to fall into the trap that most people did–allowing your face to relax into a spongy mask which would absorb even the smallest amount of anxiety in your thoughts, and turn it into an expression that would cry out "I'm lonely" or "I'm nervous" or–and this was worst of all– "I'm sad." No, the trick was to look lively, as if you were cocking your ear to listen to something interesting on the radio, to show the world that you were open to whatever possibility life could present. Suddenly there was a loud fanfare and some clapping–the stripper had appeared on stage. George stood up and walked around the bar to have a look. The routine had not changed since the year before. A muscular young lad from Las Palmas would strip down to his jockstrap and then force some poor OAP to rub baby oil into every bit of his body, except the one that the old josser really wanted to get his hands on. There were so many balding, grey-haired heads in the way that George was unable to see much. He glanced back at the table and was surprised to see Mark sitting there. As he approached the younger man smiled.

"Don't let me spoil your fun," he said.

"I've seen it a dozen times before. He's a nice looking lad, but I wish he'd vary his act a bit for those of us who come here regularly." Mark laughed.

"I wish they'd vary the whole show. Maybe every so often they could please the other half of their clientele by getting an older guy to come and strip for them." George considered the possibility.

"It would certainly be a novelty," he admitted.

"For sure it would. And once the word got out, I reckon he'd become an international celebrity. There'd be magazine interviews, TV chat show appearances. People would be queuing for hours to get in." George wasn't so sure.

"Then why do you think they haven't done it already?"

"They don't have the imagination–all they think about is what will keep these old guys happy day in, day out." It was George's turn to laugh.

"And a good thing for you they do, because it's young guys like that who bring older men into this bar. If it was some old josser, we'd all be horrified and go somewhere else. Then where would you be with your fancy ideas?" Mark sighed.

"I suppose you're right. Just one time, though, I'd like to see an older guy do a striptease." George leaned forward, speaking low and with a mischievous purr.

"I know one man who might be prepared to do it for you–a special private show in his hotel room. He's staying at a place not far from here." Mark pretended that he hadn't caught on, lowering his eyes and becoming coy.

"It must surely be the island's hottest nightspot."

"And the most exclusive," said George. "So exclusive, in fact, that you're the only person on the guest list."

"Sounds wonderful. Can you take me there?"

"It'd be my pleasure," said George. Right outside the bar was a staircase leading up to the next level of the Yumbo Centre, which would take them away from the chaos that was going on in the central plaza. They paid the waiter and strolled outside, happy to be heading in the opposite direction to the crowds squeezing in to see the finale of the carnival.

*

TERRY had retreated to a leather bar upstairs called Contact which was usually pretty quiet until after midnight–and where he thought he would be unlikely to bump into anyone he knew. It was karaoke night, and there was always the remote possibility that the sight of big hairy blokes doing Judy Garland impersonations might lift his spirits. His plan to remain anonymous evaporated almost as soon as he walked through the door, however, because sitting at the bar was Clive–the bearded charmer who'd stolen the older man away from him in Hummel Hummel the night before. Clive had an older lover, but he was rarely with him. Terry would see the boyfriend– whose name was John–hanging around the bars looking a little lost, or he would bump into Clive in the dunes, stalking the bushes like a big game hunter. John would be back on the beach looking after the bags. Terry often wondered why they were an item–they seemed to spend so little time together. He had always quite fancied John and one afternoon on the beach while Clive was away they had struck up a conversation. The older man was gently flirtatious, and when Terry put his hand on his leg had laid his own on top, giving it a gentle squeeze. The pair of them were sitting there quietly enjoying the excitement that was building up, when Clive suddenly returned, rather irritably demanding that his friend pack up his things and go back to Playa del Ingles with him. The most promiscuous men were often the most jealous! But despite that Terry was quite fond of Clive, in an almost grudging way. He was always very friendly, and their shared passion for older men gave them a fun, slightly competitive camaraderie. Anyway, it was too late for Terry to bail out now because Clive had already seen him.

"Darling!" he shouted, leaning back on his barstool. "What's the matter? You're smiling–but it's like a pretty design on a cracked plate."

"Nothing." Terry was instantly rattled. "I'm just tired. Too many late nights and too much booze. Where's John?"

"Back at the hotel having a quiet night. Said he couldn't be bothered with all this carnival nonsense." Terry smiled inwardly, thinking that John was probably under lock and key in a silent tower somewhere, like Rapunzel. He fantasized for a few moments about breaking the older man out of captivity and disappearing off into the mountains with him. The barman walked over and Terry asked him for a brandy, downed it quickly and ordered another. Clive arched an eyebrow.

"You sure you're just tired? You're putting that away pretty quickly." Terry scanned the bar with a world-weary look. He saw people cruising one another, hopeful faces looming out of the shadows. The guy running the karaoke, a rotund leather daddy with a grey beard and a shiny black waistcoat, was having trouble getting people up on the tiny stage to perform. The leather daddy's helper, a waif of a man dressed in a skin-tight black plastic body suit, was fiddling with the wires hanging out of the PA system.

"I don't know. I'm just a bit sick of this whole scene. The looks, the smiles that promise so much, the disappointment when Mr Right turns out to be just another loser." Clive tutted.

"Don't be like that. You know how this place is—just relax and have a good time, somebody else is bound to come along." Terry laughed bitterly.

"Yeah—and then get snatched away by someone like you. How was that guy last night, by the way? The one who you went off with after I spent an hour chatting him up."

"Oh." Clive looked slightly embarrassed. "Who told you it was me? If it was that bloody Paco, I swear I'll..."

"It doesn't matter how I found out—I'm just trying to say that I may not be cut out for all this. I need something more, some sort of commitment."

"But hang on, old chap. You've had your chances. Everybody on the island knows about what happened with you and that Danish guy, Alex. Whose fault was that?" Terry looked at the spluttering flames of three big church candles that had been placed in a cluster in the middle of the bar, and had become joined together by the rivulets of hot wax that had solidified around their bases.

"That was just unfortunate. I lost his phone number."

"Sure you did–but the point I'm making is that all these things are highly uncertain, and no one can legislate for anything. We're all just making the best out of it that we can, and that's the way the gay scene is."

"Well I've had my fill of it–this is the last time I'm coming here, or Sitges, or Benidorm, or Fort Lauderdale, or any of these places." But Clive was not going to be put off so easily.

"What about all the men who made the mistake of thinking that you were Mr Right? The poor old sods who thought they'd landed the catch of the day? It strikes me that you're happy enough to play the game as long as things are going your way, when you've got the whole of this island wrapped around your finger. It's only when you get a couple of disappointments that you can't stand the way things are." Clive was laughing now–and Terry was getting more needled by the second. The booze wasn't helping.

"What about you? You do the same thing and then go back to your friend. That's just as bad."

"Sure–but I'm not the one crying into my brandy." Terry took a deep breath and was on the verge of launching into a tirade, but then thought better of it and slowly let the lungful of air escape. Finally he shrugged.

"You're right, of course. I should stop feeling sorry for myself and get on with it." Clive pointed coyly at the cigarette packet on the bar.

"Do you mind if I have one? It's just that I'm trying to stop and I really don't want to buy a packet, because then I'll have to smoke the whole lot."

"Go ahead. I'm trying to stop too, but my life's a bit mad at the moment and I need all the props I can get."

"Cheers," said Clive, pulling one out. He lit it up and sat there, looking thoughtful as he smoked. After about a minute he spoke again. "This older man business is never straightforward. I mean, when I tell people that I like guys in their sixties they laugh and say Christ, it must be so easy for you... these old codgers must be queuing up. But it's not like that at all. John and I had been seeing each other for years before we actually lived together. My parents knew I was gay, but they weren't happy about the age gap. John has grown-up family, and he was worried about what they'd make of it–but things panned out in the end. I'm sure they will for you too."

"Thanks," said Terry–touched that Clive had opened up to him and surprised to learn that someone who seemed on the outside to be so together, so in charge of their affairs, suffered from the same difficulties as everyone else.

The leather daddy had failed to find any volunteers so he'd decided to do a number himself. A familiar tune started playing and a few seconds later he began to sing "Smoke Gets In Your Eyes". He was actually pretty good and Terry watched him up there on the podium, wondering what his life in Gran Canaria consisted of. Singing songs in bars like this a few times a week, doing odd jobs here and there–a strange existence. But then he thought of Rob–who would he stripping off in an hour or two's time in front of dozens of leering punters at the Block. Now that was a strange way to earn your crust! Terry looked at his watch. He was due to meet Rob and Helen at the Block quite soon, before Rob started his act. Helen had never been there before for some reason–and had persuaded Terry to accompany her on her first visit. Maybe I'll see Alan Reid in the crowd, thought Terry, leering at Rob's big dick. What a nightmare that would be, although the incestuousness of it seemed oddly appropriate. He gestured towards the barman, ordered another brandy, swigged it off, and then ordered another. Gran Canaria being a duty free island they were all, of course, huge measures.

"You look like you're on a mission to get your stomach pumped," said Clive. Terry nodded towards the glass.

"Do you want one?"

"No thanks–I'm in for the long haul tonight. John said he might come out later for a dance." A thought occurred to Terry as the barman returned with his change. He leaned over the bar.

"Mind if I have a look at the list of songs you can do on the karaoke?" The barman smiled. Karaoke night relied on people who became courageous after a few drinks–and this young guy was a dish.

"Not at all," he said, batting his eyelashes. "Cedric will be delighted to have a volunteer–especially such a gorgeous one." He handed over a large book bound in a flimsy plastic cover, which looked like a cross between a telephone directory and a photograph album. It had seen better days. Terry flipped it open, and started scanning down the columns of song titles. Unlike many homosexuals, old-fashioned musicals and the tunes from them did not appeal to him much. He recognized many of the names but they meant nothing. Then he came across one that struck a chord. A musical that had been a massive hit in the cinema when he was a child, about the ups and downs of a group of teenagers at an American high school. He moved his finger down the list of songs, then tapped the page.

"That's it!" In his drunken state he felt that the song, which had been sung by Olivia Newton-John, perfectly summed up his feelings. He slid off the barstool and walked excitedly towards the leather daddy's helper, brandishing the songbook as if it held the answers to all the big quandaries of life. Clive looked on with amusement as the leather daddy sat Terry down and gave him the microphone, then pointed to the screen on which the lyrics would appear. The helper rummaged through a metal suitcase full of compact discs, then took one out and loaded it into the makeshift sound system that had been set up next to the stage. The leather daddy turned on the microphone.

"Okay gents," he said, "young Terry here is going to sing a great song–a particular favourite of mine in fact: "Hopelessly Devoted to You" from the musical, Grease. Give him a big round of applause." There was a small amount of half-hearted clapping as the first bars of the music started to play. Terry had never done karaoke before but he had been in the school choir so he could sing a bit, after a fashion. The leather daddy handed him the microphone as the first line of lyrics appeared on the blue screen. When the time came for Terry to sing a small white dot started bouncing along the top of the words. His voice croaked slightly as he began, and he found at first that trying to stay in rhythm while concentrating on the words in front of him was a bit weird, but he soon acclimatised to it. It was actually very easy to do—or at least it seemed that way with half a bottle of brandy swooshing through his veins. Then something rather unexpected happened. As Terry reached the first chorus people in the bar started to sing along. Now this may have been for a variety of reasons. Perhaps it was because they had noticed that the boy on stage was pouring his heart and soul into the performance; or perhaps it was just because they liked the song. The reason was unclear, but by the time Terry reached the last few verses, pretty much everyone in there was singing their lungs out, even the barman and the leather daddy's helper. When the song finally came to an end, there was a huge explosion of applause and enthusiastic shouting. The leather daddy took the microphone from Terry.

"Thanks lad," he said, then he turned to the audience and laughed. "You lot should be ashamed of yourselves—a bunch of macho men trying to look hard in all your gear, singing along with a song like that. Disgraceful." There was booing and laughter as Terry jumped off the stage and moved back to the bar, keeping his head down. Clive slapped him on the back.

"Bravo! That's the best karaoke number I've ever seen. This one's on me. What are you having?"

"A brandy please—but I may just pop to the loo first." Clive winked.

"Off to the darkroom, eh? Not so hopelessly devoted as your singing seemed to suggest."

"What do you mean?"

"You're obviously following that stunning old Dutchman who's just gone in. I don't blame you. And he's bound to go for you now that you're such a stage sensation. I saw him watching you, getting himself all worked up when you were doing your act." Terry shook his head.

"You're taking out of your arse."

Walking to the back of the bar, he passed through a makeshift curtain made out of military camouflage netting, and into an area which was lit only with ultraviolet light. As his eyes adjusted, he made out a corridor straight in front of him, with louvred cabin doors at regular intervals on both sides. He could see a pale greyish light reflecting off the wall at the far end of the corridor–and knew at once that it was coming from a television that was in the room beyond. Obviously this wasn't the way to the toilet–but now that he was here he decided he might as well have a look. As Terry walked into the labyrinth he could still hear the music and chatting in the bar–and could even make out Clive talking to the barman–but the sound seemed to be coming from a great distance, echoing more than it should given that he was only about ten feet away. He tiptoed into the larger room, and saw that there was no film playing–the television screen was filled with fizzing static. There was also an empty bath and a leather sling attached to the ceiling with chains. He walked forward and gave the sling a gentle push, watching it swing slowly back and forth, wondering about all the things that must have gone on in that room over the years. It was a rare moment of tranquility–in a few hours time the place would be heaving with bodies, the air dull and reeking. But for now, there was just a cool draft and the quiet creak of the moving sling. Suddenly Terry was struck by the ridiculousness of the whole situation–his futile love for Alan, his embarrassment over what had happened with George, his humiliation at the hands of Clive. He felt like he wanted to stay in here forever, so that he would never have to face any of those people again. He shook his head.

"What a mess," he muttered to himself.

"Actually I was just thinking how clean it was tonight," said a deep voice behind him. "Normally my sandals stick to the floor." Terry hadn't heard anyone come in behind him. He whirled around, slightly embarrassed, to see a tall figure standing in the doorway. He recognized the shape at once–it was the man who had been dressed as Zeus on the carnival float. He was still wearing his costume.

"Quite cosy though, isn't it? Just you and me," he said. "All the others are outside at their various carnival pleasures. We have the place to ourselves." Terry–still startled by the man's sudden appearance—took a few seconds to find his voice.

"I saw you this afternoon during the procession, didn't I?"

"And I saw you too, at that bar next to the roundabout, with your friends." Terry's surprise turned to amazement.

"How did you manage to spot us with all those people around?" The man dressed as Zeus chuckled quietly—it sounded like rocks being rubbed together in a sack. He was certainly all man.

"Well you know—I've got a sharp eye for a good-looking boy." He spoke English with a sort of posh foreign accent—but it was hard to place. Terry strained to make out the figure in the dimness. He had to be in his sixties although he was still very muscular, with a thick beard and a huge mop of hair, which stuck out in all directions. He wasn't really paunchy enough for the younger man's taste, but what did that matter? There was an atmosphere of danger about him that was compounded by the emptiness of the darkroom, the feeling that even though they were just yards away from the biggest party of the year, civilization was out of reach. Terry found it rather thrilling, and giggled nervously. The stranger moved along the wall into the corner, staying out of the light. His eyes looked as if they were glowing, but it must have been a reflection of the static on the TV screen. Terry felt himself being pulled into a tight embrace—and was shocked to discover that Zeus was already naked. The gravelly voice was in his ear. "That's the great thing about wearing a toga to a fancy dress party." Terry dropped to his knees.

*

ALAN cursed the crowds as he fought his way from bar to bar, looking for Terry. He had already completed one circuit of the Yumbo Centre, and felt a bit like someone trying to reach a train that was due to leave, on a platform at the opposite end of a railway station crowded with commuters heading in the other direction. Only instead of commuters he had to penetrate waves of boisterous carnival revellers dressed as military commandos, psycho nurses, alien warlords, smurfs and bondage slaves. It was all quite unsettling. Alan approached Na Und—a bar he knew to be one of Terry's favourites, and therefore a good place to check. It was still pretty quiet, although within the next couple of hours it would be hard enough just to get past the people hanging around outside, never mind into the bar itself. The waiters, who all knew him, waved and said good evening, but no one asked if he wanted a drink because it was quite obvious that he was looking for somebody. Alan walked to the empty dance floor at the back of the bar, but there was no sign of Terry. A slow, smoochy number from the 1930s was playing–it struck him as slightly sad that there were no couples there to enjoy it. Beams of light from the glitterball caressed his shoulders as he headed back into the plaza. Turning left outside Na Und, Alan walked past Construction. In front of it there was already a large crowd of men, mostly bearded or with shaved heads, wearing denim or obeying some obscure dress code or other that Alan was unable to understand. He thought of the huge darkroom and the things that went on in there–and said to himself that if Terry had gone into a place like that, there was no way he would be able to find him. As Alan walked on through the crowds, something that George had said to him a few minutes ago drifted back into his mind. It all depends on what you want. What did he want? Inexplicably, Alan's mind turned to something that had happened in Na Und several years before. A suave Spaniard who had been smiling across at him for some time–but who was really a bit long in the tooth for Alan's tastes–had eventually come and asked him for a dance. The guy had turned out to be pretty good and they stayed on the floor for the best part of an hour, dancing mostly waltzes. The Spaniard was affectionate and seemed as the dancing went on to be getting more and more worked up. He was sweating a lot too and as they moved around the floor, Alan had noticed a few times the sharp smell of body odour, which increased his sense of physical repulsion. Then, at the end of a slow number, throughout which Alan had felt a hand caressing his bottom, the stranger had moved his mouth towards Alan's ear.

"Do you give love?" he whispered. Although Alan understood perfectly what the Spaniard was asking, he found the odd wording of the question quite funny–so there was a rather inappropriate smile on his face as he stepped back and responded that no, he didn't. The Spaniard, utterly offended, stalked away and never so much as looked at him again. But for some reason, his crudely worded question had clung to Alan like a curse–and now he had to admit that it wasn't as absurd as it had originally sounded. Did he give love? Could he give love–or had he become so emotionally closed off that all he was good for was the occasional grope in a darkroom?

Alan turned left into the busiest stretch of the Yumbo Centre, where the bars and cafes were all lined up in two rows, facing each other. It was where he and George liked to stop for a coffee after their dinner, and they had nicknamed it the Golden Mile because it was always so busy. It seemed that sooner or later, everyone in Playa del Ingles walked along here, to see and to be seen. The crowd was a little less dense now because many people had moved into the plaza to watch the grand finale of the carnival. The tables outside the bars and cafes were still packed, though. He walked slowly down one side, carefully scanning the faces, but felt slightly perturbed by the fact that many of the people sitting there seemed to be watching him just as intently. Some were even (quite rudely, he thought) smirking or laughing. Alan had to admit that such scrutiny was probably not the norm–but what on earth could be so amusing about someone searching for a friend? For all they knew, he might be terribly short sighted. He reached the far end of the Golden Mile and turned around, to walk past the bars on the other side and see if Terry was sitting outside any of them. To his horror, the amused reactions continued. Something wasn't quite right. Alan spun around quickly, and came face to face with a little clown who had been walking along just behind him. The clown–whose face was painted a shocking white and who had a big red nose with a flashing light inside it–had obviously been following him and mimicking his actions. Actually, Alan had to admit that from the glimpse he had seen, the impersonation was pretty good–right down to the hands clasped behind the back, and the fact that he had been leaning forward, craning his neck to get a better view of the people at the tables. But Alan was in no mood to laugh at himself. Enraged, he raised his fist and shook it at the blighter–who let out a high-pitched scream and scampered away. Of course, the customers outside the bars found this bit of slapstick even more amusing. There was laughter and clapping, and some people even booed at Alan, for being such a poor sport. It seemed appropriate to retreat, so he walked briskly up the stairs to the first floor and slipped into the crowd. Once he was satisfied that he was no longer being pursued he stopped and looked over the parapet into the square below. The show seemed to be reaching its climax. A group of dancers executed a tightly choreographed routine, while four well-built young men in old-fashioned bathing costumes brought out the papier maché fish, and laid it on top of a scaffolding frame in the middle of the stage. The sardine burning was about to begin. Alan decided to get a better view of the action. Up ahead on the corner was an amusement arcade that overlooked the plaza. When Alan and George had first visited the island it had been the only real drag revue bar in the Yumbo Centre, but one year later the lease had run out and the owners had been forced to move downstairs. Somehow, though, the atmosphere in their new place had never been the same, and now drag shows were ten a penny–as they were back home in England. Places like Ricky's Revue Bar packed them in every night, but the punters were mostly heterosexual. It struck Alan as odd that a bunch of people who would probably lynch a gay person under normal circumstances would queue up to see a man in high heels and sequins doing camp music hall routines.

The arcade was pretty packed with other people trying to see the show, and the sardine was well and truly ablaze by the time he squeezed through. Although he was on the first floor and quite a distance away from the stage, Alan could feel the heat from the fire on his face. He watched as the paper layers that had been painstakingly wrapped around the wooden skeleton of the fish were consumed by the flames, withering and falling off one by one in glowing clumps, then drifting lazily across the stage. There was so much smoke coming from the burning fish that he was unable to see anything clearly–but Alan was sure he had seen one of the glowing embers disappearing behind the scenery. Suddenly a couple of the firemen were running around at the back of the stage with small fire extinguishers, pointing them at the floor. The situation was obviously under control. There were cheers from the crowd as the wooden carcass fell apart; each half left dangling from the metal frame supporting it. The firemen moved forward and pointed the nozzles of the extinguishers at the remaining embers. Within seconds the fire was out. At that moment an unseen button was pressed and the firework display began. Alan watched the explosions above his head, but after a few minutes his thoughts returned to the task at hand. He turned from the spectacle and squeezed his way back through the crowd, eventually emerging from the amusement arcade. Straight in front of him was the bar that he'd popped into last night, after the young guys at the places further along were so rude to him. It had been a while since his last drink, and he fancied a beer. His search for Terry could continue in due course.

*

GEORGE and Mark were lying side by side in bed in the older man's hotel room. The sheets lay in a crumpled heap at their feet—it was warm enough without them.

"I'll bet you're a smashing dancer," said Mark dreamily.

"Why do you say that?"

"The way you make love. A lot of guys get into bed and they know exactly what they want to do, and that's it. They're not expressing themselves at all, and they're not trying to find out what you want either. It's quite mechanical. To me having sex is as much a form of communication as having a conversation. The more I tune in to what the other person wants, the better it gets—and I think you're like that too. You respond to me as if you're listening to music, trying to find the beat—but at the same time you're letting me know what you want. And you do it all with such finesse." George lifted his head and gave the lad a kiss.

"You know what they say—it takes two to tango." Through the open window they could hear the sounds of the night—music, distant cheering, and an amplified voice babbling away in Spanish. The only light in the room came from a small lamp on a table in the corner. Mark stroked George's temple, and George made a purring sound like a cat on someone's lap.

"That's lovely—you can rub my ear too if you want to."

"I'm going to need a book the size of a telephone directory to write down all these pleasure zones," said Mark. "Shame we didn't get started on this twenty-four hours ago." George half-opened an eye.

"We could have done, sunshine, if you hadn't gone off with Alan."
Mark laughed.

"That again! Well, they say that you value things more if they
take longer to come your way."

"True," admitted George. "By the way, in answer to your question,
I do love dancing. In fact, Alan's wife Marge and I ran night classes
for a while. We used to go in for all sorts of competitions, and we
won quite a few. Alan's pretty good too." Mark continued stroking
the side of George's head, concentrating intently on it.

"Blimey," he said after a while, "the way your hair catches the
light–it's almost as if it's made out of metallic thread. I can never
understand why people hate grey hair so much. I think it's the most
amazing colour of all–far more exciting than boring old brown or
black." George sighed.

"People don't like grey hair because it means they're getting past
it." He realised that his comment had sounded rather huffy. "But all
the same, I'm pleased you like it."

George would normally have been happy to lie here with Mark
all night but, rather annoyingly, as soon as they had finished making
love, his thoughts had returned to Alan Reid. He wanted very much
to know how his friend was getting on–whether he'd been able to
find Terry and patch things up. He gently removed Mark's hand
and sat up. His clothes were lying in a pile a few feet away. George
rifled through them, found his cigarettes and then grabbed his beach
towel, which was spread out over his suitcase, airing. He wrapped
it around his waist and went out onto the balcony. As he stood
looking out across the resort, the firework display at the Yumbo
Centre began. They were his favourite sort, small dots of white
light that hissed high into the sky and then exploded with a loud
boom, shooting hundreds of coloured flares outwards in a spherical
pattern, which expanded rapidly and then disappeared in a puff of
smoke. There was a certain rhythm about fireworks that made them
so majestic–despite the fact that it all happened very quickly, they
seemed to move across the sky in an unhurried way. The moon was
like a juicy grapefruit segment, sending out a pale yellow light which

illuminated the edges of the few clouds high in the sky above Playa Del Ingles. Buildings spread out in front of him as far as he could see. In the distance the big hotels were all lined up along the beach so that it was impossible to see the sea beyond. Their various names blazed out in coloured neon–red for the Riu Papayas, green for the Gran Canaria Princess, blue for the Buenos Aires. He heard Mark come out onto the balcony. The younger man walked up behind George and slipped his arms around him.

"You're thinking about your friend, aren't you?" George smiled– Mark was a perceptive lad.

"I am, yes. He's the closest thing to family that I have, and he's going through a bit of a weird time. He seems to have the happy knack of messing things up for himself."

"Do you want to go back and see what's going on?" George heard the disappointment in Mark's words, and he had to admit that the situation was slightly ridiculous. Here they were, the magic of the evening around them, fireworks exploding on the horizon, their own romance starting to unfold–and yet over at the Yumbo Centre, duty called. But he appreciated the fact that Mark had offered to go back.

"Yes I'd like to if you don't mind." Mark tightened his grip on George.

"That's fine by me," he said. "There'll be plenty of time later. It's something to look forward to." George chuckled–a guy in his twenties would never have been so understanding.

"Yes, and it'll give me a chance to get my strength back," he said. "It's sometimes quite hard to keep up with you younger ones." The night was perfectly still, with not a hint of a breeze. It was unusual for Gran Canaria–which was more or less constantly being buffeted by the trade winds that had made the island such an essential stopping off place for sailing ships in years gone by. It was also slightly humid which gave the impression that there was another storm on the way. George spotted movement on a balcony opposite theirs.

"Look over there," he hissed. "That balcony on the top floor, third from the left. Can you see that guy up there flashing at us?"

Mark peered across the dim space above the soft turquoise light of the swimming pool. He sniggered.

"Oh yes, I see. The dirty bugger!"

"He does it all the time. Alan told me at dinner that his wife caught him this afternoon and gave him a good hiding–but I see it hasn't put him off." The man was now close to the balcony wall, on his tiptoes, really trying to give them a good look.

"Pleased to hear it," said Mark. "He's not doing any harm–it's a public service in a way."

"I'm surprised she got so angry," said George. "I've seen them in Hummel Hummel together. His friends are all gay, and she sits with them while he goes into the dark room. She must know what goes on in there."

"Finding out that your husband is gay or bisexual is one thing, but finding out that he's a flasher too must be a bit annoying. But then, nothing surprises me about this scene any more. People find all sorts of ways to make things work for themselves."

"Yes," said George, "and the older I get the more I can understand that. So many people go through their lives with this conviction, this illusion that their relationships can stay the same as they were when they started. But they're fluid things and as the years go by what people mean to each other, what they need from one another, changes. I'm impressed that people like Balcony Man and his wife can face up to it and make it work. It seems to me a better way to go about things than to simply call it a day and get divorced, or split up."

"And where does your friend Alan fit in?" George looked into the distance.

"We've been friends for so long now, and I think that whatever happens, he's with me for the duration. He's not really built for the gay world but the death of his wife has left him with nothing else. It's a difficult transition that he's going through." Mark nodded.

"I know. He seemed so on edge when we were alone together.

Everything was fine when there were other people around, but once we left all that behind he withdrew back into himself. I thought I'd done something wrong at first but then I realised what was going on."

"I thought that might happen. He's got this strange guilty conscience thing going on about his sexuality. He's become a voyeur. He loves the idea of it, loves to talk about it, loves to watch–but when it comes to the crunch I'm not sure if he's actually able to enjoy it."

"That would certainly explain a lot." George shook his head.

"Look at us. Here together, apparently in need of no one else, and what are we talking about? Bloody Alan Reid. I doubt if he'd be doing the same thing if the roles were reversed."

"Don't be like that–I think it's lovely that you care about him. It makes you even better in my eyes, if that's possible." George sighed.

"You're certainly a smooth talker, young man." They began to kiss. After a few moments Balcony Man realised he was surplus to requirements, and went back into his bedroom. Flashing was only worthwhile, after all, when one had an audience. He was pleased to see that his wife was still in the bathroom, and was therefore unaware that he had resumed his forbidden activities. He pulled off his underpants and jumped into bed, picking up his book and his reading glasses, and adopting an expression that was beyond suspicion.

*

IN the dark room at Contact, the man dressed as Zeus was pulling his toga back over his head. He pushed his left arm through the appropriate hole and glanced at a huge aviator-style watch on his wrist. As he put his own clothing back in order Terry could see the pointers and numbers on its face glowing fiercely in the ultra-violet light.

"That was very nice," said Zeus. "I'd love to stay and buy you a drink but I'm meeting my friends–and I'm already late." Terry's jaw was quite sore and he felt sure that there would be marks on the knees of his white pants, which would give the game away when he went back outside, but he didn't care. No one was really in a position to judge him. He'd heard several people coming into the dark room and going out again while they were busy–but had rather shamelessly continued with what he was doing. The drink had made him brazen. He spoke quietly in case anyone was still in the room.

"Your friends, are they the people who were on the float with you?"

"Yes–and there'll be all sorts of questions to answer about where I've been. But to be honest I find the bars that they go to a bit stuck-up. I prefer to mix with real people when I can, and see some life."

"Where are you from?"

"Oh I've lived all over. I've got a place here though, up in the mountains. All my friends come out to visit me for the carnival every year. They're a freaky bunch but they blend in quite well when all this other nonsense is going on."

"Your float was incredible. The best I've seen..."

"Yes, my boys are clever, aren't they? Mind you, I have no idea what we're going to do with it now." Zeus shook his head. "It'll probably end up lying in pieces in my back yard for the next six months, and make the place look even more like a ruin than it already does."

"It's been nice meeting you," said Terry, putting out his hand. The guy gave it a shake–practically crushing the bones as he did so.

"Let me give you one of these," he said. He reached into a leather bag attached to his belt and pulled out a small card that was strangely shaped, like an oak leaf. Terry held it up to his face so he could read it in the dim light from the television screen. On it was written in gold leaf, in between two columns like the ones on the float, Zeus Leather and Rubber–Cologne, and a telephone number.

"One of my businesses," said the stranger. "Give me a call sometime. You cancome and visit me. My email address is on the back."

"Thanks," Terry said as he pocketed the card. The man walked towards the door, but stopped halfway there and turned around.

"I mean it, give me a call. And look–don't give this guy you're in love with a hard time. He's a decent chap and things will work out fine if you let them." With that, he turned on his heel and disappeared around the corner.

"Hang on!" shouted Terry. "How do you know about that?" He moved quickly to the doorway, but saw that there was no longer anybody there. Out in the corridor there were small lights built into the walls so that people could get an idea of where they were going. Terry held the card up to one of them and looked at the email address on the back. Zeus@mount-olympus.gr.

"Nah," he said to himself. "Couldn't be." He leaned against the wall, his heart beating fast, trying to work out what had just happened. Certain things that the stranger had said came to mind. I've lived all over, a place in the mountains, I prefer to mix with real people. Terry was so lost in his thoughts that he didn't see the older man who had just come in from the toilet until he was standing right in front of him. He was broadly built, with white hair and a moustache. Just Terry's type–and he was smiling.

"Nice to see you here," said the man. The accent was Dutch. "Would you like to go with me into one of these cabins?" Terry pulled himself together.

"I'd love to–but to be honest I'm a little worn out, and my friends will be wondering what's happened to me." The man shook his head slowly.

"The best ones always leave when I am arriving." Terry smiled.

"That's strange, because the best ones usually arrive when I'm leaving." The Dutchman laughed.

"Do you really have to go now?" Terry stopped and looked at the man. The experience he had just had was somewhat one-way and he was still feeling pretty horny. And the guy was very attractive. Terry glanced at his watch and saw that he still had half an hour or so before he was due to meet Helen and Rob. The karaoke, which had continued throughout the twenty minutes or so he had been in the darkroom, was starting to grate–and he was in no rush to go back and talk to Clive.

"I suppose not," he said. It was the usual situation –feast or famine.

Clive was still at the bar when he emerged some time later.

"Enjoy that, did you?" he said. "I saw that Dutch guy follow you in. I've been after him for ages but I thought I'd better stay out of the way." He eyed the marks on Terry's knees. "I see you had a good time with him, anyway." Terry looked down at his trousers. Although he had nothing to be ashamed of–he'd seen Clive doing much worse things than that–he felt himself blushing. Clive obviously knew about the handsome Dutchman, but strangely had said nothing about the Zeus character. Terry considered asking him if he'd noticed a huge, white-haired man in a toga leaving the bar but thought better of it. He began to think that maybe he had dreamed up the whole encounter. Terry picked up his drink.

"It was very nice, yes," he said, regaining some of his composure. Clive was looking at the camouflage netting. The Dutchman had still not come out. He was obviously hanging around inside, up for a bit more action.

"If you don't mind I might just go and take a look myself," he said.

"Of course–be my guest. I recommend it." Clive slid off his stool and disappeared into the darkroom. Terry turned around and saw Alan Reid walking into the bar. There was no time to do anything, to plan how to set his face, or to look elsewhere and try to remain casual and aloof. Terry was sick of those games, and besides he'd just had his own fun in the darkroom, and was still experiencing the pleasant afterglow of that. He was also embarrassed about leaving Hummel Hummel in the way he had done earlier that night, instead of going back to the table and finishing his drink with George. It had been inelegant–a silly little episode, a display of immaturity. He smiled across the bar.

"Evening."

"Hello!" Alan looked surprised. "This is the last place I'd have expected to see you."

"It's not quite as hectic as the bars downstairs—and you never know who you might bump into."

"Quite. Not sure about the karaoke, though." A chunky man in his late forties, who was naked from the waist up and sported a huge black handlebar moustache, leather chaps and nipple clamps, was singing "As Time Goes By". The way he was going at it, with his eyes closed and cradling the microphone in his hands like a dove, suggested that he believed it to be a show-stopping performance, when in fact he was hopelessly flat. Alan sat down.

"Look," he said, "about what happened earlier..."

"You don't have to explain. You're on holiday and you can do what you like. I'm just sorry I walked in when I did."

"Yes, well, the encounter wasn't much good. At least, nothing like the time we spent together this afternoon."

"Cheers—but really you don't have to say that for my benefit. I'm a big boy." Alan leaned closer and touched the younger man's arm.

"I mean it," he said. The barman appeared, and Terry ordered a bottle of sparkling water for himself. He'd already had more than enough to drink. Alan asked for a small beer. Terry put his hand on top of Alan's and smiled.

"I'm the one who should be apologizing for the way I reacted. I was tired—a lot's been going on over the past few days." It was the best explanation Terry could come up with and he hoped it would suffice. Because he had fallen in love with Alan so many years ago, and had never really put those feelings aside, his emotions concerning the older man were somewhat out of his control. As Helen had warned him earlier in the evening, events were likely to hold much more significance for him than for Alan, and if Terry started trying to explain how he felt without toning things down a bit, Alan was bound to pull back. Terry guessed that he just had to carry it on his own for now–lock it away perhaps, in a dark corner of his heart. He took a gulp of water and set the glass back down on the bar.

"Listen, Alan, I've got no idea what you want out of life–I barely know what I want myself–but it's been wonderful seeing you again and I'd love to see more of you when we get back to England. What do you think?" Alan smiled.

"I'd like that," he said. "Although there's something unsettling about this rather incestuous relationship of ours. I mean, I could have been your father-in-law, the grandfather of your children–and yet this afternoon we shared a bed. That's a lot to take in and it's all happened very quickly. When my wife died I didn't want to go anywhere, to be with anyone. But the months passed and things began to happen, and I started coming here with George and it was like a new lease of life. But I would never have expected anything like this. Can you see that?"

"Of course. You've got your life and it's all in order. I wish I could say the same for myself–but let's just see how it goes."

"Do you still have our address?"

"If you haven't moved since I knew you."

"No–still in Denmark Street. So I shall expect to hear from you when we get back home?" The younger man's face lit up.

"For sure!"

"I'll drink to that." They clinked glasses and Terry looked at his watch.

"Damn," he said. "I've got to meet my friends Rob and Helen in a few minutes. Rob's putting on another show at the Block tonight–do you fancy a walk?" Alan grinned.

"I wouldn't want to miss one of your friend's performances."

"Yeah, so I believe. But his girlfriend's going to be there tonight– so no funny business, okay?" As they walked out of the bar the guy with the moustache who had beensinging on the karaoke grabbed Terry's arm.

"Thoroughly enjoyed the show," he said in a leery sort of way. "You're a very talented young man."

"Thanks," said Terry. "It was the first time I've ever done karaoke."

"Oh good Lord," laughed the man. "I wasn't talking about that–I meant in the darkroom, with the big man in the toga."

"Right." Terry felt his face colouring with embarrassment once again. "Thanks." He turned to Alan, who of course had heard everything. The older man patted him on the shoulder reassuringly.

"You've got to take these opportunities while you can," he said. "And by the way, if you want to get your trousers cleaned, I know an excellent laundry." He pointed at his own pants which were covered with smears and sangria stains. "What a debonair pair we make!"

Outside it was thinning out because the carnival had come to an end. The families were heading home and those left stalking the Yumbo Centre's corridors and stairwells were the serious pleasure seekers, who would probably be on the go until the dustbin wagons arrived at dawn. As Alan and Terry entered the plaza they could see that things were descending into chaos. Wigs were getting crooked, heels were broken, and costumes were starting to show the strain. There was now a slightly possessed quality about the revelry.

"I think maybe I'm getting a little old for all this," muttered Alan.

"Would you rather be sitting in some old folks' home, waiting for the nurse to come round with your pills?"

The old gypsy couple who Alan had seen cleaning up their stall at about the same time the night before were doing it again. They were certainly game for their age! Alan wondered if they did it because they needed the money or because they wanted to be part of the carnival. The old lady was sweeping up bits of discarded streamers and tinsel, bottle tops and other party detritus into a neat pile near the bin. Her husband was once again cleaning out the popcorn machine–a cigarette hanging from his lips. The man looked up and recognised Alan. His heavily creased face cracked a smile and he lifted a finger up to the brim of his hat in a friendly gesture. Alan waved then turned back to Terry.

"I wouldn't quite go that far," he said. "But something tells me that drink, drugs, Spanish carnivals and strip shows at two in the morning might be pushing it at bit when you're my age." Terry giggled.

"Not to mention the hordes of hunks fighting to get their hands on your body." Alan gave the young man walking next to him a sideways look, an enigmatic smile on his face.

"Oh now that I can handle."

"I'm sure," said Terry. "That's one of the reasons I admire you and George–I hope I have the same attitude when I'm in my sixties."

"When you're in your sixties I'll be long since departed."

"Who knows? I probably won't even make it that far–but it won't matter as long as I've enjoyed what I had." Alan waved a fist in the air in a defiant salute.

"Well spoken that man! Now tell me–shall we have a quick joint and a walk around the square before we go to the Block? I feel as if I've gone off the boil a bit, and I'd hate you to think that I was slowing down."

*

WHEN Alan and Terry arrived at the Block, Helen was sitting outside at a table, chatting in Spanish to one of the waiters. Her face lit up when she saw Terry.

"Alright mate?" she glanced at Alan. "Had a good night then?"

"Yeah," said Terry, "a bit unusual. Missed the fireworks–but I'll tell you all about that later. This is Alan by the way. Alan, Helen." Alan gave a little bow as he took Helen's hand. Terry thought for a fraction of a second that he might actually kiss it.

"At your service," said the older man genially, somehow conveying in the way he looked at her that all his resources would indeed be available if she needed them. Terry could see by Helen's reaction that she was delighted by the display of charm. He grinned–you really had to hand it to these old buffers, who were able to turn it on in a way that younger men could only dream about. Terry wondered if they had this power simply because of the confidence that the passing years had bestowed upon them, or if they had always been this charming. He considered himself to be quite a good-mannered chap, but he would never have been able to come up with the chivalry that had just been on display. People would laugh. Perhaps, like the cloak laid in the puddle to keep Her Ladyship's shoes dry as she stepped down from the carriage, these skills had been trampled underfoot and forgotten as the decades passed. That would be a great shame though, because Terry admired them very much, and hoped that by the time he reached Alan's age, he too would be able to act with such aplomb. As they sat down the waiter nodded towards Alan and said something to Helen in Spanish. She raised her eyebrows.

"Juan says that you and your friend are their favourite customers, that you liven the place up." Juan continued to speak as Helen translated. "He says that most people stand around looking glum and saying nothing, but then you two come in and take the mickey out of them. He says you're always pinching young guys' bottoms and trying to lure them into the dark room." A rather self-righteous expression crossed Alan's face.

"I have no idea what you're talking about, young lady. This little rascal must have mixed us up with someone else. George and I always behave ourselves impeccably." He managed to hold the straight face for a few more seconds, then started to snigger. Helen translated what Alan had said back into Spanish. Juan scoffed as he heard the words. Terry shook his head.

"Sounds to me like Juan's got you two pretty much weighed up." Alan pointed at the waiter accusingly–but he was smiling.

"Rogue!" he shouted. "See that? You show them loyalty and they repay you with a knife in the back." Terry looked around the table.

"Fancy a drink?"

"I was just going to get one," said Helen.

"May I recommend the Flaming Inferno?" Alan suggested. "It's a heinous cocktail of liqueurs that they light up before they bring it to the table. You have a coffee with it. George and I tried them last night. The results were... interesting."

"Makes a change from all this beer and wine," said Helen. "Same for you Terry?" Terry nodded and Helen translated the order for Juan. Alan watched him disappear through the curtain.

"That bugger's just talked himself out of a tip," he muttered.

"He's a good lad," said Helen. "He was only having a laugh. he meant what he said, though–they really like you here."

"Well, they've always made us very welcome–and when you get to our age gay bars aren't always like that. They cater too much for the younger clientele." Terry glanced at his watch.

"Where's Rob?"

"You just missed him," said Helen. "He's gone in to get his gear on. He's doing his GI Joe routine tonight." Alan leaned forward.

"Tell me–doesn't your boyfriend's line of work bother you?" Helen paused for a second.

"It'd bother me more if he was stripping off in front of women," she said. "He used to when we were students, to make a bit of extra cash on the side. His stage name was The Penetrator. But one night he was doing his act and a bunch of girls on a hen-night stormed the stage and practically lynched him. He said he'd never perform for women again and I don't blame him. But gays are different–even if they're whipped up into a frenzy they won't do anything because they know the rules. Rob feels more comfortable with it–and I know he's not going to go off with a man. He would have done already if he was into that, I'm sure."

"It's not the only thing he does, though, is it?" said Terry. "He's actually writing a book. The stripping is just a sideline." Helen laughed.

"Yeah, the book! He's been writing that as long as I've known him—and that's six years. It'll be longer than War and Peace by the time he's finished. But you know even if stripping was all he'd ever done, and all he was ever going to do, I wouldn't be bothered. It's not a stressful way of life and at least he's giving people pleasure. How many of us can say that? Some of my friends back home have high-flying jobs in the city, and they hate it. Rob and I are really lucky—we've got a great lifestyle here. The cost of living is relatively low and it's far warmer than it is at home. Our Spanish has improved and we've started making a few friends here. At the end of the day we can always hop on an EasyJet flight and be back in England in a few hours if we need to." The drinks arrived. Alan placed a note on Juan's tray.

"Better blow these flames out,"he advised. "You don't want the rim of the glass to be too hot when you take a drink." They leaned forward and blew on their drinks. Helen was still lost in her thoughts.

"We'll probably get bored in the end and go back home to the rat race," she said. "But for now this suits us fine. What do you reckon, Terry?"

"Sounds good to me. People I know at home keep going on about how they're going to move abroad—but you're the only ones who've actually had the balls to do it, and that's pretty impressive in itself. But I like England though—I know the weather's a bit crap during the winter but I love having access to all the things I like. Holidays like this are all very well, but there's a lot I would miss if I lived abroad."

"I'll drink to that," said Alan, raising his glass. The others lifted theirs and they clinked them together.

"Are you supposed to down these in one?"Terry sounded slightly nervous. Alan smiled.

"I always do but George takes his time. He likes to see more of the scenery on the way, as it were. Cheers." At that moment, the loud music coming from the bar was turned off, which meant the show was about to start. Alan and Helen swigged their drinks off in unison, banging the thick-bottomed shot glasses back down on the table simultaneously. Helen shuddered and grimaced, Alan's eyes bulged and his face turned crimson.

"Christ," he said, "that'll put hairs on your chest." Helen's eyes were watering. She cleared her throat.

"Hope not–that's the last thing I need." She nodded towards the chain-link curtain that covered the entrance to the bar.

"You'd better go now if you want to see Rob strut his stuff."

"My dear," said Alan, "even though I'm an ardent admirer of your boyfriend's... art, I think tonight I will give it a miss." Terry looked surprised.

"You sure?"

"Why would I want to go and watch a strip show when I have such delightful company?" Terry picked up his Flaming Inferno.

"Here's to that," he said, downing it in one. Alan watched him, a discreet smirk on his face as if he was waiting for an explosion of coughing and gagging. Terry looked straight into the older man's eyes as he slowly placed the glass back on the table, smiling back at him. The merest hint of a tear in his eye was the only evidence of the drink's mighty impact. Alan clapped.

"Bravo! Waiter–another round!"

"Oh no," said Helen. "Just a beer for me please. I take back what I said about trying different drinks–that stuff's only good for cleaning your paint brushes." Loud cheers and wolf-whistles came from inside the bar.

"Sounds like a lively crowd," said Alan. "Your man's obviously not lost his touch." Terry waved at Juan and the lad came over to the table. As he ordered the drinks, Terry noticed how much the waiter flirted with Alan. He was slightly disturbed by it, but then he said to himself–get a grip, if you're going to be spending time with the guy, you'll have to get used to it. The jealous feeling–like the anger he felt earlier when he saw Alan in the dark room with somebody else–was a grim reminder of the depth of his emotions. But Alan didn't share those emotions and it would be some time before Terry would find out if the older man could reciprocate to the extent he hoped for. But then, he thought, at least I'm getting a chance to find out, to see if it leads anywhere–and if it doesn't, then so what? What will I have lost? As the others continued their conversation, Terry looked out across the plaza, at the night unraveling around them. A crowd of rather plump young women in tight sequinned dresses hobbled past, trying to pick their way through the mess in their stiletto shoes–that task made more difficult by the huge amount of booze they had clearly consumed. One of them muttered something in Spanish to the others in a frustrated tone, fanning herself with a dog-eared handful of flyers she'd picked up at various bars and clubs along the way. In the distance, near the centre of the plaza, a group of youths had linked arms and formed a semicircle, and were doing a can-can style dance in time to the loud music still pumping out of the big stacks of speakers at either side of the stage. One of them accidentally kicked a bottle, and there was a loud tinkling sound as it skittered across the concrete, followed by shouts and laughter. Men in overalls had begun to dismantle some of the lighting rigs opposite the stage, and take down some of the scaffolding. The party was over–but as with all holiday resorts, as one chapter was coming to an end, hundreds more were just beginning. People were arriving at the airport in Las Palmas, unpacking their bags, and heading out for their first few drinks, or having an early night in preparation for their first day in the sun. Every night in the Yumbo Centre, even without the carnival, was another festival. Terry had often sat upstairs at four o'clock in the morning, eating his chips and watching the waiters at the various bars turning off the neon lights, stacking up the tables and chairs and sweeping up. The following night, as regular as clockwork, they would set it all up again for a new set of punters. It was a vast and strange mechanism of pleasure–one that never really stopped running. You arrived, had your fun, left, arrived again. The locals always looked at you on your first night as if you had never really been away. And in the final analysis you probably never had. Once the island had claimed you, your life back home was just time spent until your next visit to the nudist beach, the bars, the dunes, and dark rooms–to the kingdom of pleasure. Terry's reverie was interrupted by a shout from Alan, who had spotted George and Mark going past. George–who always scanned the faces of the people sitting outside the bars as he walked along, just in case there was anything interesting–had already seen them.

"Hullo stranger!" As he approached the table, George noticed with relief that Terry was present, and all appeared jovial. "I thought you might be here. Mark, Alan–I think you know each other already." Mark said hello; Alan looked sheepish as he remembered the shameful details of the previous night. George continued, oblivious. "Mark, this is Terry." Mark laughed as he carried two more metal chairs over to the table and set them down.

"Yes I remember seeing you last night. I'm sure you won't remember me, though. You only had eyes for this man here." He patted George on the bottom. George looked across at Helen.

"Nice to see that there are ladies present for a change. An unusual occurrence in these parts–but one that we welcome." He put out his hand.

"Pleased to meet you," said Helen. "I've been hearing all about you."

"Good things I hope." Alan chipped in, his eyes flashing, shifting in his seat–giving the impression that his feathers were ruffled.

"That little slut Juan has been dishing the dirt on us." George looked severe–and raised his voice so that Juan, who was loitering nearby, would hear what was said.

"Oh dear–I may be forced to get the riding crop out later."

"Don't bother," Alan replied. "That's just what he wants." The waiter sauntered forward with a slightly insolent look on his face. He knew they were talking about him but was unable to work out what was being said. He stood over George chewing his gum as usual. George smiled up at him, fluttered his eyelashes and adopted a softer tone of voice.

"My dear–you're looking as gorgeous as ever. Two beers please, and whatever our friends want." Juan nodded and retreated from the table, disappearing into the bar through the chain-link curtain. George leaned over towards Alan with a wicked look in his eye.

"Enjoy the fireworks, old man?" Alan sighed. He had half-expected this.

"Yes, as a matter of fact I did. It was more dramatic than usual. When they burned the fish some of the embers drifted back into the scenery and set it on fire. A couple of firemen had to come on stage with an extinguisher and put it out."

"They can use their hoses on me any time they like," said George. Like a seasoned professional he waited a heartbeat and turned to Mark. "Sorry darling–you know I'm only joking, of course." Alan shook head.

"Degenerate to the very last. What have you been up to, anyway?" George slapped Mark's thigh.

"My young friend here is thinking about staying in our hotel next year, so of course I felt duty bound to show him what the rooms were like."

"It was the very least you could do." Alan turned to Mark. "And how did you find the accommodation?" Mark winked.

"I'm not sure–I think I need to go back later for another look before I make a final decision." Terry leaned towards George.

"I've heard good things about this hotel myself. Do you think you can fit me in for a tour?" George pulled an imaginary diary from the inside pocket of his jacket, and pretended to leaf through the pages.

"Oh yes," he said, "I'm sure we can squeeze you in at some stage. Although as you can see, I'm pretty booked up."

"Hey, you sluts!" shouted Alan. "I can do tours as well you know." They all laughed. Terry raised an eyebrow.

"Ah, now that's an offer I really can't refuse."

"Sounds like you lot have got the rest of your evening mapped out nicely," said Helen. "I just hope my boyfriend isn't too worn out by doing his show two nights running." George touched her arm and leaned in, speaking confidentially.

"I'm sure you've got what it takes to liven him up–talking of which, Alan, have you got any of those things left, or have you already smoked them?" Alan patted his pocket.

"I saved the biggest one until you were here." He took out the magic glasses case and removed a large, well-rolled joint. Everyone at the table watched as he carefully smoothed the paper with his fingers to remove any imperfections, then put it in his mouth and lit it up. Inside the bar, the music ended and there was applause.

"Sounds like the show's been a success," said Terry. "I must just pop to the loo." He got up and went through the curtain. Rob was standing at the bar dressed in a shiny Adidas tracksuit, drinking a glass of water. Punters were on the move–some leaving, some heading into the darkroom. The barman handed Rob a small brown envelope. As Terry approached he could see that his friend's hair was damp, and there was perspiration on his forehead. He looked like a young boxer who had just finished an intensive training session–but he also had that energized, wide-eyed look of someone who had just been on stage and still had the adrenaline in his system. He smiled when he spotted Terry.

"Hey–how's it going?"

"Great thanks," said Terry. "We're all outside. How did the show go?" Rob shrugged.

"Punters seemed to enjoy it–yeah. Nobody jumped the stage, which is always a relief."

"They loved it!" shouted the barman. "He's our best act by far. A guy from Amsterdam who comes in here even wants him to star in a porn film." Rob puckered up his lips in an expression of distaste.

"Porn always strikes me as rather sleazy." The barman laughed.

"Look around you mate–this is hardly the fucking Ritz!"

"Yeah but it suits me. I come in here and do a couple of shows a week, then go home to my girlfriend. I can get on with other things during the day. The money may be better in porn, but it takes over your life. You just end up hanging around with porn people all the time. I don't want that–and anyway I'm trying to finish my book."

"Fair enough," said the barman. "Do you want a beer?"

"Just a water for now please. It's surprising how parched you get even when you're dancing for only a short time. Must be those spotlights. What I really want is a cup of tea but I don't suppose you do those here." The barmen shook their heads.

"Vodka and Red Bull?" ventured one.

"Fuck off," laughed Rob. "The water will do fine." A few minutes later he and Terry went outside to join the others. Rob gave Helen a kiss, stage whispering in her ear as he looked around the table at the others.

"I hope Terry here's not been leading you astray."

"Alan, Mark, George, this is Rob," said Terry, pulling up another chair. "Alan's a particular fan of yours."

"Oh yes," said Alan, almost a little too enthusiastically for Terry's liking, "I think you're a real talent. And I'm not just being a dirty old man here."

"You are!" shouted George.

"No I'm not. He puts a lot of effort into his act. Believe me, in my capacity as a dirty old man I've seen a lot of strippers over the years–and some of them just stand there and go through the motions. But you give it a hundred and ten percent and that's very refreshing."

"Thanks," said Rob, obviously pleased. This kind of praise was unusual.

"What's the secret of your success?" asked George, handing the spliff over to Rob.

"I don't know really—you've got to appeal a little bit to everybody. I mean, they want you to be the boy-next-door, but they also want you to be a filthy sod. You've got to seem quite macho, but there's also got to be a vulnerability there too—as if they could storm the ramparts and take you, possess you."

"It also helps if you've got a dick like a donkey," said Terry under his breath. He and Alan smirked at one another. Rob, who seemed to have paid no attention to the comment, took a drag on the joint and frowned.

"What's a couple of cuddly old geezers like you doing with weed like this?" George had a shellshocked look.

"I ask myself that question every time I smoke the stuff." Terry turned to Alan, half-expecting some sort of wisecrack about what a lightweight George was. But the older man was staring into space; his eyes focused on nothing and his mouth hanging open. He had suddenly gone very pale—and the various colours of the neon lights around them settled into the contours of his face, the purples and greens and blues and yellows mixing to give him a slightly cadaverous aspect. Looking at Alan now Terry saw with an alarming clarity the age difference between them. They were both getting older, but unless Terry became ill or had an accident, death would catch up with Alan much faster. Seeing him suddenly drained of his vigour, Terry thought again about the nature of his situation, about what the future might hold. A succession of older lovers who, if he stayed with them, would die and leave him alone, searching for another—until eventually, when he himself was an old man, he might meet someone his own age and live out his final years with that person.

But then he shook himself out of the dark reverie—after all, how could he know how long he would have with anyone? The simple fact was that he, like everyone else, was unable to anticipate what might happen in the years to come. He had been on a covert quest for more than a decade, since the day he walked into the Magic

Clock, which had taken him throughout the world, always to places where older men congregated–a particular beach, a certain bar, a sauna that he'd heard about–and the trail had led back to Alan, to a man he had known even before his odyssey had begun. In the face of such perverse, mischievous fate, how could he make any plans at all? Terry turned his mind back to the present.

"Anyone fancy a beer at Na Und?" he said. Helen was deep in conversation with Mark and George was chatting to Rob. Alan snapped his head up like a wooden puppet responding to a jerk on the string from above.

"Yes dear boy, excellent idea! Sorry about that–I drifted a bit there." Alan turned to the others. "What about you lot? Shall we go along to Na Und for a nightcap?"

"Why not?" said Helen. "We've never been in even though we've stood outside loads of times and watched the men waltzing. They're really very good." George raised his eyes.

"German queens–you should try dancing with one. They bite your head off if you put a foot wrong, and the smell of cologne is overpowering."

"What?" Alan sniggered. "The place or the aftershave?" George shook his head.

"Aren't you the lively one? A couple of minutes ago I thought we were going to have to call an ambulance." Alan stood up, his expression a challenge to all.

"There's life in the old dog yet." As they wandered away from the Block, George looked up at the Sky Rider. He squeezed Mark's hand and nodded up towards it.

"What was it like?"

"At the beginning it's an amazing sensation. You feel as if you're never going to stop climbing, almost as if you're going to go into orbit. But after the initial rush it's a bit of an anti-climax. You just sort of bob around in mid-air, feeling a bit sick, waiting for them to lower you to the ground."

"Ha," said George. "Sounds a bit like falling in love." Mark stopped.

"You don't really think that, do you?"

"Of course not–it was just an easy one-liner. I've not turned bitter like some of the old queens you meet."

"I know," said Mark earnestly. "That's one of the things that makes you so great." George raised a hand.

"Please–I'm not used to compliments." Mark laughed.

"So does that mean I'm not allowed to say what I feel about you?"

"Not if it involves being too nice."

"Oh," said the younger man. "That's a shame because I planned to shower you with compliments at every available opportunity." George turned his nose up.

"In that case I think the opportunities will probably be rather scarce."

"Only joking," said Mark. "Seriously though, I really hope that we can see each other when we get back home. I think it's important to keep up the momentum, don't you? Otherwise things will just slide away, and that'd be a shame." George listened to Mark talking away by his side, amazed by the younger man's zeal. He remembered being like that himself when he was younger. Nothing seemed impossible and barriers were there to be knocked down. He had met so many men like this over the years, some of whom had pursued him relentlessly, only to disappear without a trace a month later–no doubt infatuated by a new object of desire. But his meeting with Mark had not been like that at all. There had been the false start with Alan sticking his nose in–then today a real meeting of hearts, minds and bodies. There had been no pursuit at all. It had happened in a very natural way, and perhaps that bode well in terms of whether their friendship would develop. How ironic, thought George, that in a place where there was such a lot of casual sex, where people often met and satisfied each other without even exchanging so much as a word, he would find something like this, something with the potential to grow. But then, the trees and plants and animals that thrived in the barren sand dunes of Gran Canaria were a lesson that life could flourish in the harshest of environments. And if it all came to nothing–well, he could always take up Manfred's offer and become a whore. He brought his attention back to Mark's chatter.

"Of course, you'd be welcome to come and visit me," he was saying. "Or I could come over to you–it's not that long a drive. Or we could go somewhere for the weekend if you prefer, so we're on neutral ground and neither of us gets put out. I don't want you to feel that I'm forcing things, but it would be nice to make some kind of plan if you're up for it. What do you think?" George smiled.

"I think it all sounds wonderful," he said. And he meant it–but not necessarily in the way that Mark maybe thought he did. As they headed into Na Und, George thought how strange it was that so many people on the gay scene spent their time looking for that special person, that beacon on the horizon to light their way safely into port. He had done it himself, standing in those bars alone, looking at the faces in the crowd until he saw one looking straight at him, and then there was that eternal, hopeful question–could he be the one? But now in his sixties, George believed that gay lives were different, that rather than one single, special lifelong bond, there was a fluid continuum of relationships moving through the whole thing, his various lovers had all intertwined and led inexorably towards this young man smiling hopefully at him now, as they made their way through the night time bustle. Presiding over it all was Alan–who had been through so much with him since that first moment at the Army barracks, when their fates became more or less inextricably linked, and who would remain his friend for better or for worse, no matter what should happen to either of them.

*

PILS Bar Na Und was still in full swing. There were so many people standing outside that at first glance getting in seemed impossible. The management had become wise to the fact that people liked to hang around watching the dancing, so they had set up an extra bar at the front, to sell beer to those on the periphery. Alan grabbed Terry's wrist and charged straight in. As was often the case at Na Und, it wasn't actually as packed further inside as it first appeared. Even so, the number of bodies meant that the air grew warmer as they moved towards the dance floor. Alan turned and said something, but his words were lost in the din of the music. Lights flashed in Terry's eyes, and someone stroked his bottom. As the crowd parted to let them through, faces leered and loomed into view–among them those of several men he had been to bed with during this and past holidays. He also recognised people from the karaoke bar. What an embarrassment! He continued to smile and allowed himself to be ushered onwards. A similar thing was happening to Alan. He'd spotted the "do you give love?" man being twirled around the floor by a big fat white-haired German, but looked away before the guy had the chance to make eye contact and pretend that he hadn't seen Alan–as he always did. Men both young and old looked at him admiring his face, his hair and his stature. The fact that he and Terry were together tonight seemed to intensify the collective desire, the group fantasy that could be generated around a handsome couple. They found stools in the usual spot at the back of the bar, next to the dance floor. Alan quickly checked to make sure there were no unfinished drinks lying around–it was not uncommon in here to come back from a dance and find that someone had stolen your seats, and your drinks had been cleared away. He had no wish to get involved in that kind of nonsense. He took off his jacket and folded it up; laying it on top of some beer crates stacked up under the counter. Terry leaned on his shoulder and spoke into his ear, talking about the music, the words slightly slurred.

"There's no way I can dance to this. I need something slower." Alan's response was lost as the Germans around them began singing and clapping along with the chorus. Terry spotted Mark, George and the others emerging into the pandemonium. As they crossed the dance floor a short, tubby man slipped his hands around George's waist and spun him around. Without even breaking his step, George put his arms round the guy's shoulders and fell perfectly into the rhythm.

"Now there's someone who knows what he's doing!" shouted Rob, flagging down the little waiter who patrolled this part of the bar.

"Oh yes." There was a hint of pride in Alan's voice. "George is very good. He and my wife Marjorie used to dance together professionally."

"I can believe it," said Rob. "Useful thing to be able to do–and it seems to have come back into fashion."

"We keep saying we'll go for lessons," said Helen, "but there never seems to be the time." The music changed, and the older German who had been dancing with the "do you give love?" man walked over to Terry, all smiles. His former partner saw where he was heading and flounced off the floor, with a face like thunder.

"May I have the pleasure?" said the German. Terry's face was a mask of panic. He didn't have a clue about how to dance to the tune–which he guessed was a rumba.

"I don't know," he said, looking towards Alan for help. "You'll have to ask my friend if it's all right." Alan grinned in a way that was not wholly without malice.

"Of course it's all right," he yelled, giving Terry's shoulder a gentle pat. "You go ahead and enjoy it." Alan leaned towards the frightened-looking boy. "Just follow what he does and try not to stand on his toes too much." The German pulled Terry into the scrum of fast-moving bodies. Alan watched as the young man was moved around the floor like a limp rag doll. Strangely though, as the dance went on, he seemed to get the hang of it–in fact after a minute or two he looked as if he was positively enjoying it. As the pair spun around, Alan could see Terry's hands exploring the German's slab of a back, then one hand moving down towards his rather stout bottom. Suddenly Alan's mind conjured up an image of the two men together in Na Und's tiny toilet cubicle, Terry on his knees, hands grasping the German's buttocks as he sucked his cock. The thought upset Alan more than he would have admitted. He swigged some beer as he continued to watch–thinking: what's this, jealousy? Decades had gone by since he had felt possessive about anyone–when a waiter had made a big fuss of Marge during their honeymoon. Just at that moment, Terry pushed the German away and stood back, eyeing him angrily. The German shrugged his shoulders and walked off. Terry came back to his stool.

"Cheeky bugger," he said. "His hands were everywhere, and he knew I was with you because I asked you if you minded us dancing. I told him to sod off." Alan laughed.

"Shame–you seemed to be getting the hang of the dancing." But good for you, he thought. The boy sat down next to him, and put his hand unexpectedly on the older man's thigh. Alan was normally quite twitchy about such gestures in public, but for some reason he didn't flinch at all. In fact his reaction, which was almost subconscious, was to widen the gap between his knees every so slightly, pushing his leg outwards towards Terry. The lad responded by moving his hand slowly up Alan's leg, towards his crotch. Alan was surprised to feel himself getting hard. For some time now it hadn't happened spontaneously, and quite often, as with Mark last night, it didn't happen at all. He had assumed that his abilities in that department were deteriorating with the passing years–but maybe, as George had often said, his problems were all in the mind.

"Why don't you go with the flow?" his friend would say, "instead of trying to mould things into what you think they should be?" Go with the flow–maybe that was the answer. But he had lived the life of a family man for so many decades now that it was a hard habit to break. His wife had only been dead for a couple of years and he still felt the need to be loyal to her. That was fair enough, and he could imagine many a widower living out their final years in such a way–but the real criminal act was to continue being loyal to his own delusion that he was a heterosexual. He had made the choice to marry Marge all those years ago for very good reasons. The success of their marriage, both in terms of the pleasure it had brought them and the fact that they had raised two happy and successful children, proved to him that he had made the right choice. But once he had mourned his wife, once the sympathetic phone calls had stopped and the flow of letters and cards dwindled, he had realized that on one level, a phase of his life had ended. He would continue to be a part of his children's world and they of his, but they had their own lives to lead, and he was not the kind of man who would impose.

Anyway, there had been this whole side of him lying dormant throughout a huge part of his life. And George, bless him, had been more than happy to welcome his old friend back into the fold. They had a lot of fun. Both were reasonably well-off in retirement, and they'd embarked on a voyage, partly to see the world, but also to see the world's gay places. It was almost as if, in taking Alan's hand and leading him on this journey, George was trying to remind him of his true nature, to point and say: "Look. That's what you are and that's what you always were–nothing has changed." But Alan had held back. Of course he had met some charming men during those travels, and supposed that with many of them he could have allowed something to develop. But there was a sense that to do so would somehow cheapen what had gone before. He had enjoyed looking, but had hardly touched. The torch that he carried had shed its pristine light on some wanton scenes, but it had never been extinguished. There had been little forays but like his infatuation with young Steve, they had always been conducted at a safe distance. Steve belonged to someone else, and in any case, he was so submissive that he would be unlikely to knock on the door in the middle of the night and demand a slice of Alan's soul.But now here was Terry–a young man who somehow bridged the gap between Alan's past and his present, and who might just hold the keys to his future–who Marge had looked at when he turned up in his school uniform, spotty and awkward but already a fine lad, with his cricket bat and his prefect's badge–and pronounced him a worthy boyfriend for their daughter. And who walked onto the beach this morning ten years later, broader, more confident, admired by all, and began this extraordinary flirtation. Alan felt that it would be unwise to try to suppress his true nature forever. Perhaps the time had come to let go of the past, to let the stick in the sand be washed away, to let the sea return the beach to its natural form. He slipped his arm around Terry's back and kissed him. The lad responded, his mouth still sweet despite the beers, the joints and the brandies.

There was a commotion nearby and they broke apart. The small waiter with the moustache, seeing them in their clinch, had begun dancing in front of them, celebrating their open display of love, holding his metal tray above his head and banging it in time to the music with his free hand. He continued for a minute or two then walked forward, smiling, kissed them both, and moved away. George arrived with a small tray of shot glasses.

"The landlord gave me these to hand out." The glasses were full of a colourless bitter liqueur–described by the staff as the schnapps of the house–which usually made people gasp and shiver when they drank it.

"Bottoms up," said George as he dispatched his own in one gulp.

"Much more of this," muttered Alan, "and I'll be crawling home on my hands and knees." The tune that was playing came to an end and the dance floor cleared. After a short pause, an intense Spanish love ballad began, which they played every night at about the same time. Alan and George had no idea what it was called, and the lyrics meant nothing to them because they only had rudimentary Spanish, but perhaps that added to their enjoyment of it. And it was perfect for a slow, smoochy dance. Alan leaned towards George.

"May I have this dance?" George smiled.

"You know I could never refuse you." They moved out onto the floor. Alan let George lead because he really was the better dancer. For some reason the Germans preferred the boisterous numbers, the sort of tunes that allowed them to slap the table tops and clap their hands, and sing along at the top of their voices. Slow, romantic ones pretty much cleared the floor–but there were always a few couples sitting around waiting for them, and every night at around the same time the management obliged. Alan spoke quietly into his friend's ear.

"If you'd told me the day we met that we'd end up in a place like this, forty years later, being courted by boys half our age, I'd never have believed you." The glitterball spun above them, sending out slender shafts that caressed every nook and cranny of the bar.

"Actually, I'm quite happy about the way things have ended up," said George. "It could have been a lot worse."

"Uh oh," said Alan, "we've got company." He nodded across to their left. Mark was navigating Terry around the dance floor.

"The poor boy," said George, noticing how wobbly Terry was on his feet. "What did you do to him?" Alan shrugged.

"Nothing really–I just gave him a kiss. Must be the effect I have on people." The song came to an end and they parted, as did the youngsters. In the middle of the dance floor the four of them swapped partners, so that Alan was now dancing with Terry, and George with Mark. The Blue Danube by Johann Strauss began to play.

"Oh no," moaned Terry, trying to move away. "I can't do a waltz." Alan gripped him tightly.

"Of course you can, you just did it before with that German. Stay on the balls of your feet and follow what I do. Try to keep sliding across the floor. It's a simple rhythm: one-two-three, one-two-three, one-two-three. There you go, easy." Terry was amazed to find that he and Alan were indeed waltzing–and getting away with it. He was delighted because he had always loved this tune, and they played it at least once a night here. To him it was synonymous with Na Und and its nightly dances. He grinned as they twirled around.

"How are you doing?" said Alan.

"Pretty good thanks. All the better for being back in your arms." Alan laughed, pretending to stick a finger down the back of his throat to make himself sick.

"I wouldn't joke about that if I were you," said Terry. "It might end up like that, with all this spinning around. I can't keep up with you guys at all." Alan tutted.

"You youngsters, no stamina. You'd better get in training if we're going to be seeing more of you." The crowd had thinned out a bit, allowing Terry see the people sitting at tables at the front of the bar, just beyond the dance floor. His eyes met those of a striking-looking woman, very smartly dressed in a black sequinned cocktail dress, who seemed to be ignoring her companions at the table, and concentrating instead on the dancing. She had a slightly bovine face, with pallid cheeks and dark eyes. He smiled and she smiled back. It must be strange, he thought, to look so extraordinary: he wondered whether she was a drag queen or a real woman, and tried to picture her waking up in the morning with her lover, in a run-of-the-mill flat or villa somewhere in Playa Del Ingles. It was impossible to imagine, so perfectly did she belong to this bar, to this crowd of people, to this carnival. There were some people who seemed to live only for the night.

The tune came to an end and a slower one came on. Terry and Alan moved closer together for a smoochy dance. Terry felt the contours of Alan's back and smiled. A rather handsome older man who glided past at that moment with his partner answered the smile. The next time the two couples passed each other, he looked again and winked, and Terry winked back. The guy was very good looking and even though he was dancing with the man he wanted more than any other, Terry's instinct was to flirt with him. Unbeknown to the lad, he was smiling at Frank, the older lover of young Steve, with whom Alan had committed his earlier indiscretion in the darkroom of Hummel Hummel. And Terry was also unaware of the fact that whenever the couples were facing the other way, Alan was flirting with Steve. Clive and the handsome old Dutchman were also on the floor, and Terry had given the Dutchman the glad eye several times too, unaware as he did so that Alan had been smiling at Clive. George Hope, meanwhile, was in a smoochy clasp with Mark in the corner–but had positioned himself so that he was looking outwards into the rest of the bar, over his partner's shoulder. He had exchanged lascivious looks with young Steve, Clive and–rather disgracefully–Terry. Alex the dashing Danish octogenarian and his boyfriend Dieter had turned up, and they too were on the floor. Terry and the younger guys who were dancing had all smiled at Alex, while Alan and George and the other older ones had been eyeing Dieter up. Helen and Rob sat on their stools, watching with amusement as the dance–and the shameless exhibition of flirting–went on. Helen leaned towards her boyfriend.

"One thing's for sure,' she said, "this lot certainly deserve each other." But the strange thing was that as the dance continued, the smiling faces became to Terry nothing more than a procession of ghosts. He had loved many of these men, and they had loved him, but they had never belonged to one another. If they belonged to anything at that moment, it was to this island of Gran Canaria, this resort of Playa Del Ingles and its gay scene–which had claimed them all as its own. Terry closed his eyes and allowed Alan to lead him around the floor, trusting entirely in the older man's ability to keep him out of the others' way. Through his eyelids he could see nothing but a shifting orange glow, as they moved around under the spotlights trained on the dance floor. His senses were filled with the sound of the music, the feel and smell of the man in his arms. Now he kept his eyes closed because for the time being there was really only one man whose face he wanted to look at, and it would be impossible for him to do that until the dance had come to an end.

Michael John

Older, Younger

Michael John

Older, Younger

Printed in Great Britain
by Amazon